RITES OF THE DARK GOD

Kemp watched as the magician lifted the archaic dagger from the altar and passed it thrice through the scented smoke from the brazier. With each pass, the blade seemed to gain substance. It took on a dark sheen, strange and deadly.

Then the mage held out the dagger. The king kissed the wicked blade, then knelt. The magician took up the crown, muttering in that guttural tongue. And something changed, something Kemp could not quite place . . .

The darkness became more complete, oppressive, and hostile. And the wind, which minutes before had whipped fiercely, died away to nothing. All was deathly still.

Then the magician placed the iron crown upon the king's head . . .

By Craig Mills
Published by Ballantine Books:

THE BANE OF LORD CALADON

THE DREAMER IN DISCORD

SHADOW OF THE CROWN

SHADOW OF THE CROWN

Craig Mills

A Del Rey Book
BALLANTINE BOOKS • NEW YORK

Sale of this book without a front cover may be unauthorized. If this book is coverless, it may have been reported to the publisher as "unsold or destroyed" and neither the author nor the publisher may have received payment for it.

A Del Rey Book
Published by Ballantine Books

Copyright © 1992 by Craig Mills

All rights reserved under International and Pan-American Copyright Conventions. Published in the United States of America by Ballantine Books, a division of Random House, Inc., New York, and simultaneously in Canada by Random House of Canada Limited, Toronto.

Library of Congress Catalog Card Number: 92-97046

ISBN 0-345-37280-8

Manufactured in the United States of America

First Edition: January 1993

For Mom

1

It was too hot.

The chill of the autumn morning had long since fled the face of the rising sun, and now a moist, languorous warmth smothered Tailor's Green. Kemp stood crowded at the back of the wagon, a creeping runnel of perspiration tickling the small of his back. His coat, though soiled and sadly rumpled, was of good, heavy wool; it had not been meant for this sort of weather. Unfortunately, with his hands bound behind his back with coarse rope, Kemp had no way of removing it. And he rather doubted that he could convince any of his jailers to untie him, just so that he could take off his coat.

Before him, mere yards away, the gallows stood as a stark reminder of the ultimate insignificance of his comfort. Trees massed cloudlike behind it, a high platform constructed of new timbers, a trapdoor in the center of it. The arm from which the noose hung looked disturbingly stout.

Kemp did his best to ignore the essential unfairness of his situation, fighting to stay alert. He still believed that there must be some way out of this predicament. At least, he was still trying to believe it. One look at his fellow prisoners told him that they had all but given up hope. Filthy, bedraggled, most in clothes that had not been any good even before their weeks or months of imprisonment, they gazed about them with abashed, frightened, discouraged eyes; none seemed to possess the strength even to look defiant anymore.

That was all very well for them. They were what they were, and there was no help for that. But he was *Jerod Kemp*. He could not conceive of a difficulty from which he could not extricate himself.

Kemp's quick, pale eyes flickered calculatingly about the

green. He imagined possibilities. There were a dozen guards, all dressed in the red coats of the Branion Home Guard, all armed with long muskets. Half of them were concentrating on keeping back the spectators. The rest looked tired and bored; this was routine duty for them. Kemp doubted that any of them were very alert. Their officer, a sallow middle-age man with sparse brown mustaches, stood aloof from his men, as if this assignment were beneath his dignity.

A sizable crowd had assembled for the show. *An ugly-looking lot,* Kemp thought. Dirty and ill-kempt, most of them, they appraised the prisoners and the gallows with malicious, bare-toothed, *longing* looks. Kemp could pick out a few ashen, anguished faces in the crowd. He guessed that these belonged to the friends and relatives of the condemned. He wondered if, given the chance, any of them would help him.

Probably not, he decided.

Keeping his face bland and immobile, Kemp twisted his notoriously supple hands deftly in their bonds. The ropes were tight, but he had been working on them. He thought that he might be able to pull his hands free if he could manage a diversion. *A diversion* . . .

Kemp looked speculatively at the pale, perspiring unfortunates who shared the back of the wagon with him. Who would be the first to face the noose? It occurred to Kemp that he could hope for no better diversion than a good hanging. All eyes would be on the poor victim. If the wretch should lose his composure, weep, faint, fall upon the ground, so much the better . . .

If he could just free his hands, there was a possibility that he could get away, reach the trees, or lose himself in the crowd. Something. If his six week in Tranding Gaol hadn't slowed him too much, he might just make it. True, he couldn't expect to outpace a musket ball, but the guns were awkward to use in a crowd and were none too accurate at a distance.

Kemp scowled. It was not much of a plan, he knew, but at least it was better than letting himself be led like a docile sheep to the slaughter.

Hearing a stately clattering of hooves, Kemp turned to see a small black coach coming up the road. The guards, also seeing it, began pushing back the crowd, allowing it to come up almost to the gallows. The officer straightened, brushed a hand quickly over his garments, smoothed his mustaches with a fastidious finger, and walked briskly forward to meet the coach.

The coachman clambered down from his perch. After opening the door with a slight flourish, he stood by while the occupants emerged and stepped down.

The first man Kemp recognized as Farenbras, the elderly sadist who was warden of Tranding Gaol. Dressed all in black save for his shirt, Warden Farenbras moved stiffly, his movements small and restricted, as if he were unfamiliar with the functioning of his body. His hair was grizzled, his neck thin and arched, his skin as pale and translucent as candle wax. His tiny black eyes took the measure of the officer, the guards, and finally the prisoners. Feeling the man's smug pleasure, Kemp half expected him to smile, although that was a thing Farenbras was never known to do.

From Kemp's perspective, the arrival of Warden Farenbras was unfortunate. The guards, inattentive only moments before, were now fully alert. Their easy carelessness vanished, replaced by rigid postures and glaring countenances. Tightening the muscles at the corners of his mouth, Kemp silently cursed his misfortune. This was not getting any easier.

A second man emerged from the coach, bringing a sudden chill to Kemp. Physically, he was anything but impressive—a short, dark, fleshy man, dark stubble visible on his chin—but he was dressed in cold clerical blue, his long tunic sealed with many cloth-covered buttons, crimson lining showing at the cuffs and the edge of his round collar, a silver-bound book clenched in one hand.

A priest. Somehow, the sight of him brought home to Kemp the full horror of his situation, in a way that even the gallows had not.

Warden Farenbras strode toward Kemp and the other prisoners, closely followed by the officer and the priest. He stopped a few paces from the wagon and appraised the prisoners calmly. Finally, with the tip of his gnarled walking stick, he pointed at Kemp. "That one," he said.

Kemp did not react visibly, though his heart, constricted, seemed to flutter like a bird clutched in a remorseless hand. He felt dizzy, and for a moment his thoughts slid senselessly beyond the grasp of his awareness.

Somehow, he had not counted on this, that he should be first. There was nothing he could do; he was trapped.

He would die.

"You," the officer said roughly. "Get down."

The fear, so long denied, began to break free, like an ice flow in the warm spring sun. Kemp felt the blood draining from his cheeks. *"No,"* he said, his voice husky and remote.

"Get down!" the officer repeated furiously. He caught Kemp by the front of his coat and pulled with brutal strength. Unprepared, Kemp felt himself start to fall forward, off the back of the wagon. He managed to maintain his orientation as he fell, so that he landed more or less on his feet, before collapsing to his knees.

Rough hands drew him upright. Kemp found himself standing shakily, caught between two guards. The officer stood mere inches before him, face scarlet with a rage that Kemp could not quite comprehend. "Stand, and face the consequences of your crimes, coward," he said.

Kemp snarled at him and was about to hurl a choice curse, when the guards began pulling him toward the waiting gallows. The priest bobbed alongside him, fumbling with his prayer book. "Is there anything that you would like to confess before the gods?" he asked.

"Leave me alone, Priest. I've no use for you or your gods."

Eyes narrowing, the priest dropped back a pace, then struggled to catch up again. As they reached the gallows and stopped, the priest pulled a bronze medallion from his pocket. He held it out, its long chain woven among the fingers of both hands. "Wear this," the priest whispered. "It will ease the way for you." The man drew the chain over Kemp's head and let the medallion drop down. In a louder voice, he said, "I will pray for your soul."

"Lovely. I'll remember you till the end of my days."

The priest set his face stonily at this, but said nothing more.

A guard both before and after him, Kemp mounted the gallows steps. When he reached the top, he looked out at the spectators who were gathered together on the meadow. Their avid, cruel faces brought a churning wave of sickness to him. He tried to steel himself. If nothing else, he wanted not to be humiliated at the end.

But still his mind worked, evaluating his guards, the position of the gallows, and the distance to the trees, sifting through the information his senses brought him. Useless. He could think of no reasonable course of action, no clever ploys, nothing. He had run out of room to maneuver.

He was guided to the center of the platform. Creaking, the trapdoor sagged slightly under his feet. He found himself becoming faint and realized how shallow and rapid his breathing had become.

If he fainted, would that give them any pause? Would it make them take someone else first? Kemp looked from the officer to Warden Farenbras; their faces were equally hard and pitiless.

No. They would either rouse him with a pail of water, or have the guards hold him up. Rather than allow himself to be so treated, Kemp made an effort to breathe normally.

A burly man in black came to Kemp and drew the noose over his head. "Relax, fellow, and it will go easier for you," he said. "I know what I'm doing. I'll see to it that the end comes quick." The man carefully pulled the noose tight, so that the coarse fibers scratched Kemp's neck. Studying the rope with a professional squint, the man positioned the knot to the side of Kemp's head, checked the hang of the rope. "There," he said, apparently satisfied.

"Thank you," Kemp told him. "I . . . guess."

"May the gods be merciful with you."

Kemp tried to nod. It was true, he finally knew. He was going to die. It still seemed . . . impossible.

The priest was reading aloud from his prayer book, his voice droning almost unintelligibly. Tailor's Green swam with light, heat, and anticipation. Faint laughter and rough conversation mingled together. *Unreal*, it seemed to Kemp, *unreal*.

"Ready!" came the officer's voice, hollow, distant-sounding. A pause. *"Now."*

There was a sudden clacking sound, and the floor dropped out from under Kemp's feet. For one terrible, impossibly vivid instant, he fell.

All eyes were fixed upon Kemp in that moment. Some looked on with dread, some with satisfaction, some with pity, some with pleasure, and more than a few with little more than weary professional indifference. An instant later, all looked on with astonishment.

As the trapdoor dropped and Kemp began to fall, it seemed to many of the spectators that a haze had come over their sight, as if a film covered their eyes. It lasted for only the space of an eye blink, but when it cleared, all that could be seen was an empty noose reaching the end of its tether and bouncing sharply from the force of its drop.

For a moment, there was only stunned silence. The noose swung slowly over the open trap, showing no sign of breakage or defect. Kemp was nowhere to be seen.

All at once, the crowd began murmuring its amazement, Warden Farenbras shouted shrilly, and the officer bawled out orders to his men.

Several of the guards looked under and about the gallows, while the remainder restrained the crowd and prevented anyone from leaving until it could be determined that Kemp was not among them. Eventually, finding nothing, the guards moved away from the gallows, jogged off to the nearest trees, and began searching irresolutely through the brush.

Nearly an hour later, no sign of Kemp had been found, and no one could think where to look next. The man had simply vanished. Later, several of the spectators would claim that, just before the man had disappeared, they had seen a dark gap open above him and a huge hand reach out and pluck him away, but they would not be widely believed.

There were no more executions performed that day.

2

The sun was sinking below the dry, russeted hills of West Gahant, and shadows had begun to spread over the world, when Cander Ellis reached the Inn of the Three Crows, the collar of his cloak turned up against the cold. The afternoon had been warm enough, but at this time of year the day's heat faded before the sun did, scoured away by chill winds out of Trelhane.

The inn, its outlines smudged by tall beech trees, beckoned to him with its promise of food, drink, and a place by the fire. Cander intended to take full advantage of what comforts he could, while he could; who knew what demands the morning might bring?

Cander rode into the inn's central courtyard, dismounted stiffly from his hired chestnut gelding, and, after first claiming his bulging kit bag, gave the animal into the care of the waiting groom, a ragged young man with dark, unkempt hair.

After setting his plumed hat to the proper angle and straightening the fine blue coat for which he'd yet to pay his tailor, Cander entered the inn's main common room, stooping slightly to pass under the low threshold. He paused within and slowly pulled off his butter-colored kidskin gloves, a finger at a time, while he scanned the room with a careful eye.

The Three Crows was a popular, prosperous, well-appointed inn. It stood on the main road to the great Protectorate of Branion, very near the border, the only establishment of its kind for several leagues. The common room, paneled all around in dark, oiled wood, boasted many tables, the majority of which were surrounded by merchants and gentlemen of substance traveling between Branion and Gahant, and perhaps a few even to distant Cyemal. A few sat alone or stood warming themselves silently by the fire, but most were engaged in conversation of some sort, either boisterous and florid or tight-lipped and somber, depending on the natures, business, and sobriety of those involved.

Even before Cander could get his gloves off, the owner of the inn spotted him and rushed toward him with a grin and an extended hand. The man's name was Gerj Kolin. He had been a sergeant of supply in the Branion army once, Cander knew, before inexplicably amassing enough money to retire to Gahant and buy the Inn of the Three Crows. He still had the build and manner of the professional soldier he'd been, half a dozen years before. In his late forties now, his cropped, sandy hair was getting thin and grey, though his tanned face was still relatively unlined. He wore a crisp white shirt and buff-colored twill trousers.

"Ah, Cander Ellis!" he exclaimed. "Back again, I see. A pleasure to see you!"

"Good to be back, Gerj. Is my room still available?"

"Of course. You paid me well enough to keep it for you."

"Good. I've had a hard day's traveling and I'm tired."

"How long do you expect to be staying?"

"Only a day or two this time. Then it's back to Branion and the wicked city of Lorum."

The man made a twisted face. "Ah, well, if you must . . ."

"After a full summer away, I begin to miss it."

"Not me, never. Not even after these five years."

"Besides," Cander said, "I have a livelihood to earn. I fear that if I spend much more time away the public will have forgotten my name altogether."

"There is that, I suppose. It's not always easy being the famous playwright Cander Ellis, eh?"

Gerj gave a beckoning gesture to a young man who lounged behind a long, high counter of dark, polished wood. As the young man came to attention and started around the counter, Gerj said, "Timony, please take Mister Ellis' bags to room eleven."

Timony took the bags from Cander, gave the smallest of bows, and started away.

"Now," Gerj said, "unless I miss my guess, you'll want something to eat."

"If you've got a table to spare. Business appears uncommonly robust."

"Not so much so that I can't find a place for the great Cander Ellis, eh?"

Cander acknowledged this with a thin smile and cynical arch of an eyebrow. "Too kind."

"This way, then. I have a nice, quiet booth in the back."

Cander gestured with a slight flourish toward the interior of the inn. "After you, good fellow."

After seeing to it that Cander was settled with his meal, Gerj excused himself to attend to his other guests. Cander waited until the man had disappeared around the corner, then gave his full attention to satisfying his appetite. The food was excellent, as he had known it would be: tender roast pork, a savory vegetable casserole, and freshly baked bread. The beer ranked with the best he had ever tasted.

When he had finished, he sat back with a warm contentment, his second tankard of beer before him on the table. He let the murmur of voices envelop him, too lazy to sort out any meaning from the buzz of conversation. He entertained the thought of getting out his notebook and putting down some ideas he'd had on the play he was working on, but rejected the thought almost as it came to him. Why spoil such a fine mood? There would always be time for work later.

Suddenly a quiet voice from behind him said, "Enjoying yourself, Ellis?"

Startled, Cander gave a little jump. Belatedly forcing an attitude of indifferent poise, he cast a bleak look over his right shoulder at the familiar figure who stood behind him: a powerfully built middle-aged man in utilitarian grey wool coat and trousers. The man's face, deeply creased and marked with numerous small scars, was studiously neutral. His eyes, a pale blue, had fixed upon Cander with an unblinking stare that made the younger man feel exposed and uncomfortable.

"Shalby," Cander said. "I should have known that it was time for you to show up again. I was actually starting to relax a little."

"It's not your job to relax."

Cander sighed. "Don't you ever rest, Shalby?"

"Never. Nor should you."

"Right, right. Just as you say."

The faintest of smiles touched the man's lips. "There. You are looking less relaxed already. Mind if I sit with you for a moment?"

"It would be better than having to look over my shoulder at you."

"Good." Moving with a grace that was derived largely from a remarkable conservation of movement, Shalby came around and sat on the bench across from Cander, sliding to the end nearest the wall.

"I didn't see you come in," Cander said.

"Maybe that's because I was already here when *you* came in."

Cander looked at the man with surprise. "What? Where were you hiding? I didn't notice you."

"I make it a point not to be noticed." Shalby let a contemptuous glance play over Cander. "While you seem to make it a point to be completely obvious. *Look* at you, at the way you're dressed. A man would have to be blind in both eyes to miss you."

"Being who I am, it would be suspicious indeed if I tried to make myself as drab as you."

"I still don't like it."

Trying to contain his growing annoyance, Cander said, "It's not for you to judge me or my methods, Shalby."

The man shrugged, and silence settled uneasily over the two, until Cander said, "I assume that you had some purpose in seeking me out, other than to spoil my digestion?"

Leaning forward over the table, Shalby said in a low voice, "A mutual acquaintance would like to see you."

Cander took this in without expression, then nodded. "When and where?"

"Tonight, an hour before midnight, where the old South Road crosses the road to Branion."

Cander rolled his eyes. "Midnight at the crossroads? Can't he think of something a little less . . . melodramatic?"

"That is the place and time," Shalby said flatly. "I'm sure you'll be there."

"I'll be there. *Of course* I'll be there."

"Good," Shalby said, rising. "I'll leave you to your digestion, then."

Saying nothing, Cander watched the man move across the room with that peculiarly balanced, phantomlike stride. Distracted by a sudden burst of laughter from a nearby table, Cander glanced away for a moment; when he looked back again, Shalby had somehow managed to disappear completely. Cander suppressed the foolish urge to pursue the man, to find where he had gone, or merely to satisfy himself that he hadn't simply vanished into the smoky air. Instead, he settled back with the appearance of cynical indifference and sipped at his beer. From where he sat, he could see out into the main room. It was getting late, and a number of the tables were unoccupied now. He still had an hour or so to kill before he had to leave to make his assigned rendezvous.

With an appreciative eye, Cander watched a young, blond serving maid move among the tables. After a few minutes, he caught her attention, gestured her over to him, and ordered a pot of jafar, a spicy, stimulating beverage from the newly discovered lands to the east. When she returned with the brew, he detained her with some well-practiced chat. She seemed just as happy to stay and talk as to return to work. He thought that, with a bit of effort, he might be able to entice her into his bed.

Cander discovered that her name was Alsimae, that she was a local girl, and unmarried. She was attractive, beyond a doubt—though not in the least elegant. Dressed simply in a long skirt and full blouse with short, puffed sleeves, she had freckled, slightly plump upper arms and an ample bosom. Honey-colored hair partially concealed an affable oval face, the lips small and pale, the eyes wide and full of that knowing innocence common to country girls. Her manner was alternately bold and shy. She laughed easily.

At length, Cander found himself inviting her back to his room. "I have to go out for a little while, but when I get back perhaps you'd like to come up with me. I have a bottle of a very nice wine that I've been waiting for an occasion to open."

Alsimae wrinkled her nose playfully. "Oh, I don't know if I should . . ."

"Come, there's no harm." He displayed his most appealing smile.

Alsimae reached out and touched the back of his wrist. Her hand was small, almost childlike. "We'll see. I'll think about it, I will. Right now, though, I really must get back to work."

As she turned to leave, Cander said, "Yes, do think about it. A good time will be had by all, I promise you." He watched the woman's receding form, until it finally disappeared into the back room. He gave a small sigh and dug into a waistcoat pocket, then, to draw out his watch—an expensive extravagance, but a useful one. *Time to go.* After slipping the heavy watch into his pocket, he drank what was left of his jafar, put down a generous tip, and got up to leave.

Intensely colored sparks showered through a darkness that seemed to shiver and twist like a living thing. Bewildered, dislocated, Kemp felt himself falling, or rising, or flying—or perhaps all three, one after another, or all at once. His stomach churned ominously. Fear froze time, sliced it into a series of separate eternities. Kemp tried to cry out, but no sound escaped his lips. There was only that high, wildly oscillating whine that seemed to pierce his nerves in a thousand places.

Where was he? He remembered standing on the gallows, the rope tight on his neck, feeling the floor drop beneath him . . . and then, the extraordinary sensation of being grasped about the middle, as if by a colossal hand, and pulled into . . . into this bright darkness.

I must be dead, he thought. *I must be.* If so, that meant there was a life beyond death, despite his previous certitude to the contrary. The thought worried Kemp, worried him deeply. Was this all there was to it, an endless hurtling through a formless void? If it was, he didn't know how long he could stand it.

Can a dead soul go mad? he wondered.

Even as this dismal thought came to him, he noticed a cloudy, amorphous disk of light growing before him. He realized suddenly that this was his destination, that he was being guided toward it, somehow. That there *was* a destination should have made him feel better, but even this could not lighten the burden of terror he felt. The disk expanded rapidly, going from the size of a small coin, to that of a midsummer sun, and finally to that of a beckoning doorway. Dim shapes appeared within it, but there was no time to recognize any of them. Hurled into the light, Kemp was falling for real, the weight abruptly returned to his limbs. He twisted, trying to catch himself, but his hands were still bound behind him. He came crashing down on one shoulder onto a hard, flat surface.

For one terrifying moment, he saw a glowing spectral hand hovering over him, projecting from what seemed a quivering black pool in the center of the ceiling. Before he could even be sure of what he saw, the hand withdrew into the blackness. The pool itself shivered; its edges drew inward, and in barely an instant, it shrank and vanished, leaving nothing to show that it had ever existed at all. Kemp heard a sound like receding thunder.

It took a moment for him to recover his breath and his nerve. Awkwardly he got to his knees and rose to his feet. He saw then that he appeared to be in large room, square, windowless, sparsely furnished. The light was dim, emanating from a pair of oddly shaped candelabra that stood on the floor near one wall.

The wall was of yellow-painted plaster; it appeared grimy and streaked with age. There was a smell of brimstone in the air.

Two figures occupied the room with Kemp. The nearest one was tall, thin, and slightly stooped; it wore dark crimson robes and a cowl that completely hid its face. It held a smoking brazier in one white hand, a strangely shaped dagger in the other.

The next figure appeared reassuringly human: short, rather portly, and balding. It was clearly a man, his features large and blunt. The mouth was particularly prominent; it appeared hard, nearly inflexible, with deep creases on either side of it. He wore a good coat of brown wool, cut straight across the bottom in front, with short tails in back, a maroon waistcoat, and breeches that terminated just below the knee.

Kemp swallowed, trying to find his voice. "Wh-where am I?" he asked the less daunting of the figures.

The portly man smiled. "Where? Why, in hell, of course."

Stunned, Kemp stared at the man. There was an icy void in the center of his stomach. "Hell?" he repeated.

The man gave a harsh, metallic laugh. "No, that's just a trifling joke of mine. Actually, you are safe and alive, at my house in West Gahant, near Liln."

Kemp blinked, relief mixed with confusion, mixed with anger. He said only, "How . . . did I get here?"

The figure in the crimson robes put down the brazier and thrust its dagger into the cord that bound its robe at the middle. White hands reached up slowly and flipped back the cowl, revealing a man's thin face, long nose, and a bulging skull covered with grey stubble. The eyes were enlarged and distorted by a pair of round lenses in thick wooden frames. The man's face shone with a peculiar intensity, almost an exaltation. "There," he declared in a piercing, childlike voice, "I've done it. I've done it!"

"Very good, Doctor," the portly man said. "Excellent, in fact. *Most* impressive." He turned to Kemp with an oily, condescending smile. "Kemp, may I introduce you to Doctor Stahlgrave, a magician of some note. It was he, at my request, who engineered your escape from the difficulties in which you'd found yourself of late."

Kemp paused, his brain still unable to cope completely with his sudden, bewildering change of circumstances. "I guess that I'm in your debt, then."

Stahlgrave smiled, though his hideously magnified eyes remain cold. He waved an airy gesture. "Think nothing of it."

"May I ask, uh, how it was done?"

"An interesting question! If you can think of the universe as a series of interlocking spheres, each sphere a reality unto itself, yet all connected—"

"It would be best, I think, if I just give you the short version," the portly man interrupted. "Otherwise we shall be all day and into the night. At the appropriate moment, Doctor Stahlgrave called upon a tame demon—"

"There's no such thing as a 'tame demon,' " Stahlgrave said irritably. "You minimize my accomplishment! Demons are all willful and dangerous beings. They cannot be tamed."

"Well then, a demon that you have under your influence. Would that be proper to say, hmm?" Returning his attention to Kemp, the man cleared his throat, then continued. "He instructed this demon to reach through a place where the stuff of reality is weak, take you away from where you were, and bring you here, where you are now."

Kemp frowned. "All in all, I think that I'd prefer the long version."

"Nonsense! You wouldn't understand it, anyway. No one does." The man extended his hand to Kemp. "Allow me to introduce myself. I am Baron Holis Quordane."

Kemp stared at the outstretched hand. "If you want me to take that, you'll have to untie me first."

"Of course, how stupid of me. Doctor Stahlgrave, may I borrow your knife for a moment?"

Frowning, Stahlgrave shook his head. "This is a consecrated knife. It is not for cutting rope."

"Oh, very well." Quordane plucked at the heavy gold chain that spanned his middle from one waistcoat pocket to the other. The end of the chain slipped out of the pocket, bringing a fancy gold penknife with it. Kemp watched suspiciously as the man moved behind him with the knife, and a moment later he felt the rope give way.

Bringing his hands in front of him, Kemp flexed his numb fingers. He shrugged his shoulders, letting the abused muscles relax. It was a relief to have his hands free. He felt immediately more confident and at ease.

"Now," Quordane said, "while Doctor Stahlgrave finishes up here, why don't we retire to my study? You look like you could use a drink."

"Fine."

"This way, then." Quordane led him from the room, up a

narrow stair, and finally down a corridor wainscotted with dark wood. Here, Kemp noticed, the house looked less forlorn than below, though it still showed signs of age and a lack of maintenance. Quordane stopped in front of a door and took a brass key from his pocket. After turning the key in the lock, he opened the door and ushered Kemp inside.

Kemp looked around him at a small room dominated by a large oaken desk, beyond which were two narrow windows. A tall bookcase was set into one wall—but, Kemp noticed, it contained few books.

Quordane took two short crystal goblets from the bookcase, put them on the desk, and sloshed a small quantity of an amber liquid from a matching decanter into each of them. He settled in the chair behind the desk, cupping one of the goblets in both hands. "Draw up a chair, Kemp. Relax. You are safe and among friends now."

Kemp pulled a rickety wooden chair up to the desk and sat gingerly. Grasping the other goblet, he took a cautious sip. The liquid was a harsh, peppery-tasting brandy, he found.

"So,' Quordane said, "you are Jerod Kemp. I'm pleased to meet you at last. If I may say so, your exploits are legendary."

"Mm," Kemp said. "I'm flattered."

"Not at all, not at all. Rumor has it that you were the thief who stole the Chalice of Tears from the Althian Temple in Lorum. An impressive piece of work, that. Tell me, is that true? Were you the one?"

Kemp shrugged. "I've always felt that a successful theft should be treated like a night spent with a married woman—the wise man does not talk about either afterward."

Quordane gave him a sly smile. "I believe that I have my answer, yes."

Kemp shifted nervously. There was something unsettling in the way that Quordane kept looking at him. "Look, I don't want to sound ungrateful, but why did you save me from the gallows? Somehow I can't believe that it was solely because of the tremendous admiration you have for me."

"Now, what could I possibly want from you? Why don't you think about that for a moment?"

"You want me to steal something for you?"

"They *told* me you were clever."

Kemp studied Quordane for a long moment. He was beginning to develop a definite dislike for this man. "And if I should decline?"

"Oh, you wouldn't want to do that. *Believe me*, you wouldn't. Think of the Power that delivered you from the noose. That same Power could just as easily be turned against you."

"In other words, you're not giving me any choice in the matter."

"I wouldn't say that. You have a choice. An extremely limited choice, it's true—but you do have one."

"Well, I suppose that I'll just have to do as you wish."

"As I said, clever."

3

The moon hung above the trees, a slender crescent partially obscured by wisps of drifting cloud. Cander stood at the crossroads, watching his breath plume in the frigid night air. Damp from the mist, his cloak pulled heavily on his shoulders. The old wheel-lock pistol stuck into his belt rubbed uncomfortably against his ribs.

A faint stirring emanated from the woods behind him, where he had left his horse. He ignored it, focusing instead on the clattering hooves and heavy jostling that was closing quickly on him from the south. In that direction, the road stretched over sharply rolling land, and Cander caught only brief glimpses of the small coach as it topped each rise like a ship in swelling seas.

Cander touched his pistol, loosened his sword in its scabbard, and flipped his cloak back over one shoulder, so that it would not hinder his movements. He did not expect to have to defend himself, but such forlorn places as this made him nervous. *Anyway, best to be prudent*, he told himself.

Not for the first time, Cander found himself wondering what he was doing here, in this place, on a cold night. Why had he allowed himself to get drawn into this business? He had work waiting for him, his true work, and here he was, embroiled in this nonsense . . .

At last, the coach appeared over the last rise. Iron-bound wheels crackling over the stone-strewn road, it rolled into the crossroads and drew to a halt beside Cander. The coach was a handsome thing, elegant and well made, its sleek lines glimmering satin black in the vague moonlight. The coachman, swathed in a full cloak with a high standing collar, a wide-brimmed felt hat pulled low across his face, sat high on his box, the reins held loosely in his gloved hands. He stared straight ahead, paying Cander no attention, the perfect picture of discretion. A long-barreled musket stood beside him.

Cander stepped up to the coach and pulled open the door.

Two men occupied the coach, sitting opposite each other in the soft glow of the small brass lamp burning by the opposite door. The first was Shalby, still dressed in his plain, monochromatic garments. His eyes met Cander's without emotion. On the comfortably padded seat next to his right hand was a small, unornamented pistol.

The other man was older and less imposing physically. His clothes were elegant and immaculate—a fashionably cut coat of the finest wool, white shirt, green silk waistcoat, and crisp, spotless cravat of white linen. He was thin, though in a tough, sinewy way. His hair and his neat, pointed beard were silver, his face remarkably smooth. He hardly bothered to glance at Cander, preferring to gaze out the opposite window with seeming disinterest.

"Well, Spy," he said in a dry, almost metallic voice, "what news do you bring me?"

Cander drew his mouth into a taut line of displeasure. He started to protest that he was not—well, at least, not *primarily*—a spy, but he caught himself. He had tried to fight this battle before; he knew how useless it was to argue.

"Protector Walthorne," he said with the faintest edge of sarcasm, "always a pleasure."

Walthorne shifted with restless irritation. "I'd rather not spend the night exchanging pleasantries. Do get on with it."

"As you say, Protector Walthorne. Would you mind if I got into the coach with you? Or would it please you more if I just stood out here and shivered in the cold?"

"Do what you will, Ellis—only be quick about it."

After putting a foot on the bar that hung under the coach, Cander drew himself up into the passenger compartment. He sat beside the man in grey, smiled at him, and winked. "Hello there, Shalby. Talkative as ever, I see."

The man gazed back unresponsively. "Fools and nances talk a great deal, I've found. It doesn't usually amount to much."

"Stop it, both of you," Walthorne said, an ugly edge to his voice. "I didn't come to this forsaken place to listen to you two match wits, such as they are."

"I'm certainly not the one who insists on always meeting in deserted places at these appalling hours," Cander said.

"It is a necessary inconvenience," the older man said with exaggerated patience. "If we were to be seen together, people *might* begin to suspect that there was some connection between us. They might even begin to think that you were working for me. You wouldn't be of much use to me then, would you?"

"I know that, Protector Walthorne," Cander said with a sigh. "That doesn't mean that I can't complain about it."

"Complain on your own time. What have you learned?"

Holding his cloak closed at the chest, Cander leaned back heavily into the padded seat, thrusting his legs out as far as he could, crossing them at the ankles. Short of yawning, he did all he could to create an attitude of unconcern.

"It seems that the reports you had were correct. The royalists are indeed massing troops along the border. Small units, for the most part, but there is at least a full regiment of calvary a little north of here. I got myself into a dice game with one of the junior officers, and he let slip the fact that they were expecting to be reinforced by a regiment of foot soldiers and several companies of dragoons."

Walthorne considered this with narrowed eyes. "This is disquieting news."

Cander shrugged. "Maybe. Even so, the royalists don't seem to have gathered nearly enough strength to be a serious threat to the Protectorate. Perhaps they're just preparing for an exercise, or something."

"Did your dicing partner have anything to say about that?"

"No. I got the impression that he didn't really know what they were doing there himself."

"That in itself seems suspicious."

"As to that, I can't say."

"Is there anything else?"

"One thing, perhaps. While I was keeping an eye on the royalist troops, I saw somebody pass through their lines. It was somebody who I recognized."

"Who?"

"One Doctor Stahlgrave."

"The magician? Now that *is* interesting."

"I decided to follow him. He led me to a country estate south of Liln. I asked around and found out that the estate belonged to one of the local gentry, a Baron Holis Quordane."

"Holis Quordane?" Walthorne asked, a sudden tension apparent on his face.

"Yes. Why? Do you know him?"

"All too well. Quordane was once a peer of Branion and was a royalist of the worst, most obdurate kind. He went into exile when King Carelinas the Second was taken and beheaded. He is known to be a strong supporter of Carelinas' son, the pretender Lalerin."

Cander shrugged. "All before my time, I'm afraid. I've never heard of him before." This was true. Cander had been three years old when the war against the king began, and only five when Carelinas found his final justice. He knew, of course, that Prince Lalerin and many of his supporters had escaped to Gahant and Cyemal at the end of the civil war, from where they continued to menace the Protectorate that now ruled over Branion. The Protectorate, controlled by the five Lords Protector who had led the revolt against King Carelinas, had been intended as a temporary means of governing Branion, but the constant threat of the royalists had kept it in power for more than twenty years now.

"There's no reason why you should have heard of him. It is sufficient that I have. What transpired while Stahlgrave was with Quordane?"

"Your guess is as good as mine. I only know that he remained there quietly for two days. He never went out, as far as I could determine. I made inquiries around the town, however, and found out that Doctor Stahlgrave has visited Quordane several times during the last year."

Walthorne and Shalby exchanged significant looks. "Hmm," Walthorne said, "interesting. Where did Stahlgrave go next?"

"East, to the border of Cyemal, where he was met by a pair of royalist officers and escorted away." Uncrossing his ankles, Cander sat up straight. He gave a small sniff. "That's all."

Walthorne fixed him with an icy stare. "You did not think to see where he went after he crossed the border?"

"I didn't have a passport for Cyemal. Besides, I had the unpleasant feeling that Stahlgrave was starting to suspect that he was being followed. I stayed on his trail as far as I safely could."

Shalby stirred and said, "There are those who wouldn't have let such trivial concerns hinder them."

"Well and good," Cander said. "Next time, why don't you have one of *them* do your dirty work? Or were you speaking of yourself? Even better. As for me, I find it distressing enough to be forced into service as a spy. Imagine my feelings about being executed as one."

"Coward," Shalby stated. "Worthless."

"*Enough*, Shalby," Walthorne said with a warning glance. After a moment, he looked at Cander, and his face suddenly softened into something that was nearly a smile. It gave Cander a chill. "Very well, Ellis. You've performed . . . adequately."

"Your high praise makes all my efforts worthwhile," Cander said dryly.

Ignoring this, Walthorne let the pleasantness drain slowly from his face. "Where are you bound now?"

"Back to the city. I have business of my own to take care of."

"Good. I'll get in touch with you there if I need you."

"Just don't make it too soon. I still have a play to finish."

"We'll see."

Cander gave Walthorne an even smile. "Perhaps this would be a good time to discuss finances. I'm out of pocket a tidy bit on this trip."

"Yes, yes," Walthorne said impatiently. "Submit your expenses in writing, and I shall see to it."

Still smiling, Cander reached into his breast pocket and brought out a folded sheet of stiff brown paper. "I've already taken the liberty." He passed the paper to the other man, who took it with paltry enthusiasm.

"Well, well," Walthorne said. "I'll review this later, in better light."

"Of course. Is our business complete, then?"

"For now."

Giving a stiff nod, Cander stood as much upright as he was able to in the confined space. He grasped the headerboard over the door, swung himself smoothly out of the coach, and dropped to the ground, taking the impact with flexed knees. After catching the edge of the door, he flung it shut.

As he backed away, he saw Walthorne reach an arm partway out of the window and rap on the darkly glistening side of the coach with the head of his walking stick. The coachman twitched the reins; the coach lurched away, gathered speed, and was soon lost to the darkness.

Kemp lay propped up on the rickety old bed in the small room, watching the light of a single candle dance on the grimy wall. He was wearing, along with his own trousers, a shirt that he had borrowed from Quordane while his own was being washed. The borrowed shirt was so big on him that it seemed more like a nightshirt. It was clean, at least, though a bit threadbare and grey at the collar and cuffs.

Quordane. Kemp rolled the name around on his tongue silently. It left a bitter taste. He did not like the idea of having anything to do with the likes of Quordane, but it appeared that he had no choice in the matter. This was a new sensation for him, and he hated it. He'd just have to see what he could do to remedy the situation. First, though, he needed to get a better idea of who this Holis Quordane was, what he was after, and what powers he served.

Kemp lay very still, listening to the sounds of the house, the creaks, the small thumps and bumps, and the distant, unintelligible voices, until little by little they died away. When a long time had passed since the last significant sound, Kemp sat up slowly, swung his bare feet over the edge of the bed, and stood.

He padded over to the door of the bedchamber. Quordane had ordered a servant to lock him in the room for the night, which Kemp thought an almost endearingly naïve gesture.

Kemp listened there at the door for a moment. Hearing nothing, he smiled to himself. Nestled in the palm of his right hand was a slender bit of metal that he'd worked loose from the bedframe and shaped to his own purposes. He inserted this into the lock, then carefully probed and turned it. The lock was an old, simple mechanism; it had never been intended to stand up against a determined professional thief. There was a faint *click*, and Kemp felt the mechanism move in that particular way that he'd trained himself to recognize.

After withdrawing the piece of metal, he slipped it into a trouser pocket. The doorknob turned easily now, as he had known it would. Kemp eased the door toward him, then peered cautiously out into the hall. The darkness was turned a vague mottled grey by the light of his candle.

He moved out into the hall, closing the door behind him. What little light remained came faint and diffuse from the end of the hall, where a narrow stair descended. Walking with a quiet tread, Kemp went toward the light. He set first one foot on the stairs, then the other. The darkness was not much of a handicap to him; he'd been careful to memorize the way when they were bringing him up.

Silently he went down the stair. He paused at the bottom, staying well within the shadows, saw nothing moving, and eased out into the corridor. He followed the hall directly to Quordane's study. After listening at the door for a moment, Kemp used his improvised lock pick to let himself in.

The study was dark, except for the ruddy light given off by a low, guttering fire in the hearth. Kemp got a thin splint of wood from a copper container by the fireplace and stuck the end of it into the coals, until a small flame flowered from it. After cupping the flame in his hand, he used it to light the oil lamp that stood on the desk, then threw the splint into the fire.

As the light from the lamp quivered and grew brighter, Kemp settled into the hard leather chair behind the desk. There was an untidy pile of papers on top of the desk. Kemp shuffled through them, but found nothing of interest—just personal accounts, bills, indecipherable notes, and innocuous letters. He had expected little more.

The desk boasted five drawers, of which one, the central one, was locked. This seemed the most logical place to start. He quickly mastered the lock and opened the drawer.

Lined up along the front of the drawer were seven large medallions, five bronze and two gold. Kemp picked up one of the gold medallions and inspected it. The face of the medallion was etched with an complicated, twisted pattern. There were some peculiar characters inscribed around the rim, which Kemp did not recognize. At first he thought that he had never seen its like before, but there was something strangely familiar about it. *I've seen one of these*, he thought. *But where?*

He considered this for a moment, and suddenly it came to him. Kemp placed the medallion down on the desk, reached up, and pulled off the chain that the priest had given him at his execution. He held the medallion that depended from the chain before him and studied it. It was the *same*, the same pattern, the same unreadable lettering.

Kemp felt a vague chill of apprehension. What could this mean? What did Quordane and a priest working at Tranding Gaol have in common?

After a moment, Kemp drew the chain back over his head. He hesitated, then slipped the gold medallion into his pocket. Whatever it signified, he knew that it was valuable. Something told him that he should hold on to it.

Reaching farther back into the drawer, Kemp came out with several sheets of thin, almost transparent vellum. The sheets were slightly curled up at the edges, as if they'd been rolled up and then straightened again. Kemp spread them before him on the desk and studied them one by one.

The first two sheets seemed to be inscribed with the plans for several floors of a building, with many rooms and corridors, large and small. The building looked familiar, somehow, but try as he might he couldn't quite place it. After a minute or two of trying, he put aside the first two sheets and confronted the last.

It seemed to be a map of the city of Lorum. Straddling both sides of the Lorum River, it was a complicated pattern of twisting streets and small lanes, most of which Kemp knew by name; he had been everywhere in that great city. And yet, it was not quite the same as he remembered. There seemed to be some additional byways marked that did not exist in reality. Impossible, of course . . . But in a world where Stahlgrave could rescue him from the gallows in Lorum and spirit him across more than a dozen leagues in a matter of moments, could he say with certainty that *anything* was impossible?

Kemp noticed that the map bore on its lower right corner the seal of the First Secretary of the Protectorate of Branion, Jey Cordelay. It must have come from the Protectorate's own archives. What could he make of *that*?

Kemp leaned back in his chair and squeezed his eyes shut, thinking. The medallions, the maps: What could they mean? Reality had become far stranger than he once could have imagined. His confidence, which had always been the one great asset that he knew no circumstance could rob from him, was deeply shaken. If he no longer knew the rules of the game, how could he make the right moves when the time came? All he could do was watch and wait, he knew, and hope that his instincts would guide him where knowledge could not.

For now, though, Quordane had him. Kemp could not risk crossing him. Eventually his chance would come, and he would reclaim his freedom. Until then, he would have to resign himself to being Quordane's servant.

It does not do for a servant to be caught searching through his master's things, Kemp decided. After putting the vellum sheets back into their original order, he returned them to the drawer. He considered replacing the medallion he had taken, but decided against it. Even if Quordane noticed that it was missing, he would be unlikely to take any extreme action against him—yet. The baron seemed to need him and his peculiar skills. As long as he appeared willing to do what Quordane wanted, he should be safe enough.

With but this single thought to cheer him, Kemp locked the drawer, blew out the lamp, and left the room at least superficially as he had found it.

* * *

Shortly after returning to his room and locking himself back in, Kemp heard noises outside his window, out in the narrow court wedged between the three wings of the house—voices . . . and horses, it sounded like. Curious, Kemp went to the window and peered out through the rusted iron grate.

A number of men on horseback were below in the courtyard. They were dressed all alike, in full breeches and long-skirted buff coats. Gold-hilted sabers hung at their sides, suspended by red sashes. All were beardless, although several wore long, dashing mustaches. One by one, the men dismounted from their horses and stood holding the reins in the gloom.

Flickering lamplight suddenly pooled within the court. Kemp saw Quordane and several lantern-bearing servants descend the steps from the main entrance. They made their way through the chaos of men and horses, until they reached the far end of the court. Kemp saw then that a large coach had pulled up in front of the gate. As he studied the coach, he caught a few glimpses of more men on horseback crossing back and forth behind it, their faces ghostly white in the moonlight.

What's this? Kemp wondered. *What's going on here?*

The coachman clambered down from his box, put a small step unit down before the coach, and opened the door. After a moment, a man slipped out of the coach and stepped down. He was tall and slender, clad in a close-fitting suit of expensive brocade. He appeared young, at least at this distance, although he had a rather frail and sunken-chested look.

The man stood there, surveying the scene with a lofty gaze, while several of the men in buff coats rushed forward and helped an elegantly attired young woman from the coach. The woman looked pale and tired; she yawned discreetly behind a delicate white hand. Finally, a boy in a brocade suit emerged from the coach and was helped to the ground. He was blond, and appeared to be perhaps three or four years of age.

Quordane dropped to one knee before the tall man, who seemed unimpressed by the gesture. The men exchanged a few words, and Quordane rose stiffly to his feet again. They then started across the courtyard, followed by the woman, the child, and several of the buff-coated men. The party climbed the steps to the main entrance and went into the house.

The coach pulled away. The remaining men began to disperse, leading their horses around the east wing of the house. Kemp heard their voices, boisterous and incomprehensible, echoing in the courtyard.

Kemp left the window. He paced the length of the room, several times, then flopped down onto the bed. *What have I gotten into?* he asked himself. *All those men, cavalry from the looks of them. And that other man. He must be important. Quordane bowed before him. That must mean . . . Kobb's boots, this is big, too bloody big!*

There was nothing for him to do, he knew—nothing but to rest and wait. When they were good and ready, they would pull on his strings, and he would dance. Maybe once he knew what they wanted of him, he would have the tool to cut himself free.

I'm Kemp, he told himself grimly. *I will find a way. Somehow, I will find a way.*

4

Cander set his horse an easy pace back to the Inn of the Three Crows, a mild euphoria expanding within him. Suddenly the gloomy countryside held a somber and mysterious beauty for him, and the cold wind brought a clean refreshment. For the first time in months, he felt free.

It was a relief to be done with Walthorne and his schemes, if only for a short time. He was tired of the intrigues and the secrecy, tired of the alternating periods of danger and tedium, especially since much of the time he was not even sure which was which. It would be good to get back to the reassuring pettiness of his own life, he thought.

After arriving at the Inn of the Three Crows, Cander made sure that his horse was taken care of, then entered the inn. By contrast with the cold night air, the common room seemed uncomfortably warm, even though the fire had burned low. Cander's cheeks burned; an itch worked its way down his spine. Standing just inside the doorway, he unfastened his coat, pulled off his gloves, and tucked his hat under his left arm. He mounted the stair that led up to his room and climbed slowly to the top. There was a short hall there, dimly lit and carpeted with a faded rug. Cander walked by a number of locked doors until he found his room. After taking out his key, he put it in the lock, yawned, and turned it. The key made a complete circle without catching the lock mechanism.

The door was already unlocked. Frowning, Cander withdrew the key and pocketed it. Perhaps the boy, Timony, had left the door open when he'd brought up the bags. Still . . .

Cander drew the pistol from his belt, leveled it before him, and cocked the hammer. It was already loaded with shot, and the pan was filled with powder. Reaching out with his left hand, he quietly unlatched the door, paused a moment, and pushed it open.

A single lamp burned on a small, round table directly opposite the door; moonlight glimmered through dusty windowpanes. A large cherry-wood wardrobe stood beside the door, preventing Cander from seeing much of the room to his right. He found himself holding his breath, and so forced himself to relax a little.

Would Timony have left a lamp burning? It didn't seem likely. He considered a moment. *What to do?* He could back out right now, or . . .

As quietly as possible, he moved into the room, easing past the wardrobe. Someone was there, all right . . . on the bed, ankles crossed. Cander smiled and lowered his pistol. "Alsimae," he said, "how did you get in?"

Alsimae reached over to the nightstand, picking up a long key. "I work here. I had a key. I hope you don't mind that I let myself in. I've come to sample your wine." Her eyes locked on the pistol, and she gave Cander an inquiring look.

"Mind? Not at all. Quite the contrary—What a delightful surprise!" Holding the pistol off to one side, Cander eased the hammer off. He put the gun down on a small, round table, took off his hat, and set it upside down next to the weapon, stuffing his gloves inside the crown.

After opening his bag, Cander got out the bottle of wine and uncorked it. It was really no better than an average vintage, but he didn't suppose that it mattered; the wine itself was nothing more than a polite mutual excuse. Conscious of Alsimae's eyes upon him, Cander moved to the bed. He sat, touching the curve of the woman's hip. "I don't have any glasses," he said.

"No matter." The woman held out a hand and took the bottle from Cander. Giving him a sidelong look, she drank from the bottle, then passed it back to him. "Mmm, good."

Cander sipped from the bottle. The wine, a full-bodied red, really wasn't half bad. He put the bottle down on the table beside the bed. "So," he said, "are your people from around here?"

"Nearby. I come from a town about half a league from here."

"Do you like your work here?"

She shrugged. "It's all right. It got me out of my father's house."

"And that was important to you?"

"I had to get out. My father wanted to marry me off to a local merchant. I suppose it would've been a good match, but he was such a boring man, and so fat!"

Cander smiled.

"They say that you write plays," Alsimae said. "Can you really make a living at that?"

"A poor one."

"Hmm," she said, fingering the lapel of his coat and then smoothing it back against his chest, "you look like you do all right."

"Oh, yes. I do all right," he said, deciding not to burden her with the sordid details of his existence. Cander looked long into Alsimae's face. Part of him appraised her dispassionately, noting the rather too-small nose, the disordered hair, the red stain of wine at the corners of her mouth; yet another part of him saw only the beauty, that glow of life and desire, the pale satin of her skin, the dark eyes that suddenly seemed immeasurably deep. "I'd like to kiss you," he said. "Do you mind?"

"Ah, you are a gentleman . . ."

"I wouldn't count on it," he said, leaning to her and kissing her gently. She started to return the kiss, then abruptly began to laugh—a low, earthy laugh, which Cander found immensely appealing. Her hands went up behind him, and her fingers ruffled the hair at the back of his head. He laughed, too. They paused for a moment, faces still touching, then kissed again, softly at first, but then with increasing abandon.

The remainder of the night passed agreeably. Alsimae proved a vigorous and obliging lover, though at moments oddly reticent. They made love, shared some wine, and made love again. Only then, while Alsimae dozed away the hour or so before dawn, her thigh crossing his, did the ungallant desire to be alone steal upon him, as it sometimes did in this awkward situation. Passion spent, he wished for nothing but a few hours of unencumbered sleep. He was cramped and uncomfortable, yet afraid that if he moved he would disturb Alsimae. Just as he came to the conclusion that he would not sleep at all that night, however, he must have dozed off. For the next thing he knew, the grey light of morning was filtering through the windowpanes, putting its somber cast on the small room.

He was still tired, but his mounting discomfort finally drove him from bed. As he was struggling into his breeches, Alsimae awoke. She yawned and stretched. "Mmm," she said, "it's morning."

"Yes," Cander said.

She sat up suddenly, holding the sheet to her breast. "Gods, I'm late! I have to get to work. Folks'll be wanting their breakfast served."

Cander sat on the edge of the bed and stroked Alsimae's bare shoulder, then kissed it. "Must you?"

Alsimae took his hand in hers and held it to her cheek for a moment. "I wish I didn't have to."

"I want to give you something, something to remember me by."

"Will you be leaving, then? So soon?"

"I must."

Cander worked a plain silver ring from the smallest finger of his left hand. Holding it out to Alsimae, he said, "Here, please take this, as a token of my regard."

The woman hesitated. "Oh, I couldn't."

"Take it. It is little enough, the merest bauble."

"Well . . ." With diffident avarice, Alsimae took the ring, slipped it on her finger, and admired it with shining eyes for a long moment. "It's very nice," she said. She put her arms around Cander and hugged him. "Thank you."

"I'm just glad that you like it."

After Alsimae had dressed and gone, Cander washed gingerly with cold water from the pitcher on the nightstand. He ran his moist hands over the biceps and chest, taking a definite pleasure in the feel of his own hard sinews and smooth skin. It felt particularly good to wear the flesh that morning, to be a man, to be Cander Ellis. He went to his open bag, got out a corked vial, and daubed himself lightly with an expensive cologne he'd had specially formulated for him at an exclusive shop in Liln. He put on a fresh shirt, then dug around in his bags until he found a small, leather-wrapped box. Inside the box were six silver rings identical to the one he had given Alsimae. He selected one, slipped it on his finger, and returned the box to the bag.

When he had finished dressing, Cander packed his bag and ventured downstairs for a good breakfast.

The footsteps stopped outside the door. There was the sound of a key being turned in the lock. Kemp, sprawled on the bed, started to rise, to face whoever came in, but then thought better of it. *Best not to look too eager,* he thought. He settled back and tried to look at ease.

In simple truth, though, he *was* eager—eager for something

to happen, almost anything. He'd spent the day alternating between boredom and anxiety. Twice, a servant had brought him a meal on a tray, but apart from those brief interruptions he had been left to himself. His room was barren of amusements; there was nothing to do but rest and listen to distant muttering of voices, the creaking of floorboards, the occasional dull clunk of a door being shut. He was starting to feel the strain of his confinement. His accommodations were more comfortable than they had been of late, but he was no less a prisoner now than when he had lodged in Tranding Gaol.

The door opened. Quordane stood there, a leather portfolio clamped under his left arm. He gave Kemp a cold look and said, "Come, it is time for you to meet someone."

Kemp didn't move. "Who?"

"Lalerin Saphrinas, who is the rightful King of Branion."

Kemp blinked, then nodded. He was not really surprised. He had begun to suspect that the royalists must be involved in the events that had overtaken him. He remembered the tall man who had arrived in the night. Was that Lalerin? Almost certainly. "There are those who would dispute that," he said. "Most notably those who rule over Branion now."

Quordane dismissed this with a sharp jerk of his head. "Usurpers, all of them. Traitors. One day they will swing at the end of a rope."

Kemp grimaced, and the other man said, "Ah, but the rope may yet be a sensitive subject for you."

"If you'd ever felt one about your neck, it would be a sensitive subject for you, too."

"No doubt, no doubt," Quordane said airily. "I might point out that the present rulers of Branion very nearly presided over your own execution."

"Yes, that's true." He paused thoughtfully. "What does Lalerin want from me?"

"I already told you. He wants you to steal something for him."

Kemp frowned. "What?"

"The king will tell you that himself."

"I don't like being kept in the dark."

Shrugging, Quordane said, "You could be dead now. I daresay that you would like that even less."

"I daresay."

"Oh, cheer *up*, Kemp!" Quordane exclaimed heartily. "You are to be given a rare opportunity to make a difference in this world, to do something that matters. And if you succeed, you will be well rewarded for your efforts. Have a little faith!"

Kemp gave a cynical sniff. Faith had never been his strong suit, and Quordane didn't strike him as being particularly trustworthy. The stories he'd heard concerning Lalerin didn't inspire any great confidence, either. Still, what else could he do?

Best to just play along, he thought. *For now.*

"Come along, Kemp. All of your questions will be answered in due course. It does not do to keep a king waiting."

Kemp rose, straightened his garments as best he could, and smoothed his hair back with one hand. "After you, then."

Quordane led him from the room and down the gloomy hall, broken by a wide, open doorway. Kemp paused a moment to scan the large, comfortably appointed room. There were seven or eight people gathered there, two of them women, the rest men who wore the long buff-colored coats and red sashes that seemed to be the royalist uniform. The two women were elaborately coifed and dressed in satin gowns sewn with numerous little bows and frills, tight bodices cut straight across the bosom. They were young and undeniably attractive, but were arrayed in so alien a fashion that Kemp found himself regarding them as exquisite artifacts. Everyone seemed slightly drunk. They laughed too loudly, and their eyes had a pinched, unfocused look.

Quordane led Kemp on, past the door and up the long, shadowy stairway that led to the top floor of the house. As they reached the first landing, Kemp heard a woman's voice, shrill and insistent, and a man's booming laughter. There was a muffled *thump*, the sound of breaking glass. Quordane took no notice, continuing up the next flight of stairs at the same sober pace. Apparently he was not curious about the damage that was being done to his house.

They came to the top of the stairs. There, fat tapers burned brightly in ornate silver sconces and thick, colorfully patterned rugs cushioned the foot. The walls were clad in a wainscoting of dark, reddish wood. At the end of the hall were a pair of double doors, in front of which stood a pair of buff-coated men, armed with both swords and pistols.

As they started down the hall, a door on the left suddenly burst open. A young woman, wild-eyed and disheveled, staggered out into the hall and propelled herself toward the stairs, pushing her way between Kemp and the wall. She appeared to be a household maid, clad in a simple skirt and a white blouse, which was torn and askew.

An instant later, a red-faced older man came out of the doorway, laughing. He was clad only in boots, breeches, and an open shirt. "Come back here, m'lovely. You won't get away from *me* so easily. Ha!"

Kemp knew at once what was happening, and he didn't like it. He had seen too much of the world to be truly outraged, but there was something about the girl's predicament that touched a sore spot in him just then. He was tired of watching the powerful use the less fortunate for their own pleasure.

So, as the older man attempted to pursue the girl past Kemp and Quordane, Kemp contrived to thrust a shoulder to that side, blocking the way. The man stopped and started around the other side. Kemp took half a step in front of him. Outraged, the man glared at Kemp, eyes narrowed. *"Out of my way,"* he said angrily.

Kemp could tell that he had taken this about as far as he safely could. He gave the man an ingenuous smile. "*So* sorry. Clumsy of me." He stepped aside, slowly.

The man looked like he wanted to say something, but he merely pursed his lips and pushed past Kemp. By this time, the young woman was already downstairs. Kemp could hear her receding footsteps on the floor below. *I've done what I can, girl,* he thought. *Make the most of it.*

Quordane grabbed Kemp roughly by the upper arm and pulled. There was something ugly lurking in the depths of his eyes. "You should not have interfered. That was the Duke Arniat. Trifle with him at your peril. He is a powerful man."

And a lecher and a bully, Kemp supplied silently.

Quordane released him. They continued toward the double doors. The two men who stood guard watched impassively as they approached. As one, the men turned to the doors, grasped the polished brass handles, and pushed. The doors opened, and Kemp and Quordane passed into the large, brightly lit room beyond.

Kemp blinked rather stupidly at his surroundings. The chamber was paneled in rich, glossy wood. Its furnishings were expensive, though not opulent. The carpet was striped maroon and grey.

A tall man stood at the far end of the chamber. Kemp recognized him as the one who had arrived in the coach during the night. Attired in a close-fitting suit of pale lavender satin, the man had a thin face, a long nose, and narrow, colorless lips. Most would have considered him handsome, though on close inspection he appeared drawn and dried out to Kemp.

Near the window, in an intricately carved and gilded chair, a woman busied herself with a young boy, combing his fair hair with her fingers and straightening garments that were far too adult for him. She was slender, with a pleasant face, finely textured pink skin, and straight chestnut hair that was fixed in manner that seemed too plain for her silken attire.

The tall man peered distractedly at Kemp, squinting in a manner that suggested that his eyes were perhaps a little weak. "Jerod Kemp, I believe," he said in an arid voice. "I've heard much about you. I am Lalerin."

Kemp halted uncertainly before him. There was something about Lalerin that unnerved him, a remote quality that made him seem so far removed from the normal run of men that he didn't seem quite human. Perhaps he was just intimidated . . . which, of course, was ridiculous. Lalerin was king of nothing. His father had been deposed more than twenty years ago, and Lalerin himself had never ruled more than a small band of exiles. And yet . . .

Kemp was not sure how he should behave; he had never met with royalty before. He'd feel foolish dropping to his knees, or anything similarly excessive, but some gesture seemed to be required, if for no other reason than that it wouldn't hurt to humor Lalerin's pretensions. Kemp finally bowed stiffly from the waist. "Your Majesty," he said, with no perceptible irony.

Lalerin accepted this homage with an abstract nod of his head. "You are to do us a great service," he said.

"As to that, your Majesty, I cannot say. I'm not all that clear on what you want from me."

"Well, we will have to rectify that situation, won't we? My lord Quordane, did you bring the charts?"

"I did indeed, Majesty."

"Lay them out on the table over there." Lalerin gestured vaguely in the direction of a long, marble-topped table that stood against one wall. Quordane nodded. After going to the table, he opened his portfolio and removed several vellum sheets, which he spread carefully on the marble surface. Kemp recognized them immediately; they were the same charts that he had uncovered in Quordane's desk.

While Quordane busied himself at the table, Lalerin went to woman and child. "My dear," he said, "why don't you take

Gar down to your room? We shall be discussing dry matters of state for some time. You would be quite bored."

"As you wish," the woman said, her voice lacking emotion.

Lalerin glanced briefly at Kemp. "Our wife, Ceris of Trel," he explained, "and our son, Prince Garadon." Putting one hand on the boy's shoulder, Lalerin looked down and smiled. There was something in the way that he regarded his son that struck Kemp as oddly chilling. In his eyes was an emotion that did not seem to be normal love or pride. It was more like cold satisfaction.

Kemp bowed. "Madam," he said. The woman smiled, though her gaze was downcast and shy. Saying nothing, she steered the young prince from the room.

As Ceris conducted the boy out the door, Kemp could not help admiring her, for her beauty, for the loving patience she showed her son. He found himself starting to get wistful, and then realized that this was no time to indulge his sentimentality. Putting the woman from his mind, he cleared his throat and said to Lalerin, "I admit that I'm curious to learn what it is that a man of your position could want badly enough for you to go to such extraordinary lengths to get it."

"Mmm, that is a fair question. And, as it happens, probably the central one." Lalerin paused a moment, drawing a chair up to the marble-topped table. "The rebellion that ended our father's life and forced us into exile came quickly, while the Court was in the south, far from the capital. There were many valuable articles that were left behind, still locked away in the Black Tower of Lorum. Some of them have belonged to the kings of Branion for hundreds of years and carry a deep significance to our family. We wish to regain them."

"Where are these articles now?" Kemp asked.

"Where they have been all these years." Lalerin turned to the plan on the table and tapped one finger down in the midst of it. "The Black Tower."

Kemp fixed Lalerin with an incredulous stare. After a moment, he found his voice. "You must be joking. Loot the Black Tower? Me? Do I look that daft? No one has ever succeeded in breaching the Tower."

Lalerin chuckled. "Calm yourself, Kemp. You forget who we are. We can show you ways into and out of the Tower of which the current guardians of the place know nothing. We can teach you all the secrets of the place. See here? The complete plans for the building, every nook and passage detailed for you. What more could an industrious thief want?"

"If it was as easy as that, why did you people go to such lengths to recruit *me*? Why not just send one of your own people?"

Lalerin and Quordane exchanged significant looks. "Mmm," Quordane said, "a good question. As a matter of fact, we did send someone before you. He was . . . unsuccessful."

"This hardly inspires confidence! What makes you think that I can succeed where my predecessor failed?"

"You are a skilled thief, by reputation the best there is at what you do. Why else do you think we risked rescuing you from the gibbet in such an unprecedented manner?"

"If you already sent a man, and he was taken, then they will know all about your secret ways, all about your plans."

Lalerin shook his head. "No, he told them nothing."

"You think not? You forget, I have but recently been a tenant of Tranding Gaol. Let me tell you, they have all sorts of nasty little toys in there: racks, hot irons, and a number of truly *imaginative* devices. If your man was taken, he will have told them anything they wanted to know."

"Doubtlessly true—if he were taken alive. Fortunately for us—and, I think, for him—he was killed before he could tell anyone anything."

Kemp frowned. "How can you be sure of that?"

"We have our contacts inside Branion, inside the Tower, even inside Tranding Gaol."

Kemp considered the matter for a moment. "Even so, they will be on their guard."

"Probably so," Lalerin said airily. "But armed with the information we will give you, I am confident that you will be able to manage."

"I am gratified by your confidence. It seems to me, though, that you're expecting the impossible from me." He fixed Lalerin with an appraising look. "What do *I* get for risking my skin?"

Quordane gave him a hard stare. "Well, for one thing, you get the opportunity to go on living for longer than you otherwise would."

Kemp matched the man's stare. "That's not enough, not nearly."

Lalerin laughed abruptly. "Just so, Kemp, just so. Don't worry. I assure you that if you do this thing for me you'll want for nothing the rest of your life. You have a king's word."

Kemp considered Lalerin carefully. The man showed every appearance of sincerity. Why, then, did Kemp have such strong misgivings? "I really don't think I can help you, your Majesty. This plan strikes me as precarious, at best. I urge you to abandon it."

Lalerin's pleasant manner curdled by almost imperceptible degrees into something cruel and unpleasant. "Kemp, we have gone to a great deal of trouble to extricate you from your previous difficulties and bring you here. The means we were forced to use cannot help but bring unwanted attention to us at a delicate time. The least you can do is hear us out."

Kemp looked slowly from Lalerin to Quordane. It was like looking from one unrelenting stone wall to another. His spirits sagged.

"I'll hear you out," he said gloomily.

5

It was good to be in the city again. After his weeks abroad in the bucolic countryside of Gahant, Cander Ellis savored the crowds, the smells, the tightly packed buildings and winding streets of Lorum. True, the crowds could annoy, the smells offend, the buildings and streets overwhelm and confuse; but here the best of everything could be found, if one but had the wit to find it: booksellers and theaters, good food and congenial taverns, conversations both casual and clever. And, of course, women—women of all ages and estates; cool, pale women in rustling silk; flushed, passionate women in linen and wool; women with slim figures or lush. They were everywhere, a thousand delightful possibilities.

To be sure, Lorum was not everything it once was. That first spring that Cander had spent in Lorum, when he was seventeen, it had seemed a carefree place, expansive, full of energy and verve. He remembered fondly that first giddy season: the plays, the masques, the stately cotillions, the taverns full of song and good fellowship. Everything had seemed possible then. He was never quite sure why it had changed. It seemed almost that a shadow had fallen over the city, so gradually that it was impossible to see that it was happening, except in retrospect. The exuberance and good humor that Cander remembered so well had become strangely muted; there was an indefinable edginess to Lorum now, an apprehension. It was still a great city, but the constant royalist threat and the resulting rigidity of the Protectorate had taken a toll.

While the sun still glimmered below the horizon, Cander left his horse at the stable on the edge of the city where he had hired it. He took a small barge up the wide, placid river that divided the city. He stood on the flat deck and watched the first light of day glimmering on the grey-green waters and the beaten bronze spires old Holyrod Palace, where the kings and queens of Branion had once lived. Then, feet on solid ground again, he trudged along streets that were quickly filling with working folk: carters, smiths, fishmongers, chandlers, and their apprentices.

Cander had lodgings in a small house near the river, in a district known as the Tareval. It was by no means a fashionable address, but it was comfortable and cheap, and it suited Cander well enough. He felt an immediate sense of ease as he crossed into the narrow, crooked streets of the Tareval. In a cheerful mood, he strode along, his bag weighing on his shoulder, until he entered the court where his house stood. The buildings here were all alike, modest three-storey houses with grey stone façades, steps leading to a central door. His own building stood at the far end of the court, distinguished from its neighbors by the bronze window boxes projecting from under the second-storey windows. At this time of year the window boxes were empty except for a few sere brown wisps.

Walking down the center of the quiet court, Cander felt in his voluminous coat pocket for his key. Finding it, he held it ready as he ascended the short flight of steps. The common front door was unlocked, as it often was during daylight hours.

Inside was a small, gloomy foyer and steep stairs leading up. Cander climbed the first flight of stairs, then stood listening at the bottom of the second flight. Sometimes particularly persistent creditors would wait outside his door, and he didn't want his homecoming spoiled by an ugly scene. Hearing nothing he padded up the stairs. He was gratified to find the hall empty. After going to the door of his apartment, he turned the key in the lock and let himself in.

"Hello," he called out. "Is anyone here? Vaddick?" Unanswered, his voice echoed back to him. *Curious,* he thought. He had loaned the flat to Vaddick Komin, a player with the Chandler's Company; he knew that Vaddick rarely got up before noon.

Cander closed the door behind him. The apartment was more disorderly now than when he had left it, but it didn't appear to have been actually ransacked. He supposed that he should be grateful for that. You take your chances whenever you lend anything to a player, he knew.

Moving around the room, he looked it over more thoroughly. The flat was only scantily furnished, as he preferred an open and uncluttered space to a room jammed with furniture. Everything was still as he had left it: the pair of matched chairs by the fireplace, the tall cupboard and square table near the window overlooking the river, the old-fashioned standing clerk's desk against the far wall.

Cander noticed that the table supported a single plate covered with cheesecloth. Lifting the cloth, he saw that the plate had a quantity of sliced bread and cheese neatly arranged on it. Cander had the impression that someone had just prepared lunch and wandered away for a moment. Except . . . he could tell that the plate had been there for some time, several days at least. The bread was hard and dried out; the cheese was discolored and curled at the edges, oil beading up from the middle.

Cander pondered this for a moment, then moved on to the bedroom. "Vaddick," he said, "are you here?" There was no answer, and he found the bedroom unoccupied. The bed was tousled and unmade; there was no way Cander could tell when it had been slept in last. After setting his bags down beside the bed, he took off his cloak and hung it on a peg on the wall. He opened his wardrobe and was relieved to find that his clothes were still there.

It was very odd, he thought. From the look of things, Vaddick had left several days ago, at least, and had not returned. Why would Vaddick prepare a meal and not come back to eat it?

Cander hung his hat on the same peg as his cloak, then went back out into the outer room. He opened his cupboard and checked out what Vaddick had left him. No food, of course, except for a few spices and a crock of preserved cabbage. As he had expected, Vaddick had drunk most of his good wine, leaving in its place half a jug of cheap red. Fortunately, he'd had the foresight to hide all of his best wine in a secret place under the floorboards.

After resting for a time before the cold fireplace in his favorite chair, he decided to go out for an early lunch. Cander grabbed his cloak and hat, then locked the door behind him and went downstairs. Once out on the street, he decided that he might as well drop by Chandler's Theater. He was curious to find out how everything had been going in his absence. Besides, he owned a small stake in the Company, so it was possible that he was owed some money, which he could certainly use.

The Chandler's Theater was just on the other side of the river, over the Kantelon Bridge. As he walked, Cander decided to go by the theater first, then have lunch. There was a tavern on the other side of the river that served up good, cheap food, and the walk would give him a chance to work up an appetite.

The Kantelon was one of over a dozen bridges in the city that crossed the Lorum River, and was among the least notable of them. It was a narrow, graceless stone span that crossed the river where it was most shallow and slow. Cander traversed the bridge slowly, enjoying his view of the river and the small boats and barges traveling along it. It was cold enough that the rank smell that often hung over the river in this spot was thankfully absent.

The other bank of the Lorum was less densely built, making it seem more expansive. The streets were wider, though rougher. The buildings were plain and unornamented, for the most part. Many were warehouses, although there were also scattered houses, shops, and taverns. To the southwest, the infamous Black Tower dominated the skyline, rising over every other structure—crude, square-walled, and built of old, dark stone.

Most of the city's remaining theaters were of necessity located here, on this less eminent side of the Lorum, where they were beyond the attention of the increasingly humorless city fathers, who saw mass entertainments of this kind as corrupting, at best, and probably subversive.

The Chandler's Theater was located in an extensive grey stone building, which had once housed a chandlery. It had a narrow, austere colonnade in front, but aside from this one halfhearted attempt at style its façade was plain and unimposing.

As Cander approached the theater, he could see at once that something was wrong. The main doors were chained and padlocked, and a large, official-looking notice was rudely tacked to one of them. Frowning, feeling strangely exposed, Cander moved under the colonnade, close enough to read the notice. It was written in an clear, official hand on heavy stock. It read:

Let all take notice!
These PREMISES are declared CLOSED and SEALED.
Let none enter, under pain of LAW.
By order of the Protectorate of Branion
AND the Great Council of Lorum.

The notice carried two scrawled, officious signatures at the bottom. The seal of Branion was stamped in red on the lower left corner.

Cander read the notice twice, disbelieving. He felt an oppressive chill settle over him. *What could this mean? Why in the world would the Protectorate close the Chandler's?*

He felt suddenly vulnerable. He glanced quickly about him, but there was no one nearby. After a moment of indecision, he went to the side door, which was down a gloomy alley. The door was weathered and discolored, with a small diamond-shape window in the middle of it. Cander rapped uncertainly on the door. When there was no answer, Cander perched himself on his toes and peered through the dusty window. He saw the cramped, cluttered office belonging to the company manager, Lor Brunnage. It appeared deserted.

What had happened? Cander's association with Protector Walthorne had always insured that the Chandler's remained free of official interference. What could have changed this? Did Walthorne think that he was no longer of any value to him? No. If that was true, Cander was confident that he would now be dead or imprisoned. He knew too much to be allowed his freedom if he wasn't still useful.

He considered charging off to find Walthorne at once, but quickly dismissed the idea. Before he tried to play that kind of game with a man like Walthorne, he better have *some* idea of what was going on.

The tavern where he'd been planning to have lunch was not far from the Chandler's. He knew that many of the Company frequented the place. Someone there would surely know what had happened. Cander set off briskly toward the tavern, taking care not to appeared overly concerned, just in case he was being watched. Those few people that he saw in the streets seemed to be ordinary folk going about ordinary business. He knew, though, that an agent of the Protectorate would look and act just so.

After a few minutes, Cander came to the tavern. It stood on a bleak corner, where a cold wind came gusting off the river. It was a small structure, its green paint almost entirely weathered away, tiny windows set very high, most of them covered.

Approaching the tavern door, Cander glanced discreetly around him. Seeing no one, he pushed his way into the tavern. The light within was dim, so that the shaft of brightness that came in behind him from the doorway made the far corners of the interior seem black and formless. When the door shut behind him, it took a few moments for his eyes to adjust to the lack of light. As they did, he saw that the tavern was unusually empty. A few working men sat dourly eating or drinking beer at some of the tables, but none of the Chandler's players was present. This was odd, because he knew that some of them practically *lived* here. Indeed, he recalled, several members of the Company did in fact live here, in some of the upstairs rooms.

Cander noticed the landlord of the place, a man called Palter, standing beneath a high counter of scarred, murky-colored wood. Cander drew himself up to the counter, gave a subtle gesture to the man, and said quietly, "A moment, Palter. I need to talk to you."

Focusing on Cander, Palter looked surprised and perhaps a little fearful. He was a large, sloppy-looking old man. He wore stained, patched breeches. A white shirt and a canvas apron were stretched tight across his big, soft chest. *"You,"* he stated without pleasure. "What are you doing here? I thought they'd rounded you all up."

"Rounded up? Why?"

Palter licked his lips nervously. "I shouldn't be talking to you."

Reaching into his pocket, Cander came out with a big silver coin. He slapped it down on the counter. "Talk to me, Palter."

The man hesitated. "Money won't do me no good in prison."

Cander pushed the coin across the counter toward the man. "Just tell me what's happened. Why is the Chandler's closed? What's become of the Company? Tell me, and then I'll go."

The man put his fingers on the coin and pulled it toward him. He spoke in a low, hoarse voice: *"Treason.* That's what they said. Your people were putting on a treasonous play. They shut down the Chandler's, arrested everyone they could find. Them that didn't get arrested made themselves scarce pretty quick."

"Treason?" Cander said, confused. "What play?"

"I don't know. That one about that old king Gallion."

"You mean *The Demon Scepter*?"

Palter nodded emphatically. "Aye, that be the name, all right."

"You must be joking."

"No."

"Well, *someone* must be joking, that's certain," Cander muttered. He knew the play well. It was a hoary old chestnut about the overthrow of the Trelhanian tyrant Gallion. There was nothing treasonous about it; it wasn't even a very good play.

"One last thing," Cander said, after a moment's pause. "When did all this happen?"

Palter appeared to consider the question, adding the days up in his mind. "Must have been a fortnight ago, or a little better."

A fortnight ago . . . If that was true, then Walthorne must have known all about it the last time they met. Cander felt a quickening anger.

"Well," he said, "I'd better try to straighten all this out somehow. Thanks, Palter." He turned and started toward the door.

The other man's low-pitched voice followed him. "If you'll take my advice, Cander, you'll stay well out of it. Lie low for a while, until things cool off a bit."

Palter gave sound advice, Cander thought. Unfortunately, he had no intention of taking it.

In his mind's eye, Cander saw himself forcing his way into Walthorne's office, pounding on the desk, and demanding immediate answers to all of his questions. He would have enjoyed that. It was a shame that life just didn't work that way. In the first place, he would not get past the anteroom if he tried to approach Walthorne directly. They weren't supposed to know each other; Walthorne would never acknowledge him in public. And, in the second place, Cander knew well that he had to be careful with a man like Walthorne, who was fully capable of having him thrown into someplace exceedingly dark and nasty if ever he became more trouble than he was worth. He wouldn't be able to do anyone much good rotting in Tranding Gaol.

He had little choice but to follow the regular procedure for contacting Walthorne, slow and tedious as it was. He went to a small copyist's shop on Bank Street, around the corner from the huge granite-grey building that housed Walthorne's offices, and placed a sheet of paper before the old man behind the counter. The sheet was folded and sealed; Cander had inscribed the outside flap with a special mark. The old man looked down at the sheet, studied the mark, then looked up at Cander with an expression of casual appraisal. "Can I help you?" he asked.

"I'd like to have this copied—in *official* script, if you please."

The man nodded. His inkstained fingers caught the folded sheet of paper and swept it under the counter. "Very good, sir. There'll be a slight wait. Perhaps you'd care to come back later."

"Certainly. How long will it take? It is rather important."

"Perhaps an hour."

Leaving the shop, Cander bought a meat pastry from a street vendor and munched it as he browsed through the book stalls near Selden Square. With a curious mixture of pleasure and indignation, he found that a minor printer had published the text of his last play, *The Tragical History of Emund Goodnight*, and had placed copies in most of the stalls. On the one hand, it was good to see his play achieve some kind of life off of the stage, long after the last player had stripped off his wig and washed the text out of his head with cheap beer. On the other hand, the play had been published without his knowledge or consent, and it irritated him to know that someone was making money off of his hard work, while paying him nothing. Paging through the flimsy chapbook, he also found that it had been published with numerous errors and infelicities of language that had not been present in the original. It seemed to him that it must have been imperfectly reconstructed from someone's memory, perhaps one of the players'. This was a common occurrence, he knew.

He thought, *Perhaps I can make a deal with a printer for my next play, provide a full copy in exchange for a piece of the profits. Probably won't see much money, but at least I can keep it from getting mangled.*

My next play . . . It suddenly occurred to him that unless he cleared up the mess with the Chandler's, there might not *be* a next play. Checking his pocket watch, he found that most of the hour had elapsed. Walking at a moderate pace, he returned to the copyist's.

The old man looked up as he entered the shop. "Hello, sir," he said. "Bad news. I haven't been able to fill your order yet."

"Do you know when?"

"Check back tomorrow, around ten."

"I'll be here."

Sunk in pensive anxiety, Cander went back to his apartment. Either Walthorne had not been in his office, or he had been unable or unwilling to see him. This did not necessarily mean anything; Walthorne did not exactly come whenever he beckoned. Sometimes it took days to get in to see him. Now, though, he had an evening to live with troubling questions for which he had no answers. Did Walthorne think that he had outlived his usefulness? If not, why had Walthorne permitted the Chandler's to be shut down? They had a deal, after all: He worked for Walthorne, using his position and his skills to gain information that would otherwise be difficult to get; in return, the Protectorate left the Chandler's alone. At a time when the Protectorate had shown itself to be increasingly willing to suppress writers and performers, the Chandler's—and Cander—had been left free to thrive. But now, something had changed.

Cander spent a restless night alone in his apartment. He could not sleep, try though he might; and when he tried to write, standing at his old clerk's desk in the dark hours of the morning, no words would come. He could not escape the feeling that the act of writing may have become pointless.

The next morning, at the appointed hour, he made his way again to the copyist's shop. The old man behind the counter looked up when he came in, and said, "Your order has come in. Perhaps you'd care to step into the back room and look it over."

"Yes." Equal measures of relief and trepidation in his heart, Cander stepped around behind the counter, went behind a dingy curtain and into a short corridor crowded with shelves stacked high with papers. At the other end of the corridor, there was a narrow, battered door. Opening it, Cander let himself into the room beyond. This room always came as something of a surprise to him, no matter how often he came here. Unlike the rest of the shop, it was of generous dimensions. It was also clean and well appointed, with an expensive rug on the floor, and a divan and several solidly made chairs stationed about the walls. At the far end of the room was another door. Cander had always assumed that it masked a secret way into Walthorne's offices, though he had no way of knowing this for certain.

Walthorne was already there. He sat on the divan, leaning forward slightly, his hands cupped over the gold head of his cane. "Ellis," he said with a slight nod of the head. "You have something for me?"

Cander closed the door behind him. "Only questions."

The man sniffed. "Perhaps you have misconstrued the nature of our relationship. I ask the questions, you give the answers. Everything is much tidier if we keep it that way."

"Not this time. I want to know why the Protectorate has shut down the Chandler's."

"Oh, that. We had no other choice, really. They were presenting a subversive drama."

"Subversive? *The Demon Scepter?* Pure nonsense!"

"The play is about a cruel and repressive tyrant who is overthrown by an exiled prince, is it not?"

"Well, yes."

"Don't you see where an awkward parallel might be drawn with the current situation in Branion?"

"I . . . suppose. But, really, you can't blame the Chandler's for presenting a play that happens to contain a few accidental parallels."

"They were far from accidental," Walthorne said stiffly.

"Of course they were. The Chandler's Company isn't political. It never has been."

"No? You weren't here at the time, so perhaps you don't know . . ."

"Suppose you enlighten me."

"Very well, I will. Not only did the Chandler's revive that particular play, which might well be considered suspicious in itself, but they also made certain additions to the text—not too subtly, I might add. These additions made the seditious intent of the play painfully clear to even the dullest observer. In deference to my association with you, I had allowed the play to go on without first assessing its content. Suddenly, though, I started getting reports that virtually every known dissident and malcontent in the city had begun to frequent the Chandler's Theater. Concerned, I sent several men to audit a performance, and they were appalled by what they saw. Before I could draft an order closing the play, however, a mob that had just attended a performance decided to arm themselves with makeshift weapons and converge, several hundred strong, on Holyrod Palace. The Protectorate had to call out the Home Guard to put them down. *That* is why the Chandler's was closed. We had no other choice."

Cander listened with mounting disbelief. It was unlikely that Walthorne would lie about something that could so easily be verified—but, still, it seemed implausible. "But why would they do such a thing? Why would they take such a risk? I can't understand it."

"Nor I, Ellis."

"What's happened to the members of the Company?"

"Some are in custody. The rest have scattered."

"Did any of them take part in the march on Holyrod?"

"Mmm, no. Not that we know of."

"Well, don't you find that odd? I mean, if there are dissidents in the Company, wouldn't you expect that some of them would have taken part?"

Walthorne shrugged. "I really couldn't say."

Cander mused over the matter for a moment. "Something's not right here. I'd like to look into this on my own."

"Fine. I was going to suggest that myself. The Protectorate has an interest in getting to the truth of this thing."

"The manager of the company, Lor Brunnage, was he arrested?"

"What do *you* think?"

"I'd like to talk to him."

"I'll have word left with the warden of Tranding Gaol. There shouldn't be any problem with that."

"Thanks."

Walthorne bent his bloodless lips into a cold smile. "You *will* inform me if you discover anything interesting, of course."

"Of course."

Casually Walthorne pointed the tip of his cane at a leather pouch that sat on the table across the room. "There's something for you on the table. Your expense money, minus a few items that I assume you included only for the amusement value."

Cander picked up the pouch and weighed it in his hand. It was lighter than he had expected, but he refrained from making any complaint. He found that he had mixed emotions about taking it at all; under the circumstances, it felt as if he were taking blood money. This was absurd, he knew, but he could not entirely suppress the feeling.

Besides, he needed Walthorne's goodwill more than money, now more than ever. Slipping the pouch into a coat pocket, he started toward the door, then stopped and turned back to Walthorne.

"One last question," he said. "You knew all about this more than a fortnight ago. Why didn't you tell me?"

"Quite simply, you were doing a job for me. I saw no reason to distract you with extraneous matters."

6

A cold, grey morning dawned, the sun a wan disk climbing into a cheerless overcast sky.

Yawning and dispirited, Kemp stood in the courtyard of Quordane's house. The court was a melancholy space wedged between two wings of the crumbling manse. Weeds grew between the crooked flagstones that paved it. The brown, skeletal remains of a shrub stuck from the mouth of a huge decorative stone urn beside the door; the matching urn that should have stood on the other side was missing. Rusted wrought-iron grates covered all of the first- and second-storey windows. Even if Kemp had felt better, it would have been a depressing sight.

A full hour before dawn, Kemp had been rudely shaken awake and told to get dressed by one of Quordane's servants. As his meeting with Lalerin had kept him up until well after midnight, he was now seriously short of sleep.

He already felt hungry again. Breakfast had been stale bread, jam, and weak jafar. His stay in Tranding Gaol had left him with an appetite that such a paltry meal could not begin to satisfy.

Baron Quordane came out of the house, swathed in a brown tweed greatcoat, an expensive hat with an upswept brim perched on his head. The portly man paused on the top step, sipping something from a silvered hunting cup.

"Quordane," Kemp said, his voice coming out husky and barely audible. He cleared his throat, then called the name again. The man looked in his direction with scant interest.

Kemp moved forward, finding himself limping for some reason. He stopped at the bottom step and said, "What's going on here, Quordane? Why are we up at this impossible hour?"

Quordane looked down at Kemp, moving only his eyes. His

head kept its haughty upward tilt. "We're leaving. No time to waste, eh? You're going home, Kemp."

Quordane descended the steps slowly. He paused momentarily to scan Kemp's face. "You look terrible. A restless night, hmm? Here—" He held out the silvered cup. "—drink this. You may need it."

Kemp took the cup as the other man brushed by him. He peered suspiciously into it, then sniffed it. It seemed to be a fortified wine.

"Come along," Quordane called without a glance back. Kemp gave him a look of keen resentment. Pride told him that he should empty the cup on the ground. As Quordane was paying him absolutely no attention, however, this seemed a useless gesture. Kemp shrugged and drained what was left in the cup. It was sweet and potent, with a rough undercurrent. Not bad; he wished there was more of it.

Looking around, Kemp saw no place to put the empty cup, so he simply tossed it into the urn beside the door. He hurried to catch up with Quordane.

Outside the courtyard gate, two of Quordane's hirelings each held the reins to a pair of horses. They slouched there in the casual manner of men well used to waiting, conferring in low voices. Quordane gave them a brusque gesture, and they moved apart. One of the men held the bridle of the sleekest, best-appointed horse, a grey gelding with a silver-studded saddle, while Quordane awkwardly fitted a foot to the stirrup, bounced on his other foot several times when the horse shifted, then laboriously hoisted himself up into the saddle. Kemp concealed a smirk.

Quordane gave him a sharp look. "The speckled mare is yours," he said. "You can ride, can't you?"

Smiling, Kemp grasped the mare's reins and mounted smartly, pulling back on the reins to restrain the horse. "I think that I can manage," he said.

"Then let's begin," Quordane said, frowning as his men swiftly mounted the second pair of animals. He nudged the gelding with his boot heels, and they all set off along a narrow, weed-grown road, the low, grassy hills of Gahant rising before them. As the road curved around the baron's estate, Kemp saw that there was a small encampment of royalists out on the windswept fields. The quivering tents and smoky fires looked forlorn and melancholy under the lowering grey sky.

A dozen or more cavalrymen were conducting exercises on a

nearby slope. They had erected several rickety-looking scaffolds, in a staggered line, and had hung a large sack stuffed with straw from each of them. Sabers drawn, the horsemen charged one by one down the hill, taking cuts at each of the sacks as they passed it. Some of the cuts connected with the intended target, some didn't. At the end of the course, each man returned to the top of the slope, where he would drink from a shared bottle, laughing and contesting with his fellows while the next man took his turn. Apparently they had been at this for some time. All of the sacks showed numerous rips and cuts; one was split wide open, the better part of its contents spilled out on the ground. The men went about this exercise with considerable energy and enthusiasm, but with little apparent discipline. They did not much impress Kemp. They struck him as the kind of soldiery who, in order to prove their bravery and élan, would make charge after charge against a strongly fortified enemy position, until they were cut to pieces, though it endangered their cause.

Were *these* the best hope of the royalist cause? If so, Kemp would put his money on the Protectorate, without hesitation.

Kemp continued to be perplexed by the royalists. Here they were, playing their martial games, while their king squandered precious resources to loot a few family heirlooms from the Black Tower. *Ridiculous*. Did they seriously think that they posed any threat to the Protectorate?

And yet there was something about them that frightened Kemp, on an almost instinctive level. He knew well that they could command extraordinary powers when they wished; the realization that those powers could reside in such feckless hands was unsettling. Kemp kept reminding himself that there had to be more going on than was immediately apparent. It could be that the royalists weren't as foolish as they seemed.

The road arced gently to the north, cutting over the barren hills. Eventually it led down into Liln, a dreary port town on the Gulf of Trelhane. Leaving the horses at a red brick stable near the center of town, Kemp and Quordane went on foot to the docks, followed by the baron's two men. After boarding a waiting ship, a modest two-master, they set sail with the tide.

The Gulf of Trelhane was grey and unsettled, and the small ship rode uneasily over its surging surface, brisk wind swelling the sails. This was a new and awesome experience for Kemp. He had never sailed out on the open waters before, though he remembered that once, as a child, he had wanted to be a sailor, before his life had taken another direction. Fascinated, he gazed out over the surging, turbulent waters for a very long time, while the sharp, wet winds beat all sensation from his face. It was not hard for him to believe that it went on forever, that all the land and all the problems of those who dwelt upon the land had simply vanished. He listened to the shouts and songs of the sailors, and he half envied them their simple lives and their mutual brotherhood.

At last, the sun declined below the horizon, the light of day faded from the overcast sky, and a blackness more profound than any he had known before sealed the ship into a forsaken solitude.

Kemp spent that night in a small berth belowdeck, on a thin straw pad, a thin blanket covering him. It was not the best sleep of his life. The ship creaked and groaned, men snored, and the sea outside slapped languidly against the hull. The smells of hemp, of cooking, and of men living together at close quarters mingled into an almost overwhelming presence. The constant motion made Kemp queasy. When finally he opened his eyes and saw dawn's light spilling down the stairs, he was relieved.

Eventually Kemp went up on deck. It was a gloomy morning. The sun could not be seen, thought it lit the overcast sky with a painful glare. Kemp saw that land lay off to the east, a long, barren strip made gloomy and indistinct by a low mist. As the morning progressed, the land grew nearer and more prominent, until the details of the shore became obvious, twisted cypress growing along the tops of the cliffs, a tiny fishing village, all weathered wood and grey stone, gnarled outcroppings of sea-ravaged rock.

At about this time, Quordane came up on deck, looking irritatingly smug and well rested. He had spent the night in the captain's cabin. He paused to exchange a few words with a tall, blue-clad man—either the captain or the first mate, Kemp supposed—then strolled over to stand beside Kemp.

"You look dreadful," the baron commented. "You really should try to get some rest. You'll need to be on the top of your form when we get to Lorum."

"And when will that be?"

"Not long. See there? That's the lighthouse that marks the entrance to Lorum Bay."

Following Quordane's gaze, Kemp saw a narrow tower rising from the center of a small island. It was three storeys tall, the top storey boasting a number of large windows. No light showed from the windows now, of course; it was broad daylight, and the fog was thin and gauzy. Gradually the tower drifted astern, as the ship entered the mouth of the bay.

Kemp and Quordane wandered the deck for a while, careful to stay out of the way of the crew, who appeared frantically busy. They stopped to stand near the prow of the ship. Ahead, Kemp could see a shore crowded with tall buildings.

"Not long now," Quordane commented at length.

Kemp grunted. His misgivings were becoming acute. Certainly there was a bit of comfort in knowing that he was coming to a place he knew well, territory that was his. He could not forget, however, that his last memories of that place involved imprisonment and a hanging. What if the wrong person should recognize him? He might quickly find himself back in the same awkward straits.

That he was being forced to undertake a difficult and dangerous task, with questionable allies, only served to heighten his natural apprehension.

The distant jumble of buildings slowly resolved itself into a city, and then into that particular city, Lorum. Kemp recognized the cruel, archaic thrust of the Black Tower and the fanciful minarets of the old palace. The harbor grew before them, the docks and warehouses, the ships and long boats, the stone quays and the austere colonnade of the Customs House, ever-watchful and untrusting.

The ship rode the grey-green bay waters into the harbor, where it joined other merchant vessels and a sleek naval ship. The sails were lowered, and the anchor was dropped.

Staring at the grim façade of the Customs House, Kemp drew a deep breath, balled his hands up at his sides, clenched them, relaxed, and clenched again.

He was home.

Cander had known his share of menace in his life. He had frequently walked the darkened back streets of the worst parts of town, places where you could never know what might be stalking you from behind, or what might wait just ahead. He'd spent long nights in rough, sinister taverns, where arguments were settled with fists or knives. In Walthorne's service, he had often found himself in tricky and dangerous situations, where death could come from any failure of judgment or nerve. And yet, in all of his years, nothing had ever filled him with such crawling dread as descending into the depths of Tranding Gaol and hearing its massive doors clang shut behind him. Was there anywhere in Branion that was more generally feared than Tranding Gaol?

Holding a brass box lantern out before him, the guard led Cander down a short flight of stone steps and along a long, dismal corridor lined with locked iron-bound doors. Several echoing, disembodied voices babbled incomprehensibly. Somewhere, someone was sobbing, loudly and without cease. The air had a peculiar greasy dampness to it; it made Cander want to go take a bath. The smell of the place was indescribably foul.

At last, the guard paused in front of one of the cell doors. After consulting a scrap of paper held in his palm, he wrestled with a key on a large ring, turned it in the lock, and pushed the door open. "This be the one, sir," he said. "I'll be nearby when you need me. Give a shout." He paused a moment, then handed the small lantern to Cander. "Here. You'd better take this."

Cander nodded. "Thanks." With deep trepidation, he entered the cramped cell. He heard the door shut with a heavy thud behind him and he cringed inwardly.

Holding the lantern out before him, Cander let the light play over the four slimy walls of the small cell. There was a low bunk set against the far wall, covered with a thin straw mattress and a single filthy blanket. Lor Brunnage sat there, blinking at the light with a dazed and dejected expression. His cheeks were sunken, and his grizzled hair was disordered. He had lost a good deal of weight, so that his soiled garments hung loosely on his frame. "What—what is it?" he asked in a voice that was cracked and pitched too high.

"It's me, Lor—Cander."

"Cander!" he exclaimed. "So, they got you, too . . ."

"No, Lor. They didn't get me. I'm here to see you."

The man mulled this over for a moment, his doubt readily apparent. His stay in Tranding Gaol seemed to have stripped away his inner restraints, making his emotions poignantly transparent in a way that they had never been before. "But how did you get in to see me? My own wife—" He broke off and shook his head.

"Let's just say that I had to call in an old debt."

"That must have been quite some debt. They haven't let anyone in to see me until now. Have you not heard? I am a dangerous man, a traitor, a revolutionary!" Lor gamely assayed a chuckle, but it turned almost instantly into a dry, hacking cough. As the cough subsided, he rose slowly from the bunk and lurched forward to embrace Cander. "But it is good to see you. At least I know that I'm not completely forsaken, eh?"

Lor's embrace was shockingly feeble, and his smell was quite dreadful. Cander pressed his lips into a hard line, afraid that his own emotions would become transparent, his pity and, yes, his disgust. "No, you are not forsaken, Lor. Don't worry, you still have many friends."

Lor drew back from Cander, and his gaze regained some of its former intelligence. "Can you get me out of here, Cander?"

"I'm working on it, Lor. You're in a pretty deep hole right now, but not so deep that you can't be hauled out again. I'll need you to tell me exactly what happened, and then we'll see what can be done." He held out the canvas sack he had brought with him. "First, though, here are some things that I bribed the guard to let me bring you. It isn't much. There's a flask of wine, some bread, cheese, and fruit."

Lor's eyes glistened with sudden tears. *"Oh!"* he said. "You *are* a good fellow, Cander. The food in this place is . . . indescribable."

"Yes, I can imagine," Cander said gently. "So sit, eat. Then you can tell me all about how you found your way into this unpleasantness."

Nodding, Lor lowered himself back down onto the bunk. Cander looked around for a place where he could put the lantern. Not finding any better place, he set it down on the floor of the cell. This caused the light to show at a weird angle that made the cell and its contents appear even more ominous, but he was tired of holding the thing. When he looked back at Lor, he found that the other man had already dug into the bag of provisions; he was gnawing on a heel of bread and washing it down with sips from the leather wine flask.

"I still can't understand it," Lor said. "We didn't do anything wrong, really. Nothing I can think of. We put on a play, is all."

"*The Demon Scepter*, yes?"

"Well, yes."

"I understand that certain critical alterations were made to the script. True?"

"Yes . . . but they seemed harmless enough."

"Apparently it was strong enough stuff that it inspired a large group of malcontents to riot."

Lor stopped chewing for a moment. He looked genuinely confused. "I know, I know. And I just can't fathom *why*. For the life of me, I can't. It was just a *play*. Who could have guessed?"

Who indeed? "All right, why were the changes made to the script? Surely it wasn't done on a whim?"

Lor frowned. "No, it wasn't a whim. The truth is that we were *paid* to present that particular play, with those changes."

Now it was Cander's turn to frown. "Paid, you say? Unusual. Unheard of, I'd almost be tempted to say."

"It happened, though no one seems to want to believe it. No one at the Chandler's had anything to do with it. It was bought and paid for, simple as that." After reaching into the bag, he pulled out a small yellow cheese and meticulously broke it into several large pieces. "Wish I had a knife. I suppose that would have been out of the question, eh?"

"Completely. Now, Lor, who paid to have *The Demon Scepter* performed—and what possible reason could this person have given for wanting to do it?"

Lor nibbled thoughtfully on a piece of the cheese. "Maybe I'd better just tell you exactly what happened. Shortly after you left on your trip, I was approached outside the Chandler's by a young gentleman. He said that he thought *The Demon Scepter* was a neglected masterpiece of the theater and that he wished to mount a new production of it. I was, ah, cool to the idea—for, as we both know, that play is no masterpiece of *anything*, not by any stretch of the imagination. But then he told me that he felt strongly enough about the play that he was willing to underwrite the costs of mounting it. This caught my interest. As you know, much of our audience leaves the city in the summer, to avoid the heat and the yearly plagues. The idea of having all the costs of a production picked up by somebody else had a certain appeal. I could tell by the young man's clothes and his manner, not to mention his fine gold-headed walking stick, that he had money. We retired to my office and there arrived at an agreement. As part of the agreement, he provided the script and had the actor's sides copied out. I noticed that he had made some changes to the piece, but when I questioned him about it, he just said that he had made some improvements to the play. Well, he was paying for the privilege of having the play produced. How could I complain if he wanted to make a few niggling changes? It all seemed harmless enough."

"I see. What name did this man give you?"

"He said that his name was Rensloe Fant. He claimed to be the scion of a rich shipping family."

"Hmm. I've never heard of any prominent shipping family by the name of Fant."

"Nor have I. Then again, I've never had quite the same fascination with wealth that you have."

Cander smiled. "People who control great wealth exert an inherent fascination. Wealth gives them power. They can therefore be most useful—or most dangerous. At the least, it is always a good idea to know who in this world to placate or avoid."

"If you say so, Cander. Me, I've always just taken people as they come."

Cander did not have the heart to point out that the ultimate result of Lor's ingenuous practices had been to land him in a dark, filthy cell deep inside Tranding Gaol. "Is there anything else that you can tell me about this Rensloe Fant? Do you know where he lives, where I might be able to find him?"

"No," Lor said sheepishly, "I don't have any idea of where to find him. He never told anyone where he lived, and he disappeared several days before the Home Guard came and arrested me."

"There must be *something* that you can tell me about him. Think! If I'm going to get you out of here, I need to find this Fant. You have to give me a place to begin."

"I wish there was something more that I could tell you, but there isn't. There just isn't."

"Can you at least describe the man for me?"

"I guess that I could give it a try. He was young—no older than thirty, I'd say. Average height, slender. His hair was blond, worn rather long, in the new fashion. He had a smallish nose and not much chin. He dressed well, if somberly."

Cander shook his head. "Not much to go on there."

"No, I—Wait, I just remembered something else. Maybe it will help. I remember that he wore a small charm on the end of his watch chain, a gold triangle with a rayed sun in the middle. You know, the kind that members of that lodge, the Society of the Dawning Sun, like to affect."

"Hmm. Well, that's *something*, I guess. If he is a practicing member of the Dawning Sun, he might just turn up at the local temple sooner or later."

Lor brightened a little. "Yes, I suppose that he might."

"It's worth a try, anyway. Is there anything else that you can think to tell me?"

"No, nothing comes to mind. So, do you think that you can get me out of here?"

"I can but try, Lor. It might take awhile. I'm afraid that you'll have to hang on here until I can come up with something."

Lor nodded unhappily. "That's easy enough, given that I don't have any other choice in the matter. I'll at least know that you are working for my freedom. I'll have hope. I am grateful."

"Well," Cander said, uncomfortable at the thought of being Lor's one hope. "Well, I suppose that I better get on with it."

"Yes, yes, I suppose that you'd better." Lor rose slowly from the bunk. He gave a dry cough and attempted to smile. "Don't worry about me, Cander. I'll be all right."

"*Of course* you will."

"Oh, I almost forgot to ask—have you finished your new play yet?"

Cander stared at the man. "What difference can that make *now*? The Chandler's is locked up tight, the company is scattered or imprisoned—"

"You *haven't* finished it," he said with a disapproving shake of the head. "I tell you, Cander, I despair of you sometimes. You've real talent—almost as much as you *think* you have—but you waste so much of your time on women, and clothes, and who knows what else!"

Cander grinned. "What can I say, Lor? It doesn't *seem* like I'm wasting my time."

"You should settle down, get married, stay home nights. Find somebody you can love. It would do wonders for you, it would."

"Lor," he somberly, "look at me. Do you really see me living that kind of life? What do *I* know of love?"

"I wonder."

Cander picked up the lantern and called to the guard through the iron grate in the door. He turned back to Lor. "Is there anything else that I can do for you?"

"Perhaps you could check on my wife and see if she needs anything? This must have been hard on her, poor woman."

"I will. Don't worry about Riala, Lor. I'll see to it that she's taken care of while you're here."

"Thanks, Cander," the man said huskily. "I owe you one."

7

Standing outside the grim, lichen-blackened walls of Tranding Gaol, Cander heard the massive, iron-bound doors slam shut behind him. He felt the heady relief flow through him like a strong brandy. Not looking back, he walked away from the place at a brisk pace, as if he were a sneak thief afraid of being caught for his crime. He was several blocks away before he slowed to a more sedate pace.

On Old Market Street, one of the city's main thoroughfares, he flagged down a cab and rode downtown, cocooned by black-lacquered wood and worn leather upholstery. He had the driver drop him near Selden Square, then snaked his way skillfully through the noontime crowds, making sure that he wasn't being followed. When he was certain that he was alone, he went to the Bank Street copyist's shop, wrote out his request for information on Rensloe Fant and the Fant family, and left it with the old man minding the counter. He wasn't wildly optimistic about his chances of finding out anything by this exercise, but it was worth a try.

At a crowded tavern down by the river, Cander took his lunch, a grilled fish and a flask of pale wine. He lingered over his wine for a long time, pushing a few discordant facts around in his head. According to Lor Brunnage, this person, this Rensloe Fant, had commissioned the Chandler's Company to perform *The Demon Scepter*, complete with his alterations. Cander assumed that he must have had some reason for doing this, but what was it? Had he merely wanted to stir up trouble? If so, he had most certainly succeeded. But it seemed to Cander that the man had gone to a lot of trouble and expense, just to whip up an abortive, doomed assault on the Old Palace. Or perhaps matters had gone farther than he had intended . . . Perhaps he'd only wanted to shape public opinion against the Protectorate. If that was the case, however, Rensloe Fant was more naïve than Cander was prepared to believe. The Protectorate had agents everywhere in Lorum, and there was no way that they would allow a clearly treasonous play to go on for long. That much was commonly understood.

Knowing as little as he did about Fant, it was difficult for Cander to assess his motives. The man had been clever enough to play on Lor Brunnage's greed, and yet his likely goals seemed anything but astute. Something about this just didn't add up.

After lunch, Cander took a cab to the westernmost edge of Lorum, to a place where the countryside began to impinge on the city with its verdant spaciousness. Here there were numerous small cottages surrounded by lush gardens, where roses bloomed, and ivy and flowering vines rambled over low stone fences. Cander had the cab pull up in front of a weathered old cottage with a big elm in front. After telling the cabby to wait, he went up to Lor Brunnage's house, knocked at the yellow-painted door, and was met by Lor's wife, Riala.

Riala was a tall, fierce, vigorous-looking woman with a sallow complexion and a head full of disordered straw-colored curls. She stared at Cander with a startled expression. He could understand why she might be surprised to see him on her doorstep; they had never particularly liked each other. "Cander," she said. "What are you— Did you hear what happened?"

"I heard, Riala. I've just come from seeing Lor in Tranding Gaol."

"*Oh*. How—how is he? I mean, is he all right? I mean—"

"He's fine. Really. He, ah, asked that I come to see if you needed anything."

"No, nothing. Except to get Lor out of that awful place."

"Yes. I'm working on that."

The expression on the woman's face told Cander that she was not overly impressed with that. It was no secret that she had always considered him to be a near-useless human being. Riala was a stolid, practical sort of woman; she had little patience for those of a more imaginative and free-spirited nature.

"I have good hopes that he will be released soon," Cander said, feeling a slight flush of embarrassment and resentment come to his face. Suddenly he noticed that another face had appeared in the doorway, peering out from behind Riala. It was a little girl, no older than five, solemn, wide-eyed, with tangled yellow hair. Lor's daughter.

"I hope you're right. They—they won't let me see him. Is there anything that you can do about that?"

"I don't know, Riala. I'll try."

"Good." A pause. "Thank you."

They stood there for a long moment, uncomfortable, avoiding each other's gaze. Eventually Riala said, "Would you like to come in? I could make you a cup of jafar."

"Um, no, thank you. I have a coach waiting, and I should be about my business."

The woman looked vaguely relieved. "Well, all right."

Cander forced a smile, which he hoped would be reassuring. "Let me know if you need anything. And—don't worry."

Riala nodded abstractly. Cander turned to go. As he neared the waiting cab, she called, "I still don't understand what he did that was so *wrong*."

Cander turned back to her. He shrugged helplessly and said, "A misunderstanding, that's all."

It took some trying, but Kemp finally managed to get the jammed window open. It was old, it had been sealed shut with innumerable coats of paint, and the casement was warped and swollen by time and dampness. It required patience and strength to work it open.

The air that wafted in through the opening was dank and cold; it brought with it the vague odors of garbage and stagnant water. Kemp wrinkled his nose as he stuck his head out the window and tried to make out the way down into the darkened alley below. It wasn't much of a drop to the pavement—Kemp's room was only on the second storey—but he could break something if he wasn't careful. As his eyes adjusted to the darkness, he saw that there was a vague suggestion of a ledge several feet below the window, eroded and spotted with pigeon droppings. Near the corner of the building, a bronze drainpipe ran all the way to the ground. Kemp smiled, thinking *Ah, the drainpipe. The thief's best friend, the philanderer's last resort. What would we do without it?* If he wanted to, he could work his way along the ledge, climb down the pipe, and then reverse the process whenever he wished to return.

Kemp stepped away from the window and stood listening at the door to his room for a moment. The rest of the house was silent, so he assumed that everyone else was asleep and therefore would not miss him if he went out for a while. Kemp let his gaze play over the small, shabby room where he had been confined since returning to Lorum, two days before. Was it really such a good idea to leave it now?

The idea of *not* leaving it brought an intolerable surge of restlessness to him, he found. "Oh, why not?" he muttered to himself. Upon returning to the window, he caught hold of the sill and backed out the lower part of his body. He found the ledge below with one foot, then the other. He felt the outer margin of the ledge crumble a little under his weight, and suppressed his apprehension. Keeping a firm grip on the sill, he edged slowly toward the corner of the building, until, finally, the drainpipe was within reach. He caught it with one hand, then carefully moved over, until he could straddle the pipe and clasp it with both hands. From there, using the drainpipe to support himself, it was easy enough to clamber down into the alley below.

Furtively he moved to where the alley opened onto the street, then started walking quickly away from the grim-faced, two-storey building. After he was a block away, he turned the corner and began to relax a little.

The house where he had been held was in the midst of Seephar District, not far from the waterfront. Kemp maintained a small apartment only a few blocks away, one of several that he'd kept for those occasions when he was particularly unpopular with the law in Lorum and needed to lie low. He hoped that it was still as he left it. It should be, he thought; he had paid a year's rent in advance.

It was late, and the streets were nearly deserted. Kemp strode along purposefully, as he always did on darkened streets. After a short while, he found his way to the old, soot-stained building that stood next to the Dog and Wheel Tavern. He went up to the front door, tried it, and found it locked. He did not have his key, but he still had that piece of metal that he had made into a lock pick. The lock was a simple one; he had it open in less than a minute. Then it was down the hall, up a flight of stairs, to the door opposite the landing.

He let himself into the room and was reassured to see that everything appeared just as he had left it. It was a small room, sparely furnished. There was a narrow iron bed, painted brown, a chest of drawers, and a round table bearing a cheap tin oil lamp and a box of matches. There were several pegs on the wall, from which various articles of clothing hung. The lone window was shuttered.

After closing the door behind him, Kemp lighted the lamp

and saw the rising light fluttering on the white plaster walls. With an odd sense of urgency, he stripped off his old, soiled clothes and threw them in a heap on the bed. He went around the room then, selecting fresh clothes: linen and shirt from the chest of drawers; coat, waistcoat, and trousers from the pegs on the wall; and a pair of soft boots from under the bed. He dressed neatly and methodically. It was a relief to be rid of his old clothes, he found. Smelling of his confinement and fear, they had oppressed him more than he had realized. He knew that by changing his clothes he would be making it obvious to Quordane that he had gone out, but he did not care. In fact, the thought rather pleased him. Perhaps it would give Quordane something to think about.

Going to the bed, Kemp searched the rumpled old coat for the gold medallion that he had taken from Quordane's desk—he still wore the bronze one around his neck. He couldn't help thinking of it as good luck, even though he suspected that there might be more ominous implications attached to it. Upon finding the gold medallion, he transferred it to the pocket of the coat he now wore.

There was one more thing. In the top drawer of the chest, there were several objects, hidden under multiple layers of linen. Kemp brought them out and studied them for a moment. The first object was a leather case containing a special set of lock tools. The second was a small purse heavy with coin. He pocketed these, then contemplated the remaining object. It was a dagger, a slender stiletto in a leather sheath. He drew the triangular blade partway from the sheath and regarded it wistfully. He did not much like knives and guns; he always tried to avoid physical conflict, in all its forms, preferring whenever possible to achieve his aims through indirection and guile. Everything was so much tidier that way. Still, there were times when violence was unavoidable, and it seemed that there was a strong likelihood that he was fast approaching one of those times.

Shrugging, Kemp bent over and tucked the sheathed dagger into the top of his boot. He straightened. He felt less vulnerable now; he had his sting.

Kemp glanced about the room once more. There was no reason to tarry any longer. He opened the door and peered out into the hall. Seeing no one, he left the room and shut the door quietly behind him.

Out on the street, he paused. He heard laughter. A pair of disheveled drunkards had come out of the Dog and Wheel. They ambled down the street, singing a popular song in wavering voices.

Kemp thought about it for a moment. *Why not?* he decided. *I can do with a drink.*

After crossing the street, Kemp entered the tavern. It was a poor establishment, old and rundown. The beamed ceiling was low and sagging, and the wooden floor had long since had its finish scuffed away by the passage of innumerable unsteady feet.

Disreputable as it appeared, the small tavern was crowded. Kemp made his way up to the bar, squeezing in between a man in an overlarge tweed coat and a dove-breasted matron in a faded dress. He ordered a pint of ale from the tavernkeep, a harried man in waistcoat and shirt sleeves, and paid him with a two-copper coin.

Sipping at his ale, Kemp stared straight ahead and tried to pick up the conversations going on about him. It had been months since he had been privy to the word on the street; he was curious to learn if there were any new common concerns that he should know about.

Kemp quickly dismissed most of the conversations he heard as inconsequential. He centered his attention on one discussion going on at the end of the bar. There, two middle-age men were talking in loud voices.

"I tell you," the first man was saying, "enjoy yourself while you still can. I hear that the Council is going to start cracking down on the taverns any day now. They're going to make them all close down early in the evening. *And* they're going to put a stiff new tax on beer."

"I don't believe it for a moment. Well, maybe the part about the tax. The Council is always looking for ways to make money from the few pleasures of the simple man. But the rest? Why would they want to close the taverns early?"

"They don't want us getting together too much. We get together, we might start having ideas, see? Can't have that. Besides, they don't want us wasting our time drinking. They want us all home, getting a good night's sleep, so that we can work all the harder, make them that's got money even richer."

"Well, there might be something to that," the other man conceded.

"Might be? *Might* be? I'm *telling* you . . ."

The two wrangled on for a few minutes more, then fell silent. Kemp finished his ale, ordered another, and drank it thoughtfully. Did the first man really know something, he wondered, or was he just blowing off hot air? It was hard to say, but it had an authentic ring. Kemp had spent much of his adult life trying to keep from being boxed in by the powers that ruled Branion. He knew as well as anyone that the liberty of the ordinary man was hardly foremost in the hearts and minds of his rulers.

Kemp felt himself getting light-headed. Evidently his tolerance for drink was not what it once was. After draining his mug, he turned and made his way out of the tavern. Outside, he stood for a moment and let the chill night air rouse him.

Maybe the royalists aren't such a bad lot, after all, he found himself thinking. *Maybe the Protectorate should be overthrown. Could Lalerin be any worse?*

Some lingering core of sobriety within him answered immediately: *Yes. As bad as things are now, Lalerin could make them much, much worse.*

As Kemp made his way back to the Seephar District house, it occurred to him that the man in the inn might just have been a royalist agent, spreading dissension among the people of Lorum. Or, at any rate, he might have been repeating rumors that the royalists had planted elsewhere.

Kemp felt a vague ache working at the front of his skull. It was all too much to keep straight.

Early in the morning, Cander returned to the Bank Street copyist shop. The old clerk took one look at him and pushed a folded and sealed piece of paper across the desk. "There you are, sir," he said with a cold grin.

"Thanks," Cander said, taking the sheet and breaking the seal with his thumbnail. He glanced quickly over the paper. As he had suspected, Walthorne's office did not know anything about Rensloe Fant, or any prominent Fant family. At the bottom of the sheet an addendum had been scrawled in Walthorne's own hand. "Keep me informed," it said.

Scowling, Cander refolded the sheet and held it out to the clerk. "Will you dispose of this for me?"

The man plucked the sheet from his hand. "Certainly, sir. Always glad to oblige. Come again, sir."

After leaving the shop, Cander went to the riverfront tavern that was fast becoming a favorite. He found a table, and ordered a pot of jafar and a pastry. As he ate his breakfast, he tried to decide what to do next.

His only hope of clearing Lor Brunnage and the Chandler's Theater depended on his finding the man who called himself

Rensloe Fant. This was the problem. There was little enough to go on, just a bare description, which could easily fit a hundred other men in Lorum, and the fact that the man wore a charm that the members of the Society of the Dawning Sun customarily affected. It made sense, then, to start there, with the Dawning Sun. This in itself presented difficulties. He did not know that much about the Society. It was a shadowy organization, crossing all national boundaries and social classes. It was notoriously close-mouthed about its goals and its membership, so Cander assumed that he could not just march up to the local temple and demand answers to his question. He supposed that he could always stake out the temple and wait for someone of Rensloe Fant's description to show up, but that might take days or weeks. He did not relish the thought of standing out in the elements for all that time, even if he had the time to spare.

No, there had to be a better way. If only he could talk to someone inside the Society of the Dawning Sun, someone who knew Rensloe Fant . . . The trouble was, members of the Society simply did not talk to the uninitiated about anything that went on within it. Those who did were known to vanish abruptly from all human commerce, which tended to discourage the practice.

Suddenly it occurred to him that there was *one* person he knew who might be both able and willing to tell him what he wanted to know. Talmis Digrippa, the renowned magician, had been a member of the Dawning Sun, until a recent falling out with them. The Society had not moved against *him*, probably because he was too powerful and well connected for them to touch. It might be that Digrippa would be willing to talk.

Cander had known Talmis Digrippa for several years now, having sought him out when he was researching the background for *The Tragical History of Emund Goodnight*, his play about the doomed Trelhanian magician. They'd gotten along well enough and had kept up a friendly relationship, though they were not on intimate terms.

Cander knew where Digrippa lived. So, after breakfast, he flagged down a cab and rode to the southern end of the city, where Digrippa had a big, old, ramshackle wood-framed house, near where the river slowed and spread into a wide delta dotted with low, sandy islands. The house stood at the end of a dusty lane, amid a ruinously overgrown lot.

Standing outside the house, as the small coach trundled away from him down the street, Cander straightened his hat and coat, wishing that he could order his thoughts as easily. Talmis Digrippa was a brilliant man, but he could be impatient and difficult. It was hard to keep up with him sometimes.

Cander went up the front path, which was so crowded by unruly shrubbery that it was nearly impassable. He knocked at a door that was weathered a pale grey. Waiting, he inspected a wavering cobweb that hung from the scalloped eaves over the door.

After a moment, he heard footsteps. He felt himself being scrutinized through the hidden peephole. The door opened, then, and Cander was met by Digrippa's servant, Vedrai, a small, dark-skinned southerner with secretive eyes that betrayed no hint of emotion. Cander asked to see Digrippa, and he was conducted into the small foyer. "Wait here," Vedrai said in his soft voice. "I will see if the master is available."

The servant disappeared into the interior of the house. Cander stood in the gloomy foyer and tried to think of a word to describe Vedrai. He started with "mysterious" and eventually settled on "slippery."

After a few minutes, Vedrai came back. "This way, sir. The master will see you now."

Cander followed the man from the foyer. They went down a long, wainscoted hallway and into a snug little room, white-walled and dominated by a large window that overlooked a wild-looking garden. Near the window was a table and chairs, substantial constructs of yellow oak. At the table, breakfast dishes before them, sat Talmis Digrippa and his sister, Eveline. Digrippa, in a red-and-black checked robe, his long, pale blond hair hanging loose, half rose when Cander came into the room. His thin, elastic lips twisted into a smile that might have been sardonic, or might not; it was difficult to tell with Digrippa.

"Cander," he said, "this is a pleasant surprise. Have you had breakfast yet?"

"Yes."

"Well, sit down with us, anyway. Have a cup of jafar, if nothing else."

"All right, thanks."

Cander took his place at the table. Eveline took up a fresh cup, filled it from an elegant silver pot, and passed it to Cander with a serene, remote smile. She was an attractive, fine-boned woman in her late twenties. The structure of her shoulders and ribs, in particular, seemed unusually delicate, making her bust seem perhaps larger than it actually was. Her complexion was palely luminous, her hair a reddish gold, her features regular and definite. She wore a full skirt, in a dark forest green, and a tight bodice trimmed with gold. Over one eye she wore a velvet patch. Curiously, this did not mar her appearance, to Cander's mind; rather, it added another level of interest and intrigue to a face that otherwise might have been too blandly perfect. She looked at Cander with her uncovered eye, which was grey, brushed back a lock of hair, and said, "Would you like some honey, Cander?"

"Hm?" Cander had at that moment been speculating, rather vividly, on what it might be like to kiss Eveline, to make love to her. Her sudden question brought him up short. "No, thanks. I'll drink it as it is."

The woman gave him such a penetrating look then that Cander felt himself flushing slightly, thinking that she must know what was on his mind. He told himself that this was impossible, but in fact was it? He remembered that Eveline and her brother were from Trelhane, that land of bleak crags and barren wastelands where the old races and their strange ways still lingered. It was widely held that many of the women there retained uncanny powers. Some said that they could even see into a man's mind. Ordinarily Cander considered this superstitious nonsense, but in the presence of Eveline he could almost believe it.

Cander was still endeavoring to make his mind center on something more innocent, when Digrippa said, "So, what brings you here today, Cander?"

Relieved, Cander said, "I need to ask you a few questions."

Digrippa speared a last fragment of sausage with his fork, smeared it around on his plate, and popped it into his mouth. "That doesn't surprise me, somehow. What do you want to know?"

"I believe that you used to belong to the Society of the Dawning Sun?"

"I would have thought that that was common knowledge."

"I was wondering if you could identify a man whom I believe belongs to the Society." Quickly Cander described Rensloe Fant, as Lor Brunnage had described him.

Digrippa frowned, his gaze suddenly cool and piercing. "Why do you want to know?"

Cander took a moment to think about it. He saw no reason to hide anything from Digrippa, except, of course, the fact that he worked for Protector Walthorne. He explained about the closure of the Chandler's and Rensloe Fant's part in it, concluding "Unless I can find this man who called himself Rensloe Fant and get him to reveal why he did what he did, Lor Brunnage and the Chandler's are in serious jeopardy."

"Mmm. I don't think that I can help you."

Cander felt his spirits sag. He had not counted on this. If Digrippa couldn't help him, he did not know what he would do next. "You don't know him?"

"Didn't say that. As a matter of fact, I believe I do know him. I just can't help you."

"Explain, please."

"It's quite simple, actually. When I was initiated into the Society, I swore an oath that I would never reveal its secrets. The identities of the members is one of those secrets."

"But you are no longer a member of the Society."

"That's not exactly true. Once a member of the Society, always a member. I simply do not participate in its business and rituals anymore. And even if I were no longer a member, that wouldn't relieve me of my oath."

Cander took a sip of jafar and set his cup aside. Brushing a few crumbs from the table in front of him, he chose his words carefully. "Talmis, I certainly don't want to make you break an oath, but this *is* rather important."

Still frowning, Digrippa took his watch from his waistcoat pocket and consulted it thoughtfully. "Hm, I must attend to an experiment in my workshop. Care to join me?"

"I suppose."

Eveline said, "I'll come along, too. I'm curious to see what progress you've made."

They rose from the table. Digrippa led the way along a short corridor and down the stairs into the basement. At the bottom was a small space filled with neatly stacked wine casks, a stout oak door at one end. Digrippa took a key from his pocket and unlocked the door. He stood aside and said, "After you."

Eveline went first, then Cander. Digrippa closed the door behind him. "You've been here before, haven't you, Cander?"

Cander nodded, as he took in the room with one sweeping gaze. It was a vast space, encompassing most of the area that was split into separate rooms on the floors above. Large as it was, however, much of it was crowded with numerous long tables of uniform height, each supporting a bewildering array of apparatus: jars and bottles filled with strange substances, oddly shaped glass vessels, some heated by the steady blue flames of small alcohol burners. There were books of all sizes and descriptions, in tall stacks, or alone, some lying open. Complicated hand-drawn charts outlining who-knew-what processes were pinned to the walls. There were many other devices and artifacts about the room, the natures and function of which Cander could not begin to discern. Small barred windows set at ceiling level illuminated the space, though gloomily. "Yes," he said, "once or twice." He was, he found, deeply intimidated by this room, where there was so much that was strange, so much that he did not understand.

"Come," Digrippa said. "I just have to check on something."

He led them down a long aisle between two ranks of tables, past clear vessels of colored vapors and restlessly motive liquids. A rapid succession of smells assaulted Cander, some sweet, others acrid or fetid. In combination, they made him feel dizzy and light-headed.

Digrippa finally halted in front of an intricate and, to Cander, baffling mechanism. It looked a little like a small iron stove that had extraneous bits added to it in a seemingly random fashion: brass tubes and attached flasks of thick blue glass, a strange system of articulated lenses, a bellows that kept puffing away at a steady rate despite an apparent lack of anything to drive it. An iron pipe ran from the egg-shaped body of the thing to the ceiling.

"What do you think?" Digrippa asked.

"Impressive. Words fail. Perhaps if I knew what it was, though . . ."

Digrippa leaned over his extraordinary contrivance, swiveled several of the lenses into place, and peered through them into the belly of the thing. "Aha!" he exclaimed at length. "Caught some!"

"Let's see," Eveline said.

"Here," Digrippa said. He stood away, and the woman took his place. Her long hair obscured her face as she looked into the lens.

"Yes, you've got quite a few of them this time, Talmis. Your best take yet."

Cander stood by patiently through all of this. Either Digrippa would explain, or he wouldn't. Cander was just stubborn enough not to ask.

After a moment, Eveline straightened and stepped aside from

the device. "Take a look, Cander," she said. "You might find it interesting."

"All right, thanks." Putting his hands on his knees, he looked through the thick lenses. There was some distortion at the edges of his vision, he found, but if he concentrated just on the center everything seemed clear. At first, he saw nothing remarkable, just the empty interior of the contrivance, illuminated by a vague reddish light. After a moment, however, he was able to pick out a number of moving specks, tiny even under magnification. They looked rather like gnats.

"Here, this may help you to see," he heard Digrippa say. A hand came over and flipped another lens down. Cander blinked, trying to focus. Then he drew a sharp breath.

Those specks had been suddenly revealed as the most remarkable creatures that Cander had ever seen: vaguely manlike in shape, though hairless and winged and apparently sexless. They had faces that looked like frozen, distorted masks of human emotion: rage, terror, anguish, and disdain. They seemed to be crying out, but Cander heard no sound. "By the gods!" he exclaimed. "What are they?"

"*Ulthants,*" Digrippa said. "They are a minor kind of demon—or perhaps a variety of elemental. No one seems to know for sure. They can be found almost everywhere, particularly over cities, though of course they are too small be seen with the naked eye, and so generally pass unnoticed. It is thought that they feed on human emotion."

Cander considered the fluttering beings for a moment more. "Yes, I can see where one might draw that conclusion." Straightening, he gestured vaguely at the device. "And this thing traps them somehow?"

"Yes. It's quite ingenious, if I do say so myself. See here; this is the burner. It burns off minute amounts of an essential oil derived from a rare herb that is known to attract the *Ulthants*. The scent goes up this long pipe, luring the *Ulthants* down the pipe and into the main chamber, here, where they are kept confined by a system of baffles. When I want to collect them, I just turn this rod here, and the pressure of the bellows forces them into this flask, thusly—" Digrippa turned the rod, and Cander could hear the wind from the bellows hissing within the chamber. Digrippa waited a few moments; then, deftly, he removed the flask from the apparatus and corked it. Holding the flask up before Cander, he said, "And there they are."

"Clever," Cander conceded. "But of what use are they?"

"The *Ulthants* are not without power, though it is almost insignificant in each individual creature. When many of them are marshaled together under the will of a magician, however, it can be formidable."

"How is it, then, that they can be imprisoned by nothing more than wind and baffles?"

Digrippa scowled. "For a supposedly imaginative man, you have an astonishingly restricted mind, Cander. The answer is that the *Ulthants* are mindless creatures, incapable of concerted effort unless it is enforced upon them from the outside."

"Hm," Cander said. "Of course this is all very interesting . . ."

Digrippa gave him a fierce, sardonic smile. "But it is not really the reason you came here, eh?"

"No."

Digrippa twisted the control rod again, and the apparatus resumed its original muted wheezing. Attaching a fresh flask, he said, "Cander, you must understand why it is that I cannot help you. I am not being obstinate merely. I am a magician, and a magician's strength is founded largely on his powers of will and belief. Belief in himself, mainly. He *must* believe that when he says a thing, that thing is true, beyond any doubt. To break an oath, to lie, is therefore a very serious matter, for it undermines his belief, and therefore his power."

Unable to think of any easy refutation of what Digrippa had said, Cander sighed. What could he say? How could he convince the man to do something that was obviously against his own best interests? What argument could possibly suffice? There was nothing. Sincerity was the only stratagem left him, it seemed. He said, "I don't know how to answer you, Talmis. Maybe I should just accept what you say and go away. I would, I really would, if this weren't so important."

Cander paused, not quite sure what he was trying to say. "I'll admit it; I'm at a dead end. I'm willing to listen to any suggestion. So you tell me: What should I do next? There must be *something*, but I'm at a loss to figure out what it is."

Cander saw Digrippa and Eveline studying him, more thoughtfully than he would have expected. After a moment, Eveline put a pale hand on Digrippa's shoulder and whispered something in his ear. The magician tightened his mouth and nodded.

"Someday," Digrippa said, "you're going to owe me a favor. You do realize that, don't you, Cander?"

"Anything."

Digrippa busied himself with the huffing *Ulthant* trap, carefully adjusting and readjusting several of the screws and valves. As he worked, he said casually, "Have you ever been to the Plaza of Fallen Heroes?"

"Mm, yes, of course. It is, uh, rather large, as I remember it."

"An interesting place, I think you'll agree. On the south side of the plaza, there is a building. It houses Balther's Bank. Are you familiar with it?"

Cander thought about it a moment, then nodded.

"A charming edifice, particularly when seen in the proper light—say, the light just before the sun goes down behind Holyrod Palace."

"Well," he said tentatively, "I'll have to give it a look sometime."

"Do so. I think you'll find it most rewarding." Through all of this, Digrippa had seemed to remain mostly absorbed in his work; now he seemed to have dismissed Cander altogether from his consideration.

Cander stood by uncomfortably for a moment. Finally he said, "Thanks, Talmis. I do owe you that favor."

Digrippa glanced up with a distracted expression, looking at Cander as if he had never seen him before. "If you say so, dear fellow." He returned his attention to the *Ulthant* trap.

Eveline smiled and held out her hand to him. "I'll see you out, Cander," she said.

8

Cruel. It was to be a cruel day. Kemp could tell that from the moment one of Quordane's underlings woke him from a pleasant dream and brusquely ordered him to get dressed. Bleary-eyed, still half asleep, Kemp muttered a dark curse and told the man to go away. He tried to resume his dream. It had involved a wanton, dark-eyed woman, with the most delicious mouth . . .

"Get up, Kemp," the man growled, relentless. After seizing the blanket, he tore it from the bed, leaving Kemp exposed and shivering.

"Miserable clod!" Kemp said, writhing. *"Leave me alone."*

The man grinned remorselessly. "Sorry, Kemp. Can't do that. You got to get up and get dressed. The master wants you."

"*I* don't have a master, blockhead."

"Uh-huh. Get up, anyway."

Kemp was wretched enough by now that he would not have been able to go back to sleep in any event. He decided that he might as well embrace the moment, pockmarked and cankerous though it might be. "All right, all right. I'm getting up. See me getting up."

Kemp sat up on the edge of the bed, grabbed his shirt from the chair, and pulled it on. Last night's beer had gone stale in his mouth. It was a cheerless morning, grey and cold. The tiny bit of sky that he could see from one corner of the window was troubled and darkly overcast, with a dingy, polluted cast to it.

"When you're ready, go down to the study," the other man said. "If you're not down in ten minutes, I'll be back to fetch you."

"That won't be necessary. Just get out."

The man gave Kemp a smile that was at least half snarl, the kind of smile that told Kemp that the man would have cheerfully murdered him, were he not under orders to the contrary. "Ten minutes," he said evenly, then left the room, closing the door behind him.

Some fifteen minutes later, Kemp presented himself at the door of the study. Quordane was there, seated in a straight-backed chair, balancing on his lap a cup and saucer glazed with a murky indigo pattern, peering over a chart on the side table. Kemp cleared his throat, and Quordane looked up.

Quordane's eyes tracked the full length of Kemp's body, from head to foot, clearly noting the change of clothes. His gaze turned colder, even, than usual; his mouth tightened with sour disapproval. "You've been out," he stated.

Taking an attitude of jaunty unconcern, Kemp shrugged and said, "I needed some things. My tools—"

"You should have told me. I'd have arranged an escort for you."

"That didn't seem necessary."

The man made an exasperated sound. "Really, Kemp. We went to the trouble of locking you in your room for a reason. If you're going to break out whenever it suits you, what's the point?"

"You've got me."

"You are known in this city, remember? What if you'd been recognized? You might have ended up in Tranding Gaol again. That would have been a fine mess, wouldn't it? How can we protect you when you do these things?"

"I can take care of myself," Kemp said with a grim little smile.

"Oh, yes. Of *course*. You were doing so well for yourself when we intruded into your life."

Angrily Kemp stalked over to the sideboard and poured himself a cup of jafar from the hideously ornate silver service that was set there. He splashed some of the scalding liquid on the back of his left hand. Cursing, he shook it off and kissed the burned place. He was letting his emotions get away from him, he suddenly realized. *Careful,* he thought.

After taking up the cup, Kemp sipped carefully, gazing over the rim at the hateful Quordane.

"No quick answer to that, eh?" Quordane said. "Well . . ."

"I simply have no desire to argue the point with you."

"No, I don't suppose that you do," the baron said mockingly. Then, after a moment's pause, he conceded, "I don't imagine that any great harm has been done. And you won't get a chance for a repeat performance. The day is at hand, Kemp, the day is at hand. Tonight you will finally have the chance to earn your keep."

Kemp put down his cup with a frown of apprehension. "Tonight? It's too soon. I'm not ready. I've not even scouted out the Black Tower yet."

"But we've done it for you," Quordane said with a frosty little smile. "There's nothing to worry about, Kemp. I'll take you through the plans over and over until you'll think that you've spent *days* inside the Black Tower."

"It's not the same," Kemp protested stubbornly.

"It will have to do," the man said firmly. "The thing will be done tonight. It must be. And until it *is* done, I don't intend leaving you alone for a moment. It appears that I must save you from your own impetuousness."

Quordane turned away from Kemp and back to the charts beside him. He fingered them pensively. "Draw up a chair, Kemp," he said. "We might as well get started."

As the sun began its decline over the spires of Holyrod Palace, Cander Ellis strode across the Plaza of Fallen Heroes, his long cloak flapping at his heels. His old wheel-lock pistol was thrust into his belt, where it was well hidden by the line of his cloak; in his pocket were a handful of paper cartridges—powder, shot, and wadding all in one. Cander had no idea if this man, whom he continued to call Rensloe Fant for want of another name, was actually dangerous or not, but he did not intend on taking any chances with him.

A chill wind whipped through the great plaza, making a low moaning sound as it brushed the ornate façades of the surrounding edifices, which housed the various powers that ruled life in Branion. To the west, crouched behind stone walls and iron gates, was Holyrod Palace, once the seat of the royal house, now domicile to the Protectorate's more formal agencies; to the east, the great halls of the guilds and the merchants; to the north, the council chambers of the City of Lorum. And to the south, where Cander was headed, was the Treasury building, immense and portentously built, and beside it, Balther's Bank.

Balther's Bank was hardly "charming," as Digrippa had called it. It was an artless, constricted building, flat-roofed and trimmed with strips of black-painted wood. It seemed to exemplify restraint and dull stability. As Cander came nearer the bank, he slowed his pace, eventually pausing beside a heroic bronze of Lord Darione, depicted in a wide stance, hands on the pommel of a greatsword, a weapon that had been archaic even in Darione's time.

Cander positioned himself so that he would not be immediately obvious to someone leaving the Balther's Bank, though he would still be able to keep an eye on the steps outside the building. There were a number of people on the plaza at this time of day, mostly clerks and minor officials leaving work, so Cander felt reasonably inconspicuous.

As he stood waiting, he flagged down a passing vendor and bought a large, soft pretzel, kept warm and fresh by the tinned case that the vendor carried. Cander munched the pretzel anxiously, hoping that he had correctly interpreted Digrippa's purposely cryptic remarks. He had not thought that there was anything else that the magician *could* have meant, but as the sun began to go down behind Holyrod Palace and there was still no sign of anyone leaving Balther's Bank who remotely resembled the man Lor had described as Rensloe Fant, he began to fear that Digrippa had been too subtle for him. He thought about going into the bank and trying to spot Fant, but he knew that this would be ill advised. The very last thing he wanted was to have Fant spot him and become suspicious.

So he waited, increasingly impatient and fretful. The wind whipped about him, trying to lift the hat from his head, and toying with the ends of the false mustache he'd worn to disguise himself against the event that Rensloe Fant knew what he looked like. Dusk settled gradually on the plaza, though the last ruddy rays of day still reflected off of the high windows of Merchanter's Hall. Finally, as a ragged old lamplighter came by with his long, crooked pole and started lighting the street lamps in front of the Treasury, several well-dressed young men came out of Balther's Bank and stood chatting on its steps. One of the men fit the description of Rensloe Fant exactly—young, of average height, slender, not much chin, with longish blond hair—but was this enough to be certain that he was in fact Rensloe Fant? Cander had misgivings. Then he noticed that the man wore a watch chain across his waistcoat, with a small gold ornament depending from it.

Cander hesitated. He needed to get a better look at that ornament. If it bore the sign of the Society of the New Dawn, he could be reasonably sure that he had the right person. If he moved closer, though, the man might take note of him, which would make it difficult or impossible to follow him. *Well,* he thought, *I've got to do it. I don't want to start following the wrong man all around the city.*

Casually he moved around the statue and started to walk past the men gathered on the steps. As he came opposite them, he stopped, pulled a folded sheet of paper from his pocket—a bill from his favorite wine merchant, as it happened—and held it up in the direction of the men. Putting on an earnest expression, he appeared to study the paper, while actually peering over the edge of it, at the dangling ornament.

Yes! It was the gold triangle with the rayed sun that was the sign of the Society of the New Dawn. He was certain now; he had found his man.

The conclave on the steps began to break up just then, with the men starting off in different directions. As Rensloe Fant passed him, Cander nonchalantly moved to put the paper back into his pocket, turning slightly as he did, so Fant would not get a good look at his face.

Fant started off in the general direction of city council chambers, striding along at a quick pace, jauntily swinging a gold-headed walking stick as he went. Cander waited a few moments, then set off on a course roughly parallel to Fant's, trying to stay close enough that he would not lose the man in the crowd, yet staying far enough behind that he would not be detected—he hoped.

With an energetic demeanor, Fant marched the full length of the plaza, and then entered onto Pasewell Street, a wide, well traveled artery. Here Cander labored to close the gap between Fant and himself. At this time of the evening, Pasewell Street was packed with pedestrians and coaches, making Cander more fearful of losing Fant than he was of being spotted by him.

Fant did not let the congestion slow him. He veered buoyantly right to left, left to right, taking advantage of any gap that opened in the crowd. Cander had an increasingly difficult time keeping up with the man. His feet, confined in narrow shoes, were starting to hurt. Ruefully he was forced to admit that his shoes succeeded better as elegant objects, to be admired for their unscuffed beauty, than they did as practical footgear.

After several blocks, Fant turned onto a side street that led in the direction of the river. The crowds thinned, and Cander dropped back again. Fant walked on for another block, then ducked into a plain-faced building.

Cander slowed, just in case the man should come out again unexpectedly. Warily he approached the building. A small, discreet sign hung over the lintel, black letters on a dark green background. *The Ventures*, it read. Cander knew of the place; it was an exclusive dining club, one of several in the area. Cander was not a member, so there was no question of his following Fant inside. There was nothing to do, really, but to stand and wait, in the hope that he could pick up on Fant again when he left the building.

For a long time, Cander stood across the street from The Ventures, dejected and cold, while people passed back and forth before him, all of them going *someplace*, it seemed to him, to some warm hearth, to the company of family or friends. It was depressing.

As time passed—the better part of an hour, by Cander's watch—he begun to imagine Fant sitting at a nice table inside, in comfort, glutting himself with food and wine, and he began to hate the man deeply.

Cander began to have the unpleasant feeling that he was himself being watched. He kept looking about him, but couldn't catch anyone who was paying any attention to him. *Nerves*, he told himself.

At last, Fant reemerged. Cander tried not to look directly at the man. From the corner of his eye, though, he saw Fant flag down a cab with a wave of his gold-headed stick and climb into it. Cander felt a quickening surge of dismay. Somehow he had not anticipated this.

The coachman snapped his whip over the flanks of his horse, and the coach trundled away. Cander hastened to follow it. At first, this was not too difficult. The streets near the Plaza of Fallen Heros were congested enough at this time of the evening that the coach was constrained to a speed not much faster than a brisk walk. In a way, it was easier to follow the coach than a man on foot, since Cander did not have to worry about being noticed.

As they neared the river, however, the streets cleared, and the coach was able to go faster, eventually compelling Cander to run in order to keep up with it. Even so, he soon started to lose ground. He wondered how long he could even keep the coach in sight. Not long, he feared. Already he was struggling for breath.

Before Cander could reach the end of his endurance, however, the coach slowed to turn onto the Kantelon Bridge. A number of pedestrians were crossing the narrow bridge, one laboriously pushing a wicker cart. They brought the coach nearly to a halt, affording Cander a chance to catch up. He ran until he reached the carved posts marking the beginning of the bridge; then stopped and tried to regain his breath. Despite the cold, he was perspiring heavily. He felt giddy.

Considering the back of the coach, which was still only midway across the span, Cander asked himself, "So, Master Fant, what can you want on that side of the river? What are you up to?"

Abruptly it came to him. *The Chandler's,* he thought. *It has something to do with the Chandler's.*

It has to be.

They sat in tense, expectant silence—Kemp, Quordane, and Quordane's two men, whose names were Frazet and Rohn, Kemp had learned. After rocking and lurching over the cobbled streets of Lorum, their coach now stood idle, waiting, while long minutes ticked away. Kemp kept wishing that he could look out and see where they were. The flaps were down over the windows, though, and Kemp was wedged impotently between Frazet and Rohn, so snugly that he was obliged to keep his hands folded in his lap like a schoolboy. He knew where they *should* be, of course, according to Quordane's plan; but he did not trust Quordane to tell him everything.

Covertly Kemp studied Quordane, who sat alone on the opposite bench. The man's face revealed nothing of the convoluted thoughts that Kemp knew to be seething behind it. The pallid grey eyes stared straight ahead, focusing on nothing. It almost seemed to Kemp that Quordane, not needing it for the moment, had let his small semblance of humanity lapse, reverting for a moment to the more natural state of spiritual nullity. Broad and florid, the face maintained a vestige of its habitual expression of smug superiority, almost as if the attitude had been stamped on so thoroughly that it no longer required any active intelligence to maintain it.

Kemp was trying to keep his own emotions in check, with only limited success. He was far from happy with the situation. He was used to being in control of his undertakings, in charge of every detail of the preparation. But Quordane had cut him off from all of that, which made him distinctly anxious. How could he be sure that Quordane and his spies had not forgotten something crucial? In all the world, there was only one person in whom he could trust completely: in himself, in his own skill. All else was inherently unreliable and insecure.

Even if the raid on the Black Tower went as planned and he escaped without detection, what then? At that point, his usefulness to the royalists would be over; they would be able to dispose of him whenever and however they wished. Lalerin and Quordane had made him many promises, of course, but would they deliver on them when the time came? Kemp doubted it. He knew how men of their sort thought. They were of a lofty and exalted estate. They would not lose any sleep over betraying someone they considered their inferior.

There had to be some way out of this trap. There *had* to be. He would just have to think of it. And soon.

There came a quiet knock on the door to the coach. Quordane's gaze suddenly came back to life. The man to Kemp's left, Rohn, drew a small pistol from under his coat, lifted the leather window covering, and peered out. "It's all right," he said after a moment.

"Open it," Quordane said.

Rohn unlatched the narrow door and pushed it open. Kemp caught a sudden, abrupt glimpse of a face hovering outside in the darkness, made strangely luminous by the coach's interior lamps. The face belonged to an elegant young man, blond, slender, clean-shaven, and without much chin. The man smiled jauntily and said, "Lord Quordane, I believe? All is in readiness."

Quordane inclined his head in a stately fashion. "Splendid."

After emerging from the coach, Kemp found himself in a gloomy, unpaved alley wedged between shadowy buildings. The dank scent of the river was on the wind. Kemp stood beside the coach, removed from the others, though near enough that he could hear what they were saying. Darkness and the circumstances, unusual yet familiar, had brought a change in him. His senses had come fully alive. Eyes, ears, the very touch of the air on his skin, brought him faint but easily comprehended messages. He felt vigorous and supremely competent. Grinning, he fancied that he could actually feel the moonlight striking his teeth. He was in his element.

"The men have broken through into the culvert beneath the Chandler's," the blond young man was saying. "The way seems clear straight through to the Tower. We are ready."

He looked over at Kemp, scrutinizing him with a brazen, impersonal eye, as if he were judging the quality of a horse or a hound. "Is this your thief?"

Insulted, Kemp stepped forward with a grave dignity. "I, sir, am Jerod Kemp. And you?"

The man gave him a wide, evil grin. He looked as if he had gotten his upper lip stuck to his teeth. "You may call me Rensloe Fant, Sir Thief. Master Rensloe Fant."

Fant gave a look back to Quordane and said, "Are you sure that the thief is up to his part? Truth, he seems a weedy little creature."

Glaring, Kemp narrowed his eyes at Fant. He supposed that it had to happen sometime: He'd found someone he liked even less well than Quordane.

"I have complete faith in Kemp," Quordane said. "He is the best in the world at what he does. He himself will tell you so."

"Well," Fant said, "if you say it, Lord Quordane, it must be so. Shall we get on with it, then?"

Quordane nodded. They moved up the alley, to a side door set into the building on the right. Fant eased the door open, letting Quordane pass through and then following him.

As Kemp went in behind the two, he noticed that the door had been clumsily forced, splintering both the door and its frame. *Sloppy,* he thought disapprovingly. *Any fool could tell that someone has broken into this building.*

A step or two inside the darkened room, Kemp paused to take in his surroundings. He was in a small, cramped office. There were two large battered desks, taking up most of the space, piled high with old manuscripts and a number of peculiar curios: outdated helmets, wooden swords colored with worn gilt, and a few pieces of gaudy and obviously fake jewelry. A pair of old pikes stood crossed in the corner.

One of Quordane's men closed the outer door, and the gloom thickened appreciably, until Fant opened the door on the opposite side of the room. A faint, bluish light leaked through the opening, illuminating the thin haze of dust that was in the air.

One by one, they went through the doorway, emerging into a space where the ceiling was so high that it receded completely into shadows. Strung on wood-framed pulleys anchored to the floor by iron hooks, stout ropes ascended into the darkness, reminding Kemp of a ship's rigging. Ahead, partially hidden by a thick skirting of curtain, was an open expanse lighted by a harsh, unnatural light.

They went forward into the light, until they came to stand in the naked center of the expanse. There was an open trapdoor here, at their feet, a dark square with the top of a ladder projecting out of it. A faint echo of voices issued from below.

Squinting, Kemp peered out toward the light. He saw that they stood on an elevated stage that projected out into a large auditorium. All along the front of the stage were a number of shell-shaped brass scoops, inside of each of which was a dazzling white sphere. It was from these spheres that the light emanated.

The Chandler's Theater, he thought. He had been here before. He could recall standing out there in the darkness beyond that rim of bright spheres, watching as the players conjured up distant times and exotic places with naught but their words and gestures. He had often wondered what it would be like to stand upon this stage himself, but he had never imagined circumstances such as these.

Kemp felt stiff fingers on his shoulder. It was Quordane, impelling him toward the open trapdoor. Blinking from the brightness, Kemp returned his attention to his companions. He saw that several of them had already gone down the ladder into the darkness below. "Try to keep your mind on business, Kemp," Quordane said sharply. "You go next."

Suppressing a retort, Kemp moved sullenly toward the dark square in the stage floor. He sat on the edge of it, dangling his legs down, then twisted around and put his feet on one rung of the creaking ladder. Carefully he climbed down. He saw that he was entering into a cramped, untidy space, divided by thick posts and walled with rough stone. Several small lanterns hung flickering from the posts.

He took his feet from the bottom rung and planted them on the earthen floor. Then, standing away from the ladder, he gave a quick glance about him. It was apparent that the Chandler's used this space for storage. A mound of old furniture was stacked in one corner: chairs, tables, and brass-bound chests. Wedged between support posts were a number of large canvas-covered frames, on which various scenes had been ingeniously painted.

Ponderous and slow, Quordane descended the ladder. His massive hocks looked particularly impressive from below, Kemp noticed. After Quordane came Rensloe Fant, moving with somewhat greater assurance. When all had reached bottom, Fant pointed the way through the forest of supporting beams, and they picked their way through the cluttered gloom, until at last they came to where the floor had been dug up—and recently, it appeared. The earth that was piled up beside the hole was still dark with moisture; a pair of shovels and a pickax lay nearby.

Standing beside the hole, Kemp looked down dubiously. He heard a faint trickle of running water below, but saw nothing except a dim, fluttering light. Lashed to a stout support, a knotted rope dropped down into the gloomy cavity.

Turning to Quordane, Kemp said, "It looks like your people have been at work here for some time. How is it that they could go unnoticed?"

Rensloe Fant answered, smirking, "The Protectorate obliged us by closing the theater. There has been no one here to notice."

Quordane stared at Kemp impassively. "Down you go, Kemp. We'll wait here for you."

Kemp hesitated. "Where are the things that I'm going to need?"

"Below. Don't waste time. You *know* the plan."

Gritting his teeth, Kemp grasped the rope and tried to get the feel of its abrasive fibers. "Aren't you going to wish me luck?" he asked Quordane.

"Good luck," the man said tonelessly.

Kemp snapped the rope several times against the support beam, making sure that the knot was secure. Then he tightened his grip, shifted his weight against the rope, and, repressing his deep trepidation, slowly backed his way into the void. His boots loosened a shower of sand and gravel, which caught the lamplight for an instant, before being swallowed up by the gloom. A moment later, Kemp's feet slid away from the solid earth. He dangled like a broken puppet, until he could clasp the knotted rope with his legs. Looking up, he saw Quordane's face hanging over him, avid and devoid of all human concern.

Heart pounding dolefully, Kemp cautiously began lowering himself down the length of the rope.

9

It was a long way to the bottom.

As Kemp's eyes adjusted to the gloom, he saw that he hung within what appeared to be a natural cavern, rough-walled and spreading. Just below him was a massive ledge of grey stone, darkly glistening with moisture. Some six feet below that was the cavern floor. Through the middle of the floor, shallow water fingered its way through the sand and sediment. On a flat stone was a brass lamp, shedding a feeble amber glow. A canvas bag lay nearby.

After pushing past the stone ledge, Kemp lowered himself the remaining distance to the cavern floor. He stood there beside the rope while he caught his breath. Wiping the perspiration from his forehead with his sleeve, he glared up at the distant pool of light above him and mouthed a silent curse.

At length, Kemp moved to examine the articles that had been left for him. The lantern was small enough to hold comfortably in one hand. It had a pivoting shield over the front-mounted lens, which allowed the light to be easily regulated; a lever mounted on the handgrip raised and lowered the shield. Kemp could tell by feel that the oil reservoir was better than half full—more than enough for the evening's activities.

Within the canvas bag were the rest of the articles he had requested: a length of rope, an iron pry bar, charts of the various culverts and sewers that led to the Black Tower, and a brass-cased compass. Kemp took out the compass and charts, then slung the bag over one shoulder.

After consulting the compass, Kemp started off in a roughly northwesterly direction. He quickly came to the end of the chamber and was confronted by a deeply fissured wall of stone. A narrow passage had been carved through the rock there, its entrance shored up with stout timbers. Opening his lamp up full, Kemp pushed through into the confining passage.

It was fortunate that he was not much bothered by dark, cramped spaces, as the passage was so low that he was forced to proceed in a bent-over posture, and there was barely enough space between the two rough walls to accommodate his shoulders. The lamp was ineffective beyond a few feet ahead, past which point all was sunk in impenetrable blackness. The tiny stream that trickled through the center of the passage quickly managed to soak through the soles of his boots, so that his toes squelched uncomfortably in his sodden hose.

Later in the season, he knew, this stream would be more than a casual nuisance; he would be knee-deep in run-off from the winter rains. This passage was part of the system of culverts and sewers constructed long ago to keep the streets from flooding; that much Quordane had told him. Now, if Quordane's intelligence could be trusted, this particular culvert should run directly under the Black Tower. If it didn't, then Kemp was going to a lot of trouble for nothing.

The passage began to take an upward slant. Kemp found himself wondering how long it had been since another human being had passed this way. A generation? Two? If he should perish here from lack of air, how long would it be before he would be found? Considering this question, he felt increasingly alone and forsaken.

Legs aching, perspiration starting at his temples, Kemp labored along, coming at last to a place where the passage split into two. Pausing, he consulted the chart, shifting awkwardly to shine the lamp on it, and finally decided to take the branch to the right. As he felt his way along, he was unable to put down the fear that he might somehow lose his way. *Don't think about it,* he told himself.

The passage narrowed even more. It was getting so tight in places that he had to force his shoulders through. A larger man would not have been able to pass at all.

Eventually the passage stopped rising. A series of low arches began to pierce the dank walls, none of them higher than three feet tall. Kemp counted each in its turn. When he got to the fifth arch, he stopped. After checking the chart to make sure that his bearings were correct, he knelt beside the archway. He felt the chill water soaking his trouser legs as he shined the lamp into the chamber beyond. The chamber, its ceiling of crudely dressed stone, receded from the light, its full extent impossible to discern.

After stuffing the map and compass into his coat pocket, Kemp entered the chamber on his hands and knees, dragging the canvas bag behind him. Once inside, he tried standing, but found that the low ceiling forced him into such an awkward position that it was more comfortable to inch along on his hands and knees. His trouser legs became sodden and filthy, and he quickly developed a deep distaste for the muck into which he had to keep plunging his hands.

Finally he came to a place where the chamber's ceiling rose high enough to allow him to stagger to his feet. Looking up, he saw that he stood below a circular well, which went up perhaps ten feet before terminating abruptly in a metal cap. An iron ladder extended up the side of the well, red with rust, obviously long disused. Kemp paused a moment to wonder if the ladder was still sound. There was only one way to find out for certain, he decided.

The ladder came down only to the bottom of the well, still some four feet short of the chamber floor. Giving a sigh, Kemp shouldered the bag of tools, stretched up with his free hand, and grasped the third rung from the bottom. With his other hand, he carefully propped the lantern on the center of the rung, leaning it back against the side of the well, so it would stay put. Then he started to pull himself up, struggling to get a foothold on the lowest rung. He gasped from the effort, and the grating of his hands against the pitted surface of the ladder sent tiny bits of oxidized metal showering down into his eyes.

Eventually he managed to bring both feet onto the lowest rung. He rested there for a few moments. Then, after rubbing the metallic grit from his watering eyes, he reclaimed his lantern and continued the climb. The ladder *seemed* sound enough to bear his weight, but each time he went up another rung, he half expected it to give way and send him plunging.

Awkwardly he made his way to the top of the well, off-balance from the weight of the tool sack that kept tugging at him, his hands abraded and burning. When he made it into the metal cylinder that capped the well, he stopped and scrutinized it with care. He saw that there was a hinged door in the center of the cylinder, small and square. There did not seem to be any lock or latch.

Kemp closed his lantern as far as it would go, so that only a dim orange glow escaped from it. Bracing one forearm against the middle of the door, he pushed. At first, the door refused to budge, and Kemp feared that it had been sealed somehow. But then it gave a low, tortured groan and began to move. Slowly and carefully Kemp pushed the door open, moving up the ladder as he did so. Just before the door reached the point where its own weight might make it crash down on the other side, Kemp put his lamp down on the flat area outside the well and gripped the edge of the door as tightly as he could, holding it in place. He emerged from the well into a gloomy chamber. Keeping a good hold on the door, he stood very still for a moment, until he was reasonably certain that there was no one around to observe him. Finally he eased the door shut behind him.

He was in the basement of the Black Tower now; it would not go well for him if he were caught. Kemp took several slow, deep breaths, trying to make himself relax. An excess of anxiety now would only make a fatal mistake more likely.

At length, Kemp considered the chamber in which he found himself. Stone-walled and windowless, it was bare of furnishings; only a few scattered crates and barrels kept it from being entirely empty. A stone stairway went up one wall. At the top, a single lamp burned, beside a stout oaken door.

Checking his watch, Kemp saw that he was running behind schedule. He knew that he had to get moving, or risk being caught when the guards made their regular patrol of the Tower and its grounds. After grabbing his lantern, he made quickly for the stairway. The stairs were built of roughly dressed stone. Long use had worn shallow depressions into each step, and every surface was glossy and slick. Kemp, in his wet, leather-soled boots, was forced to climb with the utmost deliberation.

Upon reaching the landing at the top over the stairs, Kemp tried the door. He found that it was locked, but a quick inspection showed him that the lock was an antiquated piece of rubbish. It took less than a minute of patient manipulation to get through it. After opening the door a crack, Kemp listened for any nearby sound. There was nothing, so he opened the door the rest of the way and eased out into the dimly lit corridor beyond.

The corridor presented a bleak aspect. It was narrow, hardly more capacious than the tunnels below. The floors were of wood, dull, dark, and worn. The walls were all of grey stone, with only an occasional length of faded tapestry to cheer them. The doors that opened out onto the corridor were uniformly heavy, utilitarian things, lacking all style and beauty.

Kemp turned left, making his way as silently as he could. The corridor curved, as it made a circuit of the Tower, so he could never be entirely sure that there wasn't someone just up ahead, standing quietly, waiting for some unlucky thief to run into him. Kemp's heart was beating rapidly. He wished desperately that he had never gotten involved in this highly suspect scheme.

There were two stairways that led to the Tower's upper storeys, Kemp knew. There was the main stairway, which started in the anteroom near the front entrance; this would be impossible to approach unobserved, as there were always several guards stationed there. The second stairway was in the back. Originally intended for servants, it had been sealed off for many years now, since the Black Tower had ceased to have any real day-to-day function.

The Black Tower existed now primarily as a symbol of power, of legitimacy. It had been the seat of the House of Saphrinas for five centuries, though the kings of Branion had not dwelled there for generations prior to the civil war that had lost them their country. The current rulers of Branion obviously knew the value that the Black Tower had as a symbol of sovereignty; they kept it manned and in good repair, though it no longer had any utility as a fortress. Its only practical uses now were as an armory and as a repository for the treasures of Branion's history. Even these rather modest rôles could almost certainly be performed more effectively by a different structure.

At last, Kemp found the entrance to the rear stairway. It stood at the end of a short hall that branched off from the main corridor, guarded only by a locked brass-bound door. This lock was not as trivial an impediment as the last. It appeared to have been installed within living memory and was of high quality. After setting down the lantern, Kemp got out his picks and set to work. The lock proved maddeningly resistant to tampering. It probably didn't help that Kemp half expected someone to come strolling along at any moment, which made him less patient than usual.

Finally he managed to catch the mechanism and manipulate it in the proper manner. The lock gave way with a gratifying *click*. With a profound sense of relief, he pulled the door open and peered within. Darkness. After taking up his lantern, he opened it up slightly so that a thin beam of amber light caught the iron-railed staircase before him. He moved toward it, pulling the door shut behind him.

The signs of the stairway's disuse were unmistakable. There

was dust everywhere, and streamers of cobweb hung wavering from the rail. A heap of abandoned furniture partly blocked access to the stair, old-fashioned stuff, oak, solid and ungraceful. Even the air smelled like something that had been shut away from life for too long.

Kemp ascended the stair gingerly, not quite able to trust in something so long forsaken, solid as it might feel. The lantern played strange games with the shadow, bringing threatening, evanescent shapes to life. His footsteps echoed within the stairwell, making him fancy that someone else must be there with him in the darkness. By the time he reached the first landing, his nerves were feeling the strain.

The Black Tower had six storeys. The item that Kemp was to steal was locked away on the topmost storey. He was not going that far, though. According to Quordane's intelligence, armed guards blocked the obvious approach to the treasure room. Fortunately, there was another, less obvious way.

Kemp made his way up five flights of stairs, then went to the door. He was prepared to spend another five minutes picking the lock, but found that this door was unlocked. *Good*, he thought. This would put him almost back on schedule.

After again closing the lantern as far as it would go, he opened the door a crack and saw only a deserted hall, dimly lit, carpeted with a threadbare runner of maroon and gold. He moved through, silent as a shadow. Antique suits of armor lined the hall, standing a patient, motionless guard; Kemp passed them by as if he were an honored lord reviewing his troops. In a sudden fit of whimsy, he put on an exaggerated swagger, until he chanced by a full-length mirror and caught sight of himself: a disheveled little man, coat streaked with filth, trousers covered with mud, something green and mossy-looking clotted in his hair. No lord, he.

With a more subdued demeanor, he continued down the hall, finally coming to the door that Quordane had described for him. It had a distinctly forbidding and martial look to it: coarse-grained oak bound with thick iron straps, a small, barred window high in the middle of it. From the look of it, no power in the world could have forced it open. The door had one significant weakness, however. The lock that held it secure was ludicrously old and simple. It was barely enough to slow him. He was almost sorry that the door proved so trifling an impediment.

A darkened chamber lay behind the door. Shining his lantern about, Kemp saw that he was in an armory. Most of the weapons, he noticed immediately, were long obsolete. All across two walls were racks of pikes and halberds; across a third were a large number of long-barreled match-lock guns, standing stock-down in a row. In the center of the chamber, there were several long benches, each stacked neatly with assorted arms and armor: helmets and iron collars, wheel-lock pistols and powder horns, daggers and sheaths. As outdated as all of this equipment looked, however, there was only the thinnest film of dust covering it. Obviously, everything here was well cared for.

Kemp gave the chamber and its contents only a cursory inspection. What he was looking for was located rather higher. Tilting the lantern so that its light played over the chamber's ceiling, he carefully examined the spaces between the supporting beams. At last he found it: a slight recess in the ceiling, which had been patched over with a different kind of wood from the rest. There had once been a stairway here, or so Quordane had told him, which had been removed and imperfectly sealed a decade or so before. It led up into what was now the treasure room.

After clearing off a corner of the bench that ran under the sealed opening, Kemp scrambled up onto it and paused to catch his balance. He removed the prying bar from the canvas sack he carried. Moving with careful precision, he fitted the end of the bar to the superficial clefts that existed between the ceiling and the boards that patched over the old opening. Very slowly he flexed the bar, forcing up the boards. He winced at the cracking noise the boards made as they gave way, knowing that there were guards just outside the door to the treasure room.

After long minutes of work, he managed to clear enough of the opening. He rested for a moment, his arms and shoulders aching from holding the heavy bar over his head for so long. Despite his fears, he heard nothing from above that indicated that his efforts had been detected.

He put the prying bar down on the bench at his feet; it had done its work. After lifting the lantern up through the overhead hole and sliding it safely to one side, he grasped the edges of the opening and laboriously pulled himself up, scissoring his legs in a useless attempt to give himself an extra impetus. Little by little, he drew his head and shoulders through the opening. He struggled to change his grip, then pushed himself entirely into the upper chamber. Upon swinging his legs out, he caught the solid floor with his feet, then awkwardly walked the rest of his body on his hands to join them. He rested for a moment then, as quietly as he could, though his body badly wanted him to draw, ragged, noisy breaths. He heard a faint murmur of voices from beyond the chamber door. They sounded casual and unconcerned; Kemp felt confident that his struggles had gone undetected.

Rising shakily, Kemp picked up the lantern and gingerly opened it up so that only a thin beam escaped the shield. Eyes opened wide against the darkness, he moved the lantern slowly around the chamber.

Kemp drew a quick breath. Suddenly all of his weariness and apprehension fled in the face of a new emotion: pure, unalloyed avarice. All the walls of the chamber were covered with huge beveled glass cases, and the cases were filled with the most astonishing array of treasure that Kemp had ever seen: gold, gem-encrusted crowns and scepters, enormous diamond rings, complicated brooches of platinum and gold. There were unset gemstones, too—rubies the size of walnuts, star sapphires, flawless blue-white diamonds, all glittering coldly in the lantern light.

As if in a trance, Kemp assayed each case in its turn, astonished and deeply reverent. He was a good thief, the best. He'd stolen a small fortune in gold and jewels in his life—yet the gains of his entire career were as nothing compared with what he saw before him now.

He came to the last case and saw within it one object that overshadowed all that had come before. It was an unset diamond, nearly as large as an apple, round and gorgeously faceted. The glow of the lantern played within its depths, which seemed as clear and perfect as a mountain stream after the spring snow melt. *The Heart of Almenor,* he thought. He almost said it out loud, forgetting where he was for a moment. The most celebrated diamond in all the world, and here he was, separated from it only by a pane of glass. His mouth went dry, and he could actually feel his greed gathering at the back of his eyes. It was his, if he wanted it, his.

And yet, what would he do with it? Use it as a paperweight? There was nowhere that he could sell it in its present form. He could always have it recut into smaller stones, of course, but he couldn't bear the thought of that. It would be . . . criminal.

Reluctantly he put the gem from his mind. He had serious business to attend to. Checking his watch, he saw that he had already wasted too much time. In ten minutes, the guards would start their regular circuit of the Black Tower. Before then, he had to be finished and gone.

He had been told to look for a large box of black wood. He didn't remember seeing any such object during his first tour of the chamber, but he had been distracted by more noteworthy things. He examined the cases more carefully and finally found it, shoved back into the rear of one of the cases, so that it almost blended with the shadows. Good.

The case was padlocked. It was a good lock, one of the new ones. It wasn't entirely impervious, but it could take precious minutes to pick. Kemp scowled. He hated to do such sloppy work, but . . .

After slipping the thin-bladed dagger from his ankle sheath, he eased the blade under the locked hasp. Working meticulously, he wrenched the blade against the hasp, pulling and twisting, until one end came loose with a faint splintering sound. It was a common mistake, he reflected—using a good lock on a poorly attached hasp.

Once he opened the glass door, he slid the box toward the front of the case and picked it up. It was heavy, heavier than he had expected. He wondered what was in it, that Quordane and Lalerin wanted it over all of the treasures contained in this room.

As he hefted the box up and slid it into the canvas bag he carried, Kemp became aware of a strange rattling sound, slight but noticeable in the silence of the treasure chamber. It seemed to be coming from—

His pocket? Frowning, Kemp reached into the pocket, finding only the compass. Fingers communicating a constant vibration, he drew the compass from his pocket and stared at it. The needle was spinning madly, around and around, as if driven by a tightly wound watch spring.

10

There was a light rain falling.

Cander Ellis stood motionless in the shadows, wrapped in his dark cloak, watching the side door to the Chandler's Theater. He had followed Rensloe Fant here, watched him alight from the hired coach, pay the coachman, and send him on his way. He had seen him approach the small private coach and rap on its door. He had seen the four men emerge from the coach: a well-dressed portly gentleman, two wary-eyed younger men, and a small, careful-looking man who seemed to want to distance himself from the others. After a few moments, they had gone one by one through the side door into the Chandler's, leaving only the coachman, hunched miserably on his box.

Cander lingered irresolutely in the shadows, unable to figure out what was happening, or what he should do next. He thought at first that they might be coming right out again, but after long minutes passed without any sign of a reappearance, he began to suspect that this was going to take some time. What were they doing in there? He decided at length that there was only one way to find out, and that was to follow them into the theater. This, he knew, would be risky.

First, he would have to get past the coachman. Cander eyed the man speculatively. The coachman had settled back against his seat, arms crossed under his brown cloak, hat pulled low, rain dripping from its wilted brim and beading on his beard. He didn't look very attentive. It should not be too difficult to get past him.

Cander crept slowly around the coach, staying within the deeper shadows as much as he could. Finally, however, he had to step into the open in order to reach the door. The door was several yards from the coach, and slightly behind. As long as he did not make any noise, Cander figured, he should be able to make it there without being noticed.

Three gliding steps took him to the door. Gingerly he pushed it open. Lor Brunnage's office was dark, but Cander was familiar enough with it that he did not have to fear walking into anything. After closing the outer door behind him, he drew his pistol and moved forward. He could feel cold fear churning away inside of him. He was putting himself into a perilous situation, he knew.

Cander put his hand on the knob of the door that led onto the stage of the Chandler's, and felt its chill for a long moment, while he summoned the courage to turn it. Slowly he pulled the door open and quickly determined that the wings of the stage were deserted. The magic orbs that lit the stage were operative; they appeared to be set at less than half their maximum intensity. There was no one anywhere to be seen, but one of the traps was open, the one at center stage.

Odd, Cander thought. There was nothing of any use to anyone beneath the stage. As far as he could remember, it was used almost exclusively to store old set pieces and props.

This was getting stranger by the moment. Cander hesitated, not sure what to do next. He knew that he couldn't go below; if Rensloe Fant and the others were indeed down there, he could not possibly escape detection. For a moment, he considered going for help. He realized, though, that this would take too long. Fant and his friends would probably be long gone before he could return. What then? Withdraw while he still could, and hope to follow them wherever they went next? No. There was a good chance that they would split up after this. He was but one man. He couldn't follow them all.

He decided that he would just stay where he was. He did not know what he could hope to accomplish, but it seemed the best way to find out why Rensloe Fant had come here.

Glancing about him, Cander took stock of his position. He decided to move to the wall nearest the proscenium arch. He would be less obvious there, in the shadows, and the curtains that hung at the edge of the stage would mask him from any casual inspection.

Near to where Cander now moved was a cylindrical brass stand, as high as his sternum, topped by a convex disk of a white, vaguely luminous substance. The orbs that lit the stage were controlled from here by magic. Passing a hand over the disk away from the body would cause the orbs to brighten a level; toward the body, they would lower correspondingly.

The orbs and the controlling disk had been a gift of the enigmatic magician Gul Highton. They had allowed the Company to abandon its old open-air theater on the outskirts of the city and had helped to make the Chandler's the premiere theatrical company in Lorum.

Stroking his false mustache, Cander contemplated the glowing disk, considering the uses to which he might put it in his current situation.

Increasingly conscious of the need for haste, Kemp retraced the route that had brought him to the treasure room atop the Black Tower: descending into the armory, then out into the long hall where archaic armor stood vigil, down the back stairs, into the ground-floor corridor. Just as he reached the door to the stair that led into the dank basement of the Black Tower, he heard footsteps in the corridor, coming closer. The guards had started their rounds.

He ducked through the door, closing it behind him, and started immediately down the steps, knowing that some sign of his intrusion could be discovered at any moment. He would not feel secure until he was well away from the Tower.

In his haste, Kemp slipped on a step about halfway down. In attempting to recover, he very nearly dropped his lantern. After catching himself, he stood wavering for a moment, blinking into the gloom below. He was appalled by what had almost happened. What if he had broken the lantern through his carelessness? Disaster.

Suppressing a shudder, he forced himself to continue down the worn steps, going much more slowly. Before he could reach the bottom, he began to hear voices from above, shrill with excitement. Kemp gave a fierce grin. It appeared that his trespass had been noted. It almost made him wish that he had left a note: "Kemp was here."

Kemp made his way into the tunnels beneath the tower without incident. From there, he retraced the rest of his way with scrupulous deliberation. His compass no longer functioned properly, and he was afraid of taking a wrong turning in the dark and getting himself hopelessly lost.

When he finally reached the great chamber under the Chandler's, he allowed himself a small moment of relief. His lantern was beginning to flicker and smoke as it ran low on fuel. No matter. In a few minutes, he would be free of this place.

First, though, he was determined to satisfy his curiosity. After setting down the failing lantern, he slid the purloined case from the canvas bag, thumbed open a tiny latch, and lifted the lid. The case was lined with dark-green velvet that gave the impression of being very old. Nestled in the verdant folds were two objects. The first was a heavy crown of black iron, crude and archaic in form. The second was a dagger with an odd, leaf-shaped blade and a grip wrapped with dark leather. The blade was marked by four angular, runic characters, which he did not recognize, despite his extensive experience with antiquities.

As Kemp peered into the case, he was overtaken by a strange emotion, a powerful yet inexplicable horror entirely at odds with the unremarkable nature of the objects he looked upon. It was as if they exuded a malignant force that could not be seen but that somehow impressed itself on his nerves. Kemp felt a sudden chill shiver down his back.

An iron crown, an old dagger, neither of any apparent charm or value—why, out of all the treasures of the Black Tower, did the royalists want those things? An iron crown—that struck a familiar chord. Vaguely he called to mind some of the quaint old tales that his mother used to tell him when he was a boy. Some of them had mentioned, not in a pleasant context, an iron crown that the kings of Branion had worn. Was this *that* crown?

The light dipped abruptly lower, then gradually regained about half the intensity it had lost. The lantern had almost exhausted its fuel; there was no time for idle reflection. After closing and latching the case, he returned it to the bag, which he slung over his shoulder.

Grabbing hold of the thick rope that depended from the ceiling of the chamber, Kemp gave a quick look up at the bright rift above. It was discouragingly far above him. He sighed.

Laboriously he began climbing the knotted rope, careful not to look down. The rope swung slightly as he ascended; the bulky bag he carried hindered and chafed him. Gasping, swearing under his breath, he struggled to the gap in the cavern ceiling. It was a tricky matter here to pull himself through without getting his fingers pinched between the rope and the side of the hole, but he finally managed it.

Emerging into the space under the Chandler's stage, he saw Quordane standing over him, an expectant gleam in his eyes. "Well?" the man demanded. "Did you get it?"

"Someone help me up," he gasped.

Quordane nodded to his man Frazet, who grabbed Kemp's wrist with a huge, meaty hand and pulled him from the opening.

Kemp scrabbled to his feet and stood there beside the hole, wheezing slightly.

"Did you get it?" Quordane repeated with undisguised impatience.

Kemp appraised Quordane with a speculative look. What would the man do if he said no? Probably have Frazet and Rohn chuck him down the hole again. "Of course I did," he said.

"Give it here."

Kemp hesitated for the barest instant. He had misgivings about turning the case and its contents over to Quordane, but what else could he do? He took the bag from his shoulder and passed it to him.

The man seemed to hold his breath while he opened the bag and peered within. He gave the dandy called Rensloe Fant a tight smile of satisfaction. "Yes, I recognize the case."

"Perhaps we should check the contents," Fant said, giving Kemp a cold glance, "just to make sure that no one has played us a nasty trick."

"Yes, perhaps we should." Quordane reached a hand inside the bag, undid the latch on the case, and tilted back the lid. He squinted into the bag, and his expression softened perceptibly. *"Success . . ."*

With an emphatic movement, the man snapped the case shut and latched it. "Let's get out of here. No sense taking the chance of being discovered."

There were grunts of agreement. One by one, they went up the ladder, until they all stood on the stage, blinking into the blazing orbs dotting the outer edge. For reasons not readily apparent, at least to his conscious mind, Kemp had begun to feel a sharp uneasiness.

Driven by a sudden impulse, Kemp stepped in front of Quordane, blocking his way. "So," he said, "now what?"

The man raised an eyebrow. "Now we go out, get into our coach, and ride away."

"No. I meant, what happens to me?"

"I don't think that we need to worry about that. You've done all that we required of you."

"My point exactly. So now, what do you intend to do with me?"

"There will be time to discuss that later," Quordane said stiffly. "Don't be tedious." He tried to move past him, but Kemp stopped him again.

"Do you mean to kill me?" Kemp asked, studying the man's face carefully. "You do, don't you?"

"Don't be absurd. Let me by, Kemp. You have nothing to fear."

Thoughtful, Kemp stood aside. He had glimpsed the truth in the deceitful glint in the man's eyes. If he went with Quordane now, he'd be as good as dead. His body would be found in a dark alley somewhere, with the other trash.

Satisfied, Quordane grunted. "I'm glad that you've decided to be sensible. Come along."

Kemp backed away several more steps. "I don't think so. Let's just part company now, make a clean break of it, eh?"

Quordane fixed him with an ugly look. "That is impossible."

"Impossible or not, I think it is for the best. I'm sure of it, in fact."

Quordane gave an exasperated sigh. "Frazet, Rohn, it appears that friend Kemp here is determined to be difficult. You'd better kill him now, before he can cause any further trouble. Do it quietly."

Wearing grim, tight smiles, Frazet and Rohn moved toward Kemp, each from a different side. Rohn seemed particularly pleased by this development.

Kemp stole a quick glance behind him. It appeared that there was an unbroken wall there, maybe six feet away. He hadn't given himself much room to maneuver in, he realized, chiding himself for his carelessness. Not much he could do about it now, of course. He would just have to deal with matters as they were.

Kemp backed off another step, then reached down for the knife he had strapped to his ankle. As he drew it from its sheath, he saw Rohn bounding toward him. The big man moved far more swiftly than Kemp would have thought possible. He was on him in an instant, before Kemp could get the knife free.

Crouching and turning, Kemp tried to evade Rohn, but an arm thickly corded with muscle encircled his neck and pulled tight. He struggled, finally managing to draw his knife. Frazet shouted out a warning; Rohn caught the hand that held the knife in an iron grip. Kemp heard a hoarse sound of desperation escape his lips.

Rohn pulled back sharply on Kemp's throat, almost lifting him off his feet. Without ever loosening it, the man gradually worked his grip down Kemp's hand and wrested the knife away. He said, "What's this? A toy? Let's play, little man."

Kemp felt the point of the knife pierce the side of his neck right below the ear, just deeply enough to draw blood. "How do you like this game?" the big man asked, his arm choking off any possibility of a reply. "Hmm? Hmm?"

Quordane said indulgently, "Rohn, as much as I hate to disturb your enjoyment, we are in rather a hurry. Just do it."

"As you say, Baron," the man said, obviously disappointed. With relentless strength, he tightened his arm across Kemp's throat.

Unable to breathe, to cry out, even to gasp, Kemp labored desperately to free himself. Flinging his hands out behind his head, he caught his captor under the chin and tried to force him back. Rohn had the neck muscles of a bull, though; he was entirely unmoved by Kemp's efforts. Flailing out with first one leg then the other, Kemp tried to bring Rohn down, but he was at a disadvantage that was impossible to overcome. His strength was leaking away, gradually but surely; a strange darkness seemed to enter his skull.

He could not believe it. Was it possible that he had been rescued from the gibbet only to meet his end in this pointless, ungracious manner? It seemed . . . unfair.

From his place of safety, Cander watched events unfold with a growing sense of agitation, as it became apparent that he was about to be witness to a murder, if he didn't do anything to stop it. He hesitated for an uncertain moment. He was not by nature heroic and he knew that his interference could well have an unpleasant outcome. By any objective consideration, he should do nothing. In the end, however, it was pure emotion rather than rational consideration that compelled him to act.

Lips pursed in disapproval of his own actions, he cocked his pistol and ran his free hand rapidly over the glowing disk beside him. The orbs that bathed the stage in brightness abruptly doubled in intensity. The men on the stage blinked in dumb bewilderment at the sudden fluctuation, even the one who had been methodically choking the life out of the disheveled man that someone had called Kemp.

Cander stepped forward to the edge of the stage. He knew that he had a serious problem. He had only one shot with which to stop four men. He believed, however, that he had a solution. "*Stop!*" he called out in as authoritative a voice as he could muster. Four astonished gazes turned toward him, then narrowed to ill-natured appraisal. "Let Kemp be." He leveled his pistol at the portly man in brown. "Or I'll kill the fat one."

There was one uncomfortable moment of indecision. Cander was sure that he had chosen the leader of the group. He was *almost* certain, but what if he had chosen wrong?

At last, the man in brown spoke. "Rohn, do be good enough to let Master Kemp go."

With the appearance of profound reluctance, Rohn did as he was told. Kemp collapsed to his knees, gasping and choking. His face, which had been deathly pale, flushed a mottled scarlet before gradually assuming a more natural complexion. After a few moments, he managed to stagger to his feet. His eyes remained dazed and unfocused.

"Are you all right, Kemp?" Cander asked.

"*Yrz,*" the man said hoarsely, which Cander took to mean "Yes."

"Why don't you move away from the others? Take care not to pass in front of the fat one."

"I do wish you would stop saying that," the man in brown offered, frowning. "It is a highly offensive characterization."

"If you'd care to give me your name, I wouldn't have to rely on descriptive terms."

The man opened his mouth, then shook his head. "No, I'd rather not."

Staggering somewhat, Kemp had made his way to the shadowy area beyond the stage. "Here," Cander said, "come stand behind me." The man did as he asked, still wheezing slightly.

Cander contemplated the man in brown, while trying to present a stern and confident aspect. At length, he demanded, "All right, talk. What are you doing here?"

"I might ask you the same question," the man answered blandly.

"You might—if you were holding the gun, instead of me. Tell me what I want to know, or I may just put a shot square in the middle of your forehead." This was pure bravado, of course; Cander was no great shot.

The portly man gave him a crafty look, eyes glittering. "No, I don't think so."

Cander scowled. "Then I'd advise you to think better."

"No. Even were you bold enough to do as you say, you would be opening yourself up to retribution from my companions. You have only one shot."

"You have a point," he admitted, realizing that his gambit had failed. "Well, you may reckon yourselves fortunate. I have decided to forgive you your trespass here. I warn you, though. Don't attempt to follow us, or I may reconsider."

The man in brown fixed Cander with an ironic look, as Cander began to back away, Kemp in tow. They faced one serious difficulty, he knew. As soon as they turned to go out through Lor Brunnage's office, the men on the stage would draw their weapons and be after them. He would have to slow them up.

"Be ready to follow my lead," he told Kemp. The smaller man nodded. As they passed the brass stand on which the light-controlling disk was mounted, he turned to it quickly and stroked down over the face of the disk several times. The stage lights dropped and died, leaving only an eerie afterglow. The men on the stage shouted out their consternation. They would be almost totally blind, Cander knew. He was barely able to see anything himself, but he knew the Chandler's well. Pulling on Kemp's arm, he made his way to the office door. After opening it, he pushed Kemp through, and turned a glance back toward the stage. There was a sudden flash, the sound of a gun being fired, a resounding *crack*, as the lead ball struck the wooden door frame beside Cander and buried itself there. Giving out a hoarse exclamation, he propelled himself through the door, slamming it behind him.

He urged Kemp through the office as quickly as he could, then threw open the outer door. They stumbled out into the alley. The coachman had turned to see them, no doubt alerted by the gunshot. Eyes widening, the coachman pointed a long-barreled pistol in their direction and said, "Hold it there. Don't move!"

Hardly thinking, Cander aimed his pistol and fired. He missed. The ball struck the edge of the box behind the coachman, splintering the wood. It came near enough its target, however, that the coachman threw himself aside involuntarily. His gun went up and discharged, sending its shot into the sky.

The horses that drew the coach, alarmed by the noise, reared and took off at wild gallop, while the coachman grappled for the lost reins. The coach sped down the alley, then turned onto the street. It was going far too quickly for safety, and one rear wheel caught the edge of the curb. The coach flipped up on one side, and for one instant it rode on two wheels, before teetering over and crashing down on its side. Their restraining yoke broken loose by the accident, the team of horses clattered freely down the street and were lost to the night.

Fascinated by the appalling spectacle, Cander and Kemp did not move for several moments, until Cander remembered those who followed them. "Come," he said, touching his companion on the elbow. "We've got to get out of here."

"I think not," came a voice from behind. With a sinking heart, Cander turned and saw the four men emerge from the Chandler's. Two of them carried pistols, which were rudely pointed at Cander and Kemp. The man in brown glared at them, his cheeks red and mottled. "You're not going anywhere," he said thickly. "Not in this life, at any rate." He gazed mournfully at the ruined coach in the street, then seemed to collect himself. "It's a shame. I'd really like to question you in depth about your interest in this affair. I'm quite sure that you could be highly enlightening, given the proper persuasion. But you see how things are. It appears that I shall have a long walk ahead of me, thanks to you. All in all, it will be safest to do away with both of you now. And, you see, I am a prudent man."

He turned to the two men who held the pistols and waved a casual hand. "Rohn, Frazet, you might as well just shoot them. There has been noise enough already. Under the circumstances, efficiency seems more important than discretion."

Rohn grinned. "A pleasure."

Cander felt a sharp fear rising within him. His heart was beating so fast that it seemed to flutter within his breast. His extremities had gone suddenly cold, as if all the blood had been constricted from them. He tensed, ready to move quickly. Perhaps he could leap aside at the last instant, or reach the man who held the pistol before he could shoot. The odds were poor, but he had to try *something*.

At that moment, however, a new voice echoed in the alley. "*Stop!* Lower your weapons. *Now*, slowly, or my friends here may become agitated."

That voice was familiar. Cander looked around and saw four shadowy figures at the far end of the alley. As he watched, they stepped forward into the light that spilled into the alley from the street. Recognition dawned on him.

The first man, the one who had spoken, was Talmis Digrippa. He wore uncharacteristically dark garments, a wide-brimmed hat of black felt, and a stern, uncompromising expression. His slender body seemed charged with an authority that Cander had never observed in him before. Beside him was his dusky servant, Vedrai. Flanking the pair were two men whom Cander did not recognize. Except for Digrippa, all carried pistols, which were cocked and aimed at the man in brown and his followers.

"Uncock your weapons and lay them down at your feet,"

Digrippa said. "*Now.* I won't ask again." Uncertain, Frazet and Rohn looked to the man in brown, who, after a moment's reflection, nodded. The two men slowly released the hammers of the pistols and set them down at their feet.

"Now kick them away from you," Digrippa instructed. They did.

Cander watched in silence. He was thoroughly bemused. Aspects of the evening's events reminded him uncomfortably of a bad farce. It almost seemed that he had written this scene before. He half expected yet another party of armed men to come out of the shadows at any moment.

"*You!*" Rensloe Fant said, spitting the word like a mouthful of bad wine. "What are you doing here, Digrippa? You have no interest in this matter."

A look of emerging comprehension momentarily enlivened the saturnine features of the man in brown. "Digrippa? Talmis Digrippa? I've heard of you! Your reputation precedes you. Were circumstances not so awkward, I would say that I was glad to make your acquaintance . . ."

Digrippa studied the man for a long moment. "Baron Quordane, isn't it? I know of you, too. These circumstances make me especially glad to make *your* acquaintance."

"Obviously you don't know what you're getting yourself into, Digrippa. You are interfering with momentous affairs. If we might have a moment alone, I could explain everything to your satisfaction."

"I wouldn't trust him, Talmis," Cander said. "He is a slippery devil."

"I know," Digrippa said, giving him a sly glance. "I know all about our Baron Quordane." He turned back to Quordane with an avid smile. "We will talk, Baron, but not here, not now. For a fact, I do not understand exactly what is going on here, but I expect to learn all."

Quordane wiped a growing sheen of perspiration from his forehead with the back of his hand, then nervously loosened the collar of his shirt. "Really, Digrippa, you are being most unreasonable . . ."

Digrippa shrugged. "Under the circumstances, it pleases me to be so. Now, what is in that bag that you clutch so tightly? It seems to be important to you." He indicated the canvas bag that the baron had taken from Kemp.

Quordane's chubby fingers fidgeted with the collar of his shirt. "That is none of your concern."

"We shall see. Vedrai, please relieve the baron of his burden."

"No." Quordane gave a crooked little smile, as he drew an odd gold medallion from his shirt. Clenching it in his hand, he said, "I cannot say that it has been a pleasure, Digrippa. When next we meet, I expect that the conditions will be more agreeable."

Quordane closed his eyes, and his face acquired an almost fervent aspect. He pronounced a peculiar phrase that did not seem to be in any language Cander had ever heard. It sounded to him like: *"Afvar nas jerhammon, ke afvar!"*

The ground seemed to tremble, very faintly, as if something enormously heavy were being rolled along nearby. Suddenly a jagged slash of blazing light appeared over Quordane, seeming to conceal within it a rift of absolute darkness. A hot, fetid wind swept over Cander, as a huge spectral hand reached from the rift and plucked Quordane from where he stood, drawing him into the zone of darkness. The wind fell still, the rift closed, the vibrations died. It all happened so quickly that Cander felt that he would have missed it entirely if he had happened to blink. As it was, he almost doubted the witness of his own senses . . . except that Quordane was no longer there, a fact that no amount of rationalization could evade.

Digrippa scowled. "I was sure that we had him. Damn."

While everyone else still gaped stupidly at Quordane's extraordinary disappearance, Rensloe Fant tried to make a run for it. Vedrai raced after him, though, catching up with the man before he could reach the street. Leaping, Vedrai caught Fant by the shoulders and bore him down to the ground.

Digrippa acknowledged Fant's attempted escape with a disinterested glance. "Cander," he said, "why don't you make yourself useful. Collect up those pistols."

Cander nodded abstractedly. As he bent to pick up the discarded pistols, his mind was awhirl with questions. Who was Quordane? What had he wanted with the Chandler's Theater? How had he managed his spectacular disappearance? And then there was Digrippa: What was his interest in this affair?

Cradling the weapons in the crook of one arm, Cander went to stand by Digrippa. "You had me followed."

"Yes."

"Why?"

Digrippa dismissed the question with an airy gesture. "There'll be plenty of time for that later. Eveline has a carriage nearby. I propose that we withdraw to my house, where we can inquire into these matters at greater leisure."

"You have a lot of questions to answer."

Digrippa tilted back his head, to regard Cander through half-slitted eyes. "As do you, dear fellow. As do you."

There was a sudden disturbance nearby. Cander heard the unmistakable sound of a man having his breath knocked out. Turning, he saw that the big man Rohn was on his knees, clutching his stomach. Kemp stood over him, right hand balled into a fist, smiling pleasantly.

11

"I tell you, I don't *know* what's going on," Kemp said hoarsely. His voice had been returning slowly, soothed by innumerable cups of hot jafar sweetened with honey, brought to him on a silver tray by the slender, subtle Vedrai. His neck still hurt, but at least he found himself in more comfortable circumstances. He was not exactly sure what he had fallen into. He knew both Cander Ellis and Talmis Digrippa, but only by name and reputation. For the moment, it was enough to know that they were enemies of Quordane and the royalists. "The royalists abducted me by sorcerous means and forced me to steal a box from the Black Tower. Once I did that, I became expendable. They were about to murder me when Cander came along. Trust me, I was not somebody they confided in overmuch."

Cander Ellis made an impatient *tsk*ing sound. He shifted abruptly on the plush settee he occupied, his body indicating an attitude of disbelief. Cander fascinated Kemp. His face, his hair, his attitude, his attire all betokened the essence of the handsome young popinjay—except perhaps for that dark, stiff, incongruous mustache. Yet to rescue him, Cander had challenged four dangerous men—definitely not the act of the idle, ineffectual fop he appeared. Much of the time, his manner seemed languid, almost irresolute, but then he would reveal a burst of mercurial energy that was startling by contrast. Clearly, Cander Ellis was not entirely what he appeared.

"It's true," Kemp said.

"I believe him, Cander," Digrippa said. He stood in front of the small fireplace, looking restless and pent up. "You've been absent from Lorum, or you surely would have heard how a thief named Jerod Kemp vanished mysteriously from the gibbet. It has been a common topic of rumor for more than a fortnight now."

Digrippa turned to Kemp, and his shrewd eyes seemed to bore deep into Kemp's soul. "So, suppose you tell us about it in your own words. What happened to you after you vanished from Tailor's Green? What *do* you know?"

Kemp felt suddenly nervous, as if he were being expected to pass some obscure test. "There isn't that much to tell," he said diffidently. But, leaning slightly forward in his chair, he told briefly of how he had found himself in the service of Quordane, of his meeting with Lalerin, of the medallions in Quordane's desk, of coming to Lorum, and finally of his theft of the box from the Black Tower. He gave only a bare account of the facts, trimming away all of the attached emotion, which he preferred to hold for himself.

Throughout, Digrippa and Cander studied him, obviously weighing his words and applying them to what they already knew. Digrippa's gaze seemed to glitter and dance with comprehension, while Cander's remained more guarded and begrudging. Halfway through his tale, Kemp noticed that Eveline was standing in the doorway. He did not know how long she had been there—perhaps the whole while.

Knowing that the woman was watching him, Kemp felt suddenly exposed and self-conscious. He stammered over his words, and his already marginal voice threatened to constrict away to nothing. There was something in the way that she looked at him that made him uncomfortable. It was almost as if she knew him, all of him, even those parts that he did not wish to be known. It was ridiculous, of course. They had only just met. She knew nothing of him or his life. Still . . .

"And that's all," Kemp found himself saying, ending with a slight flourish of the wrist and a weary smile.

"*Excellent*, Kemp," Digrippa said. "That does fill in some blank places. Thank you. There is one thing, however. This case you took from the Black Tower, surely you looked inside it?"

"I did."

"What was inside?"

Kemp shrugged. "Nothing of any apparent value: a plain dagger and a rather sinister-looking iron crown."

Digrippa and his sister exchanged pained looks. "There," he said. "They have it. I should have realized what they were after when Cander first came to us."

Cander Ellis stood. *"What?"* he demanded. "This has all

been interesting, of course, but I find myself more mystified than ever. All that effort for a dagger and an iron crown? Why?"

"All in good time, Cander," Digrippa said tartly. "If we start rushing willy-nilly down every avenue of inquiry, all will be confusion. Let me finish my questions before you start in, please."

Cander went to the hearth and draped himself across the mantelpiece in an fashion that was both casual and artful. "I still don't understand what your interest in all of this is."

"I do not wish to go into that at this moment, Cander. Rest assured that my reasons are neither frivolous nor unseemly."

Cander narrowed his eyes pensively, but said nothing. Digrippa turned his attention back to Kemp. "Those medallions you mentioned—the one you took from Quordane's desk, and the other one—do you still have them with you?"

Kemp considered the question for a moment. He saw no reason to lie. "Yes."

"May I see them for a moment?"

Kemp dug into his pockets, found the gold medallion he had taken from Quordane's desk, and held it out to Digrippa. The magician plucked it from his hand and examined it, frowning. "And the other one?"

The bronze medallion still hung on a chain around Kemp's neck. He unbuttoned his shirt, drew it out, and pulled it off over his head. Wincing from the sharp spasm of pain that came when he lifted his head, he handed the medallion and chain to Digrippa.

Clenching the medallions, one in each hand, the magician nodded and went quickly from the room. "Wait a moment," he said, throwing the words over his shoulder. Eveline stood aside when he reached the doorway, then followed him down the hall.

Kemp and Cander were left staring uncomfortably at each other, matching reticent, sardonic little smiles. Cander looked away first, as he started to prowl about the room, eyes flitting restlessly over the furnishings. Pausing before a round, convex mirror, he seemed to study his own face. After a moment, he plucked at one end of his mustache and, much to Kemp's astonishment, peeled it away from his upper lip. Rubbing his denuded lip thoughtfully, he turned, saw Kemp gaping at him, smiled. "There, that's better," he said.

"Um," Kemp said ambiguously.

* * *

At last, Eveline returned. She stepped into the room and beckoned to Kemp and Cander with a gesture. "Come," she said. "Talmis wants to show you something."

Kemp exchanged uncertain looks with Cander, and they followed the woman from the room. Walking with a quick, light stride, Eveline led them downstairs, to a vast room crowded with long tables, all covered with strange implements and apparatus. Kemp stood just inside the door for a moment, trying to comprehend the evident mysteries of the room and its contents.

Talmis Digrippa sat on a tall stool, hunched over a clawfooted table. In his hand was a silver-tipped wand. Before him were the two medallions, set about a yard apart. A curious sort of a mirror was set behind them. Framed in black wood carved with arcane symbols, its silvered surface had an unusually dark, tarnished appearance. The mirror reflected Digrippa, the tabletop, the medallions, and . . . something else. In the reflection, complex patterns of light flickered over both of the medallions. The two patterns were similar but subtly different.

Digrippa turned a quick glance over his shoulder. "Ah, Cander, Kemp, what do you think of this?"

Cander moved closer. "Very pretty. Apart from that, I can't really say. It would help if we knew what we were looking at."

Kemp grunted softly in agreement. He fancied that he could feel the force of magic in the air, tingling on his skin—but what manner of magic, and for what purpose, he could not imagine.

"Both of these medallions have had potent spells attached to them," Digrippa explained. "I have simply caused these spells to reveal themselves. You may notice that the spells differ in slight but functionally significant ways."

Kemp studied the winking, silvery patterns in the mirror. They *were* different, though Kemp lacked the expertise to know what, if anything, the differences signified.

With a fluid, rather exaggerated gesture that seemed to belong more to a street-corner conjurer than to a master magician, Digrippa indicated the bronze medallion. "The spell that is bound to this one is by far the simpler of the two. It seems to serve as a magical beacon, allowing its wearer to be found easily. This is how Doctor Stahlgrave was able to locate you, when he transported you from the gibbet to Quordane's manse in West Gahant."

"That would mean that the prison priest who gave it to me was a royalist."

"Either that, or in their employ."

Kemp nodded absently. In the back of his mind, he had suspected this all along. To have his suspicion confirmed absolutely, though, was somehow shocking.

Seeming to divine Kemp's thoughts, Digrippa said, "It really shouldn't come as a terrible surprise, given recent events in Branion, that the Protectorate is riddled through and through with royalist agents. It is one very wormy apple. But I digress."

Digrippa touched the bronze medallion with the tip of his wand. Eyes narrowed with concentration, he muttered a foreign word. Abruptly the bright pattern reflected in the mirror over the medallion faded and died, leaving the one that remained over the gold medallion as a singular miracle.

"You may have this one back, if you wish. I can't recommend it. The spell is active. Conceivably, you could be snatched away at any time, were you to carry it."

"You may keep it," Kemp said.

"Wise." Digrippa turned to the gold medallion. "Now, this one is overlaid with a much more interesting spell. I haven't totally unraveled it yet, but I can hazard a guess as to its function. I would say that this spell is designed to call a certain demon and compel it to transport the wearer to a specified place."

He sat musing for a moment. "All in all, an impressive work. It's a tricky matter to weave so complex a spell and bind it to an object in such a way that it remains stable until called upon. Dangerous, too. Demons are unpredictable things. I don't think that any spell could be designed to control one with an absolute certainty."

Cander's face betrayed a look of dawning comprehension. "So, this Quordane fellow must have used a similar medallion when he made his remarkable escape . . ."

"*Obviously.*" Eveline, who had remained near the door, came forward now, to stand between Kemp and Cander. Kemp felt the slight pressure of her shoulder against his upper arm; he imagined that he could feel her warmth, even through the heavy fabric of his coat—a delightfully discomfiting sensation.

Digrippa studied the pattern in the mirror. "Yes, yes," he murmured, "it becomes clear. An interesting spell, indeed. It occurs to me that it might be amended somewhat, to a possibly profitable result. It would be a delicate matter, but *hmm* . . ." The magician cupped his chin in the palm of his hand, as his eyes traced over the pattern before him.

"Gentlemen," Eveline said in a muted voice, "let us retire to the sitting room. I'm afraid that Talmis will likely be lost to us for several hours at least."

Without saying anything, Kemp and Cander turned and followed the woman from the room.

"I suppose that we owe you something of an explanation, Cander," Eveline said. She sat in an erect but relaxed manner on a plush divan across from Cander and Kemp, her fingers laced around a crystal wine goblet. The effect, Cander thought, was quite breathtaking. "When you came to Talmis for help in finding the man who engineered the closure of the Chandler's Theater—"

"Rensloe Fant."

"*Not* Rensloe Fant, actually. His real name is Jursen Palintine. He is a partner of Balthar's Bank, and a royalist agent. We have been well aware of Palintine and his sympathies for some time now. When you brought his recent activities to our attention, we became curious. We decided to keep an eye on you while you pursued Palintine."

Cander considered what the woman had said; it seemed to raise more questions than it answered. "Uh, why?"

Eveline regarded him with a cool look. "Why? . . . I don't think I quite understand the question."

"Why do you and Talmis care anything about Jursen Palintine or the royalists? I can't believe that it is a mere whim."

"Let's just say that we maintain a certain interest in the subject of evil."

Cander restrained a laugh. "*Evil!* Surely you overstate your case. The royalists are hardly a pleasant lot, and I certainly would not like to see them return to power, but . . . evil?"

"Evil," Eveline said steadily. "Evil, to their very core."

Kemp cleared his throat. "It's true," he said softly. "If you'd spent as much time around them as I have, Cander, you'd know."

Cander shrugged. He had a difficult time believing in the existence of evil, but this did not seem the time for a philosophical argument. "I'll bow to your superior knowledge, then. Evil or not, the question is: What are they after?"

"That is not the question," Eveline said. "It never has been. We all know what they are after: the destruction of the Protectorate and the ascension of Lalerin to the throne of Branion."

"Mm, yes—but they seem to be going about it in a very odd

way. Why plot to have the Chandler's closed down? In order to steal a dagger and an iron crown? Why?"

"*That* is the question, isn't it?"

"Well, yes. I thought so when I asked Talmis about it. He didn't see fit to give me any answer." Cander did his best not to sound peevish, but the patronizing expression on Eveline's face told him that he had not been entirely successful.

"You must forgive Talmis. This is a complicated subject, and his mind was elsewhere . . . how shall I begin? Have you never heard of an iron crown in connection with the House Saphrinas?"

"Some old stories, perhaps. Didn't they use an iron crown in the coronation of the old kings of Branion?" Cander considered this for a brief moment. Perhaps he was being oversubtle. "Is *that* what this is all about? Do the royalists hope to somehow exploit the symbolism of the traditional coronation crown?"

Eveline smiled, and Cander marveled. "Not . . . exactly," she said, "but you're getting close. How much do you know about the early history of the House Saphrinas?"

"Only what old Master Kirth taught me in grammar school. Nasty old fellow. Smelled of mildew and fried onions." Cander knew a bit more than that, of course. He had read books dealing with the subject, but much of what he had gleaned had already sunk into the depths of his memory.

"I'll start at the beginning, then. Five hundred years ago, there was no Branion, just a collection of small, constantly warring principalities. At this time, innumerable minor princelings strove to unite all others under their own banner. Lalerin's ancestor, Volmer Saphrinas, was merely one among many."

"That much I know. I know also that Volmer was almost crushed by his enemies, and spent a year hiding in the barren hills, before returning to destroy his enemies and cement his rule over Branion."

"Yes, but you are getting ahead of the story. When Volmer was driven into hills, he was a nearly broken man. His lands and titles were lost. He had only a few dozen men-at-arms, among them his two young sons. Many were wounded or sick, all were hungry. They retreated deep into the hills, into lands inhabited only by the Gwyndi, the long-vanquished original inhabitants of Branion. They wandered there for weeks, under dire conditions. Finally they came upon the ruined remains of an old Gwyndi temple, still tended by a few aged priests. Volmer's first inclination was to kill or drive off the priests and take whatever food they had. He would have done it, too, if the priests had not offered him something he could not resist."

"What could they offer him?" Kemp asked suddenly. "Even gold and jewels would have been of limited use to him, in his circumstances."

"*Power*. Nothing more, and nothing less. They were priests of the faded god Brani, who is an old god, perhaps the oldest, and perhaps the last god to survive those dim times before people came to expect justice and mercy from their gods. They promised Volmer that if he consecrated himself properly to Brani, he would be given rule over all of Branion, in the manner of the old kings."

Cander frowned. "And he believed them?"

"I can only imagine that they showed him sufficient cause to believe."

"So, why would they offer Volmer such power? He was nothing, an interloper, a member of the usurping race, and a virtual vagabond at that."

"I can only surmise that they knew that Volmer's nature would be sympathetic with that of Brani. Understand that theirs was a dying faith. Their prayers had kept their god alive, if quiescent, but unless something was done soon, he would fade into the void of Disbelief. At any rate, Volmer agreed, and the consecration was performed."

A thought that had been flitting vaguely through Cander's mind suddenly burst fully into his awareness. "I think I begin to understand. The crown and the dagger were part of the consecration ceremony, yes?"

"Very good, Cander," Eveline said, though Cander suspected that a hidden irony was attached to the words. "You have it exactly. The iron crown is the same that was used to crown the Gwyndi kings of old. It was a necessary part of the consecration."

"And the dagger?"

The woman's expression darkened. "It, too. The ceremony required that Volmer shed the blood of his own blood . . ."

An extraordinary look abruptly moved across Kemp's face, one equally composed of realization and revulsion. "Volmer sacrificed one of his own sons," he stated in a flat tone.

"Yes."

A strange chill tingled at Cander's spine. He prided himself on his insight into the human heart, and yet he now found himself reduced to mute shock. How could any man dispassionately kill his own child?

"Volmer received the full benefit of his bargain," Eveline said. "From that time on, he was invincible. Men hastened to his banner, and his enemies fell like weak reeds before him. Fortune seemed always to smile upon him. Within a year, he had cemented all of Branion under his rule."

The woman paused and drank with tight lips from her cup. "Each of the kings of the House Saphrinas who followed after Volmer in turn reenacted the consecration to Brani, which was always conducted in great secrecy, for obvious reasons. That is, until the time of Lalerin's father, Carelinas. Now, Carelinas was no less ruthless than any of his forebears, but he hesitated to perform the bloody ritual. Perhaps he didn't believe in the power of Brani—who knows? As a result, though, he was overthrown and faced the headsman's sword."

Cander considered this for a moment. "So, the implication is that the royalists plan to perform this awful little ritual, to consecrate Lalerin."

"Yes, certainly."

Studying the woman's perfectly impassive face, he said, "Do you really believe all this?"

"Beyond any doubt. Talmis and I have documented everything very carefully."

"I don't know," Cander said, shaking his head. "I find this all extremely hard to credit."

"Do you have any better explanation for why Quordane and Lalerin would have me steal an iron crown from a roomful of priceless treasures?" Kemp asked sharply.

"No," he admitted. "But if it *is* true, then there's not much we can do about it now, is there? They have what they wanted. They will be able to perform the ritual whenever they want, if indeed they haven't already."

"Fortunately, there's more to it than that," Eveline said. "First, the consecration rite must be performed at the old temple to Brani, and that means that they must journey to Branion. Second, the ritual demands that a special incense be compounded—and Talmis knows more about this than I do—from a rare and shy plant, which these days can only be found on the banks of the Wistram River, in Cyemal. The plant must be used within a month of being harvested, I've been told, or the essential oils will deteriorate. The royalists will have to dispatch someone who knows what to look for to Cyemal; that should take at least a fortnight. We have time."

"Maybe not," Cander said, memory coming to him in a sudden flash. "I happen to know that Doctor Stahlgrave crossed the border into Cyemal more than a week ago."

Eveline swung a startled look in his direction. "*What!* Are you sure? How do you know this?"

"I'm sure. I watched him cross over with my own eyes."

"And how is it that you happened to be there at that particular moment? Luck?" She held up a interdicting hand. "No, no, you needn't answer. I don't suppose it matters, anyway. Well. This puts an entirely different complexion on the matter. We may have less time than we had thought."

"Well," Kemp said, "it seems clear what we must do, if we are to stop the royalists."

"Indeed? I am anxious to hear what that is."

"We must go to this Gwyndi temple and prevent them from performing the rite."

The woman gave him a wistful smile. "Undoubtedly that would be the thing to do, if we knew exactly where it is. Unfortunately, we don't."

"Oh."

"The Three Crows," Cander said suddenly.

Both Kemp and Eveline turned curious stares on him. "The Three Crows," he explained. "It's an inn in West Gahant, on the road to Branion. *Everyone* stops there on the way to or from Branion. Stahlgrave stayed there after leaving Branion. I'd bet anything that he stops there on his way back from Cyemal."

"Mmm," Eveline said judiciously, "interesting thought. Of course, we can't know for certain that Stahlgrave will return along the same route he left by."

"No, but it seems reasonable that he would. Besides, even if he doesn't pass that way, it is likely that Lalerin *will*. It is, after all, the only decent road in that part of Gahant. And from everything I've heard of Lalerin, I can't imagine that he would be content to jostle along some forsaken cattle path, if he had a choice in the matter."

"A good point."

"I am friendly with the owner of the Three Crows. At the least, I'm sure that he could tell us if there has been any unusual activity in the area."

"Well, it's a plan—perhaps a good one. Why don't we discuss it with Talmis in the morning? Vedrai is, mmm, *questioning* our prisoners. I expect that by morning we should know whether or not they can tell us anything of value. I don't hold out any great hope, but there is always a chance."

The woman rose. "In the meantime, I trust that you will both consent to be our guests for the night? There are rooms made up for you."

"Of course," Cander said. "You are most kind."

Kemp gave a slow nod, looking almost comically grave. "I have nowhere else to go."

12

Tucked into a narrow old bed, in a room that smelled vaguely of camphor, Cander spent a restless night. The bed, with its high, curving head- and footboards, was too short for comfortable sleeping, compelling him to keep his knees pulled up slightly at all times. Even if it were not for that, he would not have been able to sleep well. His head was too full of the night's events; the details kept floating around and recombining in weird and twisted ways. The Protectorate, the royalists, Lalerin, Quordane, Rensloe Fant, an iron crown, an ancient god seemingly out of some nightmare—it all seemed so unlikely. And yet, deep in his heart he could not help feeling that it was all true.

Cander was up early the next morning, even as the first rays of dawn were creeping through the diamond-shape panes of the small window opposite the bed. He dressed with less attention than usual, then went downstairs. He found both Eveline and Digrippa in the white-walled breakfast room, cups and a platter of pastries before them. Digrippa appeared pale and pinched; Cander could tell at a glance that the man had not slept at all. Eveline, in an azure blue dressing gown, managed to look as fresh and composed as ever.

The two looked up as Cander came into the room. Digrippa gave him a crooked smile. "Ah, Cander. Come and join us."

After drawing up a chair, Cander sat next to Eveline. He poured himself a cup of jafar, cradled it in both hands, and sipped from it gratefully.

"Eveline has been telling me of your idea about the Three Crows in Gahant. There is much to commend the notion—though, of course, it isn't entirely without flaw. Since I haven't any better ideas, however, I think that we may have to go with it."

"Your prisoners haven't been able to tell you anything?"

"Nothing immediately applicable."

"Not even Rensloe Fant?"

"Rensloe Fant? Oh, you mean Jursen Palintine. No, nothing that we can use. He knows a little of the royalist organization here in Lorum, very little else. The truth is that he was simply a pawn—though, of course, he doesn't quite see it that way."

"Well, if you're finished with him, may I have him?"

Digrippa raised an eyebrow. "Why? What would you do with him?"

"I need him. He is the key to proving that Lor Brunnage and the Chandler's Theater are innocent of treason against the Protectorate."

Fixing him with a coolly analytical look, Digrippa said, "I should be interested to know how you intend to go about proving that, simple playwright and private citizen that you are."

Cander felt the blood come to his cheeks, betraying him. What could he say? He could hardly tell Digrippa that, as an agent of the Protectorate, he had access to the highest levels of the government. "I know people," he said finally. "I know people who know people."

"Hmm, I just bet you do. Very well, you may have him if you want him."

"Good. I will give you an address. If you will bind him securely and have one of your men deliver him there, I would be most grateful." After taking out his notebook, Cander scrawled the address of an abandoned warehouse that Walthorne's agents used as a safe drop. He tore out the page and passed it across the table to Digrippa.

The magician took the page, glanced at it, and said, "All right, it will be done." He took up his cup sipped, grimaced, and set it aside. "Now, on to more immediate concerns. If we are to reach the Three Crows in time to do any good, we must leave soon. Tomorrow morning, at the latest. This evening would be better yet. When can you be ready, Cander?"

"When can *I* be ready? That . . . might prove difficult. My own business is far from finished. I don't know that I can leave Lorum right now."

Digrippa blinked at him with undisguised astonishment. "But, my dear fellow, you must! *You* are the one who is familiar with

Gahant. *You* are the one who is friendly with the owner of the Three Crows."

"It's not that I'm not anxious to help," Cander lied. "However, there are still the matters of the Chandler's Theater and the members of its Company who have been unjustly imprisoned."

"Cander," Digrippa said steadily, "if the royalists succeed in what they are about, none of that will matter. The shadow of the crown has already touched Branion, and the Chandler's Theater is only one of the things that have withered under it. If it should fall completely over the land, no one will be safe, and no aspect of life will be as it was before."

"Believe him, Cander," Eveline said, her voice soft. "He is telling you the truth. You must help us. We need you."

Gently the woman touched his hand. Cander looked into her face, seeing only sincere concern reflected in her delicate features. She really did need him.

He was lost.

After leaving Digrippa's house, Cander headed directly for the Bank Street copyist shop. There were no public cabs to be found so far from the center of the city, so he was forced to hurry along on foot for a good part of the way. It was a cold, breezy morning; even so, his heavy woolen garments were soon damp with perspiration.

Finally Cander reached a street that was busy enough to boast a few coaches for hire. Upon flagging one down, he told the driver to take him to Bank Street. He saw no reason to take an elusive route; he was certain that no one was following him. Sitting slouched in the back of the coach, as it trundled over the cobbled streets of Lorum, he occupied himself by fretting over the ominous circumstances that Digrippa and Eveline had detailed. He wondered what their stake in the matter was. There had to be something that they were not telling him. People just didn't concern themselves with vague, convoluted plots without a good reason. What reason could they have, though?

The coach drew up across the street from the copyist shop. Climbing out, Cander paid the driver, then crossed the street and entered the shop. As usual, there were no customers. After calling for a pen and some paper from the old man behind the counter, Cander carefully composed his message to Walthorne, blotted it, folded it three ways, and passed it across the counter.

"This is an extremely important job," he said. "I'll wait here until it is done."

"As you wish, sir," the man said, fixing him with a shrewd look. He took the folded sheet of paper and disappeared through the curtain into the back.

While he waited, Cander checked his watch, gently wound it, and returned it to his waistcoat pocket. By now, he figured, Digrippa's men should have delivered their charge to the address that he had given them.

After some minutes, the old man returned from behind the curtain. "The job," he said, "will require more time. I suggest that you come back in two hours."

Cander nodded. "Two hours."

When he left the shop, Cander found an agreeable restaurant several blocks away and ordered an early lunch. He had considered going home to his apartment and taking a nap, but he wasn't sure that he would be able to wake up in time to make his appointment with Walthorne. He was tired.

Cander dawdled over lunch as long as he could. Even so, after all the dishes had been taken away, he still had more than a half an hour to kill. He spent the time walking along the riverfront, letting the brisk, moist wind revive him, then returned to the copyist shop.

The old man ushered him directly into the back. After opening the door to the secret room, Cander stepped through and saw Walthorne standing with his back to the door, arms clasped behind his back.

As Cander closed the door, the man turned and gave him an imposing look. He said, "Well, Cander, you have been the busy one, haven't you?"

He shrugged. "So it would seem. Have your people picked up my little package yet?"

"Jursen Palintine? Yes. He arrived somewhat damaged, but otherwise in good order. He is quite upset with you."

"I can imagine."

"You did know, didn't you, that Jursen Palintine is a prominent person, with a number of powerful friends? He is not the sort who may be detained on a whim."

Cander stared at the man. "You didn't let him go, did you?"

The man's pale lips quirked up at the corners into tight hooks, which Cander took to be a smile. "Fortunately, none of his powerful friends know where he is at the moment. We were therefore bold enough to put certain questions to him—in, I might say, a rather athletic fashion. He has already proved extraordinarily helpful."

"*Good.* I hope that it's now entirely clear to you that Lor Brunnage is innocent of treason?"

"Certainly I believe that Brunnage is guilty of nothing more than greed and stupidity."

"I trust, then, that you will see to it that Brunnage and any other members of the Chandler's Company are released, and the theater reopened."

"We'll discuss that in a moment. First, I'd like you to tell me exactly what you have been about since last I saw you. Your written report was vague on several points."

"Very well. Do you mind if we sit? This will take a few minutes."

"By all means. Your comfort is important to me." Walthorne lowered himself stiffly to the settee and perched there like a canny old vulture waiting for something to die. Cander drew up a chair, sat down, and hesitated. This was going to be delicate, he knew. He did not know why Digrippa and his sister had involved themselves in this affair, but he was fairly certain that they would not want the Protectorate casting a curious gaze in their direction.

"*Well?*" Walthorne said pointedly. "Begin. I don't have all day to spend with you."

After swallowing, Cander began. Thinking feverishly ahead, he told of how he had located Jursen Palintine, and of the night's events at the Chandler's Theater, including Quordane remarkable disappearance. He altered the story slightly as he went along, making it sound as if Digrippa's actions were purely at his behest. This left a number of logical gaps in the story, and Cander was afraid that Walthorne, normally a meticulous listener, would notice them. Fortunately, the man seemed distracted; he accepted everything that Cander told him without question or comment.

Finally Walthorne gave a rigid nod. "I see, I see. And you think that you and your associates can intercept either Lalerin or Stahlgrave while they are still in Gahant?"

"Very likely. But there's some question of what we can accomplish even if we do find one or both of them. The royalists have assembled a potent force in Gahant. It might be better if you assigned the task to an armed detachment."

Walthorne made a sour grimace. "There's nothing that I'd like better. That would pose certain difficulties, however. You seem to have realized what I've known for some time: that the Protectorate is riddled through with royalist agents. I don't know who can be trusted anymore. Given time, I will be able to put together a reliable force—but we don't *have* time. You will have to do this thing."

"So, if I find Stahlgrave or Lalerin, what then?"

"You will just have to use your imagination. You've done well enough so far—better than I would have expected. The important thing is that you *find* them. That will give me the chance to muster enough loyal men to deal with the situation. If you can stop the royalists on your own, so much the better. If not, you are to follow them until you can contact me."

"How will I contact you? I'll be far from Lorum, in the wilds of Gahant."

"I'll send a man after you, to act as liaison."

"Who?"

"Someone you know well."

"Not *Shalby*."

"Indeed, Shalby. I know that you two have had your little differences—"

"That's putting it mildly."

"—But I am confident of his abilities. More to the point, I am confident of his loyalties. He has every reason to hate the royalists. Those scars on his face came courtesy of a royalist mortar, during the Civil War. He was sixteen. Later, his family home was burned to the ground by troops commanded by Baron Quordane, as they retreated toward Gahant. Did you know that? No, of course not. You two are always too busy sniping at each other to ever actually talk."

Cander frowned, and tried to think of some adequate answer to that. He failed. "All right, point taken," he said quietly.

"Good." Walthorne fished his watch out of a waistcoat pocket, opened the cover with a thumbnail, and consulted it. "In case something goes wrong and you can't get in touch with Shalby, look for me at Morulin, a town not far from the border. That is where I intend to assemble the forces of the Protectorate. Now, if there's nothing else, I have an appointment." Snapping the cover down, he started to rise.

"Wait," Cander said. "What about Lor Brunnage and the rest?"

"I'm afraid that there is nothing that I can do about that now. If I had Brunnage freed, it would be noted. It would bring attention where we least want it. I will try to see to it that Brunnage is made more comfortable, but that's all I can do."

Cander knew that there was no point in arguing. Walthorne was right, as much as he hated to admit it. "You expect a great deal, in exchange for very little."

"I know."

Upon leaving the copyist shop, Cander went directly to his apartment. After stripping off his garments and throwing them on the bed, he attired himself in appropriate traveling clothes: fine woolen hose, knee-length breeches, a dark-green coat trimmed with red and boasting a superfluity of brass buttons. He exchanged his shoes for his most comfortable pair of boots. Scrutinizing himself in the mirror, he saw that he cut an agreeably dashing figure. His hair needed to be cut, but there was little to be done about that now. He fastened it back with a length of red ribbon; then, after a moment's consideration, tied matching ribbons over each knee.

He got out his traveling kit, which he had not yet had a chance to unpack, and added a few articles of clothing to it. Snapping the kit shut, he looked about him and sighed. Time to go.

After closing and locking the apartment door behind him, Cander went out onto the street. He flagged down a passing cab and rode out to Digrippa's house, his thoughts gloomy. As the cab clattered away, he walked up the path to the front door and knocked. After a few moments, the door opened, and he was met by Vedrai, who greeted him with a faint, ironic smirk.

"I am ready," Cander said.

13

It was a long journey, and, for Kemp, not without its nightmarish aspects. Lurching, swaying, seeming to find every defect in the road, Digrippa's small coach raced toward Gahant. The constant movement made sleep impossible for Kemp—a problem that none of his companions seemed to share. While they slumbered, Kemp sat dourly wedged into a corner of the coach, wondering why he was even there. Of what concern was any of this to him? He could have as easily declared his part in the affair done and just walked away.

Why hadn't he?

A large part of it, certainly, was that he still felt that he had unfinished business with Quordane. The baron had used him, betrayed him; Kemp hated the thought that he would prosper from his treachery. There was something else, though. Try as he might, Kemp could not put the faces of Lalerin's wife and child out of his mind. If Eveline's story was to be believed—and Kemp did believe it, as improbable as it had sounded—then the boy was marked for death. Remembering the singularly cold-blooded look that Lalerin had given his son, Kemp felt a terrible certainty pervading his consciousness. He had no doubt: Lalerin intended to sacrifice the boy to the god of his own ambition. Was it possible that Ceris was aware of what horrors her husband had planned for their son? Somehow, Kemp couldn't force himself to believe that.

The coach plunged on through the darkness. After lifting the window flap, Kemp could see dark trees lining the road like shadowy giants, a moon that glowed dimly through the overcast sky, and gauzy curls of mist churned by the coach's passage. Wondering how long it would be before they reached their destination, he settled back, closed his eyes, and tried to at least rest, even if he could not sleep.

Shortly after the first light of dawn crept over the horizon, transfiguring the blackness into a ghostly grey, the coach rolled to a stop beside a dismal wood-framed structure. After a moment, there came a single sharp knock on the door of the coach. The door creaked open, and Kemp saw Vedrai, who was serving as their coachman, standing in the chill mist, wrapped in a bulky cloak, a cocked hat pulled low on his head. His complexion was several shades paler than normal, and his features were unusually puffy. "This is where we change to a fresh team of horses," he said. "If you want to get something to eat, or to attend to any other needs, now is the time."

Kemp's companions slowly began to rouse themselves. Cander Ellis at least had the good grace to look groggy. The playwright drew a noisy breath, rubbing the back of his hand across his eyes; his eyes did not focus right away. Neither Digrippa nor his sister showed any sign at all that they had been sleeping, however, which Kemp thought rather unfair.

"Thank you, Vedrai," Digrippa said mildly, hands cupped over the gold head of his walking stick. "We'll avail ourselves of the facilities."

Upon emerging stiffly from the coach, they stood blinking curiously at their surroundings for a moment. There were trees all around, many bare-limbed, or nearly so. Set back from the road, two small buildings occupied the top of a low rise, the largest of which was obviously a stable. In the grey light of an overcast morning, the place looked small, dreary, and forlorn. Somewhere, a dog was barking: a melancholy sound at that delicate hour.

Cander took in the scene with a wryly disdainful look. "Charming spot," he remarked to Eveline.

"Mmm," she answered serenely.

Indicating with one hand the second of the two buildings, Vedrai said, "You may wait inside. There should be a fire, and food." Kemp could only suppose that Vedrai had come this way before.

Cander offered his arm to Eveline. "Allow me," he said. The woman hesitated a moment, then linked her arm with Cander's, giving him a remote look. They strolled over to the building, followed closely by a somber Digrippa.

Kemp stared after them, giving his head a small shake. He envied Cander his smooth assurance, while at the same time wondering how any woman could possibly be deceived by it. To Kemp, it seemed so clearly impersonal, calculated. How could anyone think otherwise? Perhaps it wasn't so much that Cander was fooling anyone as it was that he was simply extending an unmistakable invitation, which a woman could accept or not, as she chose.

For Kemp's part, he was not really made jealous by the attentions that Cander lavished on Eveline. He was welcome to her. For, as undeniably attractive as the woman was, there was something about her that Kemp found eerily daunting. She frightened him a little. *Why should that be?* he wondered, as he pensively followed the others into the building.

In a small, poorly furnished common room, they were met by a massive, phlegmatic woman, who seated them at a table in the corner, took their order, and went off, without ever altering her cheerless mien. Breakfast, when it came, was a greasy egg and sausage pie. Kemp ate without enjoyment, while drinking down several cups of weak jafar. Gradually his mood brightened somewhat.

After breakfast, they emerged into the daylight again, and found that a fresh team of horses was already in harness, coats black and vaguely glistening. One by one, they climbed into the coach, and were soon underway once more.

As the sun reached its midday zenith, they finally reached the frontier between Branion and Gahant, and here the coach rolled to a halt. After opening a window, Digrippa leaned his head out and strained to see around the side of the coach. "Uh-oh," he said, pulling his head back into the cabin. "Trouble. It looks as if the Protectorate has closed the frontier."

"Hmm, let me talk to them," Cander said quickly, his face composed and unreadable. "There is an art to dealing successfully with border guards."

"Be my guest, dear fellow."

"A moment, then." Cander unlatched the door, rose to a low crouch, and heaved himself out through the opening. Curious to see what was happening, Kemp flashed Digrippa and Eveline a stiff smile and followed him out.

A small company of red-coated Protectorate soldiers commanded by a corpulent officer in a plumed hat stood before a makeshift barricade fashioned from a single log and several lashed-together braces. Standing beside the coach, Kemp watched while Cander strode up to the soldiers, his attitude jaunty and unconcerned. After drawing the officer off to one side, Cander talked quietly for a few moments, took a folded document from his breast pocket, and passed it to the man. Puffing out his cheeks, the officer scrutinized the document carefully, then refolded it and returned it to Cander.

The officer issued a curt order, and his men hefted the barricade and began to swivel it toward the margin of the road. Nodding to the officer, Cander returned to the coach. He glanced up at Vedrai, who still occupied the driver's box, and said, "We may continue now, Vedrai."

Catching Kemp appraising him thoughtfully, Cander smiled blandly and said, "Nothing to it, really. You just have to know how to handle these fellows." Grasping the edges of the open coach door, then, he pulled himself inside.

Kemp stared after him. The ease with which the man had gotten them through the blockade had caught his interest and aroused his suspicious nature. Could it be that Cander maintained some kind of affiliation with the Protectorate, which for some reason he was choosing to conceal? And, if so, what might that mean to their current mission?

Kemp had to wonder how far Cander could be trusted.

It was midafternoon before the coach finally drew to a stop in front of the Inn of the Three Crows. The sky was grey and threatening, streaked with patches that were so dark as to be almost black. Brisk and cold, the wind moaned through the treetops, bringing with it the damp smell of impending rain.

Cander disembarked from the coach, his legs stiff and tight from the long confinement. He yawned, stretching his arms up over his head for a moment, happy that they were finally there. It had been a tiresome journey, enlivened only by Eveline's presence. If there was anything good that had come from the confused and disagreeable circumstances in which he was entangled, it was that it had served to bring him into closer quarters with Eveline.

He had admired Eveline from the first, but had always before been forestalled by her habitual air of detached amusement. Now, though, thrown together by circumstances, working toward a common goal, who knew what might happen? To be sure, nothing that Eveline had said or done throughout the journey thus far had indicated that she was interested in taking him as a lover, but he was fully prepared to believe that she was just being reticent.

Cander saw that both Kemp and Digrippa had exited from the

coach, and now Eveline was starting to emerge. Hastily he moved to offer a hand to steady her as she climbed down. She gave him a swift, abstracted smile for his pains.

The four of them approached the entrance to the inn, while Vedrai drove the coach around the side of the building, where the stables were. Cander held the door for Eveline and the others, then slipped in behind them. At this time of day, the common room was nearly empty. Two men sat at a corner table—local merchants, to judge by their garments—and Gerj Kolin stood behind the counter, musing over a thick ledger. There was no one else.

Gerj Kolin looked up when Cander closed the door, his gaze blankly curious, until Cander stepped forward; then he gave a sudden grin and came quickly around the side of the counter, hand extended. "Cander Ellis!" he said. "Back so soon? This *is* a pleasant surprise." He gave a glance to the trio behind Cander. "And you've brought friends."

Cander took the man's hand warmly. "Hello, Gerj. Good to see you again. We'd like rooms for the night, if you can oblige us."

Gerj licked his lips thoughtfully. "Four rooms?"

Cander turned to Digrippa. "What about Vedrai?"

"He will stay with the coach."

Nodding to Gerj, Cander said, "Four rooms, then." He supposed that they could save money by sharing rooms, Cander and Kemp, Digrippa and his sister. Cander had hopes of instigating a rather different arrangement, though.

The innkeeper's smile widened. "Ah, is it any wonder that you are among my favorite customers? This way, everyone, and we will get you comfortably settled in."

Before Gerj could slip behind the counter again, Cander caught his arm and said in a low voice, "After we are settled, we would like to talk to you. In private."

The man's eyes searched Cander's face for a moment. "Of course, Cander," he said blandly. "That is easily done."

After agreeing to meet downstairs in half an hour, the four went up to their rooms to freshen up after their long journey. Cander, in fine spirits after seeing that Eveline had been put in the room across the hall from him, washed thoroughly with the hot water that a room servant brought him, humming all the while. He daubed himself with scent, then changed to fresh linen, brushed his coat carefully, and dressed. Checking his watch, he saw that he was a few minutes late. He hastened downstairs.

When he came to the foot of the stairs, he looked out across the common room and was horrified to see that Eveline, seated at a table, was quietly conversing with the serving maid Alsimae. Standing beside the table, Alsimae absently twisted the silver ring that Cander had given her.

Cander cringed inwardly. Alsimae and Eveline were the last two people in the world that he wanted to see together at this moment. What if the conversation should turn to his own self? Terrible complications could result. He hesitated a long moment, considering skulking back upstairs. He wasn't sure how much good that would do him, but . . .

Too late. Eveline suddenly looked toward the stair and saw him. A moment later, Alsimae followed the woman's gaze. She gave him a wide smile and a wave. He was caught. All he could do now was to try to brazen his way through the delicate situation.

Putting on a grin that he hoped didn't look too false, Cander left the stairs and went to the table where the two women waited. "Hello," he said, doing his best to project an attitude that was friendly yet restrained. He hoped that if he could keep the conversation from becoming too personal, he might come away with a result no worse than a bad case of nerves.

Eveline looked up at him pleasantly—perhaps too pleasantly? "Cander," she said languidly. "We were just talking about you."

Feeling the blood rising in his cheeks, he said, "Were you, indeed?"

And Alsimae gave him a glowing look, eyelashes fluttering slightly. It was appalling. "Well, Cander, you've come back. I guess that you just couldn't stay away for long."

"Um, I guess not, *ha*." This was not going nearly as well as he had hoped. In a moment, he thought, he would have no secrets left to him. Fortunately, at that moment Kemp and Digrippa came down the stairs, and Cander turned to them, as if to long-lost brothers. "Talmis! Kemp! Over here!"

The two exchanged looks, apparently startled by Cander's unexpected enthusiasm at seeing them. Hesitant, they came over to the table. "Is there anything wrong, Cander?" Digrippa asked.

"Wrong? No, there's nothing wrong."

"Mmm," the magician said dubiously, studying him.

The door behind the counter opened, and Gerj Kolin appeared in the doorway. "I'm ready whenever you want to talk, Cander," he said. "I thought that we could use my private parlor."

"We'll be right there," Cander said. He glanced quickly at each of his three companions. "Shall we?"

Digrippa quirked up an eyebrow, shrugged.

"Let's," Eveline said.

The woman arose, smoothing down her full skirt. Digrippa and Kemp accompanied her around the counter and into the private parlor. As Cander moved to follow, Alsimae caught his eye. Smiling, coyly twisting a curl into a lock of her own hair, she said, "I'll see you later, then, Cander."

"Yes," he said, "later."

Gerj Kolin's parlor was a small, windowless room, paneled with yellow pine and furnished in a comfortable, rustic style. Gerj served each of his guests a glass of wine, a delicate, limpid white imported from Trelhane. Then he settled in a high-backed wooden chair and asked, "Well, what is it that you want to talk about?"

A pause. There seemed to be an unspoken agreement that, Gerj being his friend, Cander should take the lead. "First, Gerj," he said at length, "it should be understood that whatever is said here should go no farther than this room."

The man stared at him, eyes cool, level. "Discretion is a fundamental asset that any good innkeeper should possess."

"Good. I just wanted to make sure that you understood."

"I understand discretion perfectly. What I don't yet understand is what you want from me."

"Just a little information, Gerj."

"Mm? What manner of information?"

"We are primarily interested in knowing if you have noticed, or heard of, any unusual movements along the road to Branion."

The man frowned. "Unusual? In what way unusual?"

Seated in the corner, Digrippa cleared his throat and said, "In *any* way unusual."

"No, not that I can think of. No."

"Are you sure? Nothing?"

"I'm sure. Nothing passes this way that I don't know about. There's been nothing remarkable." Gerj paused. "What, exactly, are you looking for?"

Cander said, "To be specific, we want to know if there have been any recent royalist movements into Branion."

"Why would you want to know that? Of what concern is it to you?" When Cander did not answer immediately, Gerj fixed him with a shrewd look and said, "Look here, Cander, if you want my help, you'll have to give me a better idea of what's going on. Gahant is a dangerous place in which to get involved in intrigues—and likely a deadly one, if you don't know whom you're dealing with."

"You know me well enough, I should think," Cander said.

"I do. But I don't know your companions at all. For all I know, they might be royalist agents, here to test my sympathies . . . no offense."

Digrippa smiled, shaking back his long hair. "The gentleman has a point," he said mildly. "Cander, why don't you do the honors? That is, if no one objects? . . ."

Cander glanced quickly to Kemp, then to Eveline. Kemp gave a cynical arch to his eyebrows, shrugged. Eveline was sitting on the divan, stroking an agitated index finger along the bottom of her eyepatch. The gesture registered as strange to Cander; he had never seen her exhibit this nervous mannerism before. "Go ahead," she said.

"All right. This is Talmis Digrippa. You've probably heard of him; he is a magician of some repute. This is his sister Eveline. And this is Jerod Kemp. I can assure you, with certain knowledge, that none of them are royalist agents."

"Pleased to meet you all," Gerj said with a nod. "I have, in fact, heard of you all. I can't help but wonder, though, why you would be interested in the movements of the royalists."

"This is a delicate question, and one that cannot be easily answered. Some night, I will tell you all, over several glasses of your excellent wine. In the meantime, I can tell you that we have stumbled across a royalist plot that endangers all of Branion. We have reason the believe that a body of royalist troops will be coming this way, and among them Lalerin himself. It is imperative that we intercept them."

Drumming his fingers on the carved arm of his chair, Gerj said, "As I have said, there has not been any suspicious activity on the road to Branion, as of yet. I will, of course, alert you should any occur. And, if you like, I can make some discreet inquiries about the neighborhood tomorrow. Perhaps someone knows something that has escaped my attention."

"That would be fine," Digrippa said. "Thank you."

Gerj jumped up from his chair and put his empty goblet down on the sideboard. "In the meantime," he said energetically, "enjoy your stay. Eat. Drink. Get a good night's sleep, hmm? In the morning, we'll see what can be found out."

Thoughtful and withdrawn, Cander and his three companions dined together in the inn's common room. In public, they could not discuss the subject that most occupied their thoughts, and it seemed too much effort to manufacture false topics of conversation. Cander tried to keep the mood light, commenting on the quality of the meal and the wine. None of the others seemed willing to be drawn into the spirit of the thing. Digrippa had entered into one of his remote and unapproachable phases; he scarcely said a word throughout the meal. Eveline, who had seemed troubled since their meeting with Gerj, was not much more responsive. And Kemp, hardly friendly or outgoing at his best, gazed at Cander with such a wry, cynical expression that Cander could not help but feel rather offended.

Finally, after the fruit and cheese were served, Cander became tired of the thief's smug attitude. In a low voice, he said to the man, "Tell me something, for I'm curious. You are supposed to be a great thief, which is why Quordane went to such extraordinary means to recruit you. Yet you were about to be hanged. How was it that you came to be in custody?"

Cander was gratified to see that Kemp's face lost its superior aspect. A pink flush worked its way up the man's cheeks. "No," he said stiffly. "We don't yet know each other well enough that I want to tell you that."

"Come, Kemp, we're all friends here! Tell us."

"No."

"But I am curious!"

"Cander," Eveline said firmly, "leave it be. If Jerod doesn't want to talk about it, he shouldn't have to. I'm sure that there's much in your own life that you wouldn't want to discuss in polite company."

Cander gave the woman a sharp glance, lost for words, not sure whether or not to be angry. In return, she regarded him coolly, unemotionally. He realized, suddenly, that he was being foolish. If he persisted, he would only succeed in looking even more foolish. "Oh, very well," he said. "I meant no offense, certainly."

Kemp looked away in an ostentatious manner, smirking slightly.

Eveline balled up her napkin and dropped it on the table.

"Well, it's late, and it's been a long day. I think that I shall retire."

"A good idea," Digrippa said, breaking his long silence. "I'll probably follow in a few minutes."

Eveline got up from the table, and the men half rose. "See you in the morning," she said.

Cander watched her walk away. He wanted to follow, but did not want to be too obvious. *Better to wait,* he thought.

Glancing about the room, he saw that it was a slow night for the Three Crows. Barely a third of the tables were occupied. He realized that he had not seen Alsimae that evening. He supposed that she was not working the dinner shift—a fact that gave him no small measure of relief.

Careful not to look hurried, Cander finished his cup of jafar, excused himself, and went off in pursuit of Eveline. He figured that he would knock on her door and tell her that he had noticed that she'd looked troubled at dinner. She might like that. It showed attentiveness. Besides, he really was curious to find out what was on her mind.

As Cander made his way to the stairs, he saw Gerj talking in hushed tones to a tall man in red beside the outer door. Catching sight of Cander, Gerj gave a quick smile and a nod. "Cander."

Cander returned the nod as he passed by. "Gerj."

Approaching the stairs, Cander noticed that there was someone standing on the small landing that came just before the stairway turned and went up behind the wall. He realized abruptly that this someone was Eveline. The woman was standing very still, partially masked by shadow, looking down the stairs in the direction of Gerj and the red-haired man. She touched her eyepatch, and for a moment it appeared that she was going to lift it. At that moment, though, she seemed to notice Cander. Lowering her hand, she turned and swiftly ascended the stairs.

Cander pursued her, taking the steps two at a time. He caught up with her in the second-storey hallway and bobbed alongside her. "Eveline, wait," he said. "Is there something wrong?"

The woman stopped in front of the door to her room. "I don't know. This place . . . Something here just doesn't feel right."

She turned, caught his arm, and searched his face. "Can't you feel it?"

Eveline's nearness to him made Cander's nerve endings tingle pleasantly. He could actually feel the warmth of her body in the air; it was a peculiarly intimate sensation. "No," he admitted at length. "Not really, no."

She shook her head, frowning. "Maybe it's nothing, then. Maybe it's just me."

"Well, these are trying circumstances."

"Gerj Kolin," she blurted out suddenly. "How certain are you that we can trust him?"

"I've known Gerj a long time. He's never given me any reason *not* to trust him. Why?"

"I can't really say. There's something . . ."

"Well, Gerj is not perhaps the most open and forthright of men, but Gahant is a peculiar place—a tiny country, caught between three great powers. Everywhere there are spies, everywhere suspicion. It is not wise to be too open and forthright here."

"That might be it," she conceded.

He gave her an even smile. "Why don't we discuss this in your room, where we can at least be more comfortable?"

Regarding him with a sidelong look, Eveline said, "I don't think so, Cander. Not tonight. I'm tired. I plan on going straight to bed."

Suppressing the obvious suggestion that came immediately to mind, Cander said, "Of course. I understand. It's been a long, wearing day." He was beginning to resign himself to the hard fact that Eveline represented a long, patient campaign, with no assurance of ultimate success.

Why should I bother? he wondered, as he turned away and put his hand on the knob of his own door. Eveline had not shown the slightest awareness of his overtures, let alone interest. There were any number of women, women of charm and allure, who would be more than happy to have his attentions. Why waste time on someone who seemed, quite frankly, indifferent to him?

Hearing Eveline opening the door to her room, Cander turned and saw her in the open doorway. Her hair, fine and smooth, caught the warm colors of the oil lamp that burned within, the reds and the rich golds. A pale flush had brushed her cheeks.

She *was* lovely, he thought, never more so than now. And yet, it was not that alone that drew him to her. There was something else, something not entirely clear to him . . . a hidden strength, a mystery. She intrigued him.

In that brief moment, Cander found himself renewing his determination to penetrate the mystery that she represented, no matter how long it took, even though that might mean forsaking all others.

Eveline caught him staring at her, and she returned his gaze, rather haughtily, over one shoulder. "Was there something else?" she asked.

"No. Sleep well," he said.

"You, also." With that, she entered her room. The door closed behind her with an emphatic sound.

Giving a small sigh, Cander unlocked the door to his own room and went inside. He looked gloomily around the room. He felt restless and thwarted. He really ought to turn in and get some sleep, he knew, but the day still seemed . . . unfulfilled.

In the end, he could think of nothing to do but relent and start getting undressed. He was already out of his coat and was in the midst of unbuttoning his waistcoat, when there was a knock at the door. *What was this?* Perhaps the evening was about to take a turn for the better.

"A moment," he called. He considered putting on his coat again, but thought that a more casual appearance might be called for. Leaving the top two buttons of his waistcoat unfastened, which was more casual yet, he went to the door and flung it open, while assuming a nonchalant pose, one arm braced against the frame of the door.

He was momentarily surprised to see Alsimae standing outside. Before he could gather his wits to him, she ducked in under his arm, saying, "At last. Would you believe it? This is the first moment that I've been able to get away. I was working the kitchen tonight."

Speechless, Cander hesitated in the doorway. This wasn't exactly what he'd had in mind, but he didn't know what to do about it. After a moment's reflection, he closed the door, rather than let Alsimae's visit remain visible to anyone passing outside in the hall.

He turned to Alsimae. "Um," he said.

The woman was beside the bed now. She wrinkled her nose and plucked at the front of the blouse. "Wet," she said. "I just *hate* working in the kitchen." With that, she pulled the blouse up over her head and draped it negligently over the back of a chair. Her undergarment was of thin, well-washed linen. It clung to her in a most appealing manner, leaving little to the imagination.

Alsimae noticed him looking at her. She gave a bold smile, shifting her weight from one hip to the other. "Hello there."

Cander was aware of a sharp conflict of emotions within him. He knew where this was ultimately headed, if he did not put a stop to it now. Being alone with Alsimae in these circumstances made his heart beat faster and his nerves tingle pleasantly. But it was Eveline who filled his imagination now. He did not see how he could freely enjoy himself with Alsimae, knowing as he did that Eveline was just across the hall. Besides, had he not just promised himself not to involve himself with another woman, until he had overcome Eveline's resistance? Ten minutes seemed too short a time to go before relenting on his promise.

He knew that he had to put Alsimae off, though the prospect hardly gave him joy. The question was, how could he do it without hurting her feelings and provoking an unpleasant scene?

"Alsimae," he said softly, "it was good to see you again, but—"

She spread her arms slightly. "Come here, and show me how good it is."

Cander considered this for a moment, giving the mental equivalent of a shrug. There could be no harm in showing the woman a little honest affection, could there? Of course not. After going to Alsimae, he embraced her, intending to give her only a brief, reassuring cuddle. Apparently she had a different idea. Wrapping her arms around him, she pulled him tightly to her, turned him so that his back was to the bed, whipped one leg behind his knee, and pushed. They toppled to the bed, sank into the soft down. Alsimae, on top of Cander, kissed him with such force and passion that he nearly lost touch with his virtuous intentions.

No, he thought hazily, *this is not good* . . . It was good, of course, it just wasn't *good*. Putting his hands on Alsimae's shoulders, he rolled her off of him and over onto the other side of the bed. "Alsimae," he said breathlessly, "listen to me. We can't. Not right now. You shouldn't even be here."

The woman looked at him and frowned, apparently unsure of whether or not she should be offended. "Why not?" she asked, a certain dire edge to her voice.

After an instant of thought, Cander came upon the most reasonable excuse he could manufacture on short notice. "Can you keep a secret?" he asked.

Alsimae perked up noticeably at this. *There are few things in the world,* Cander thought, *that could charm and distract a person more than the prospect of being told an important secret.* "Yes," she said. "Yes, certainly."

"Very well. I will tell you, then, that my companions and I are not here on any casual trip. We are on a delicate and dangerous mission."

"A mission?" Her eyes shone. "That sounds exciting. What kind of mission?"

"It is best that I don't tell you the details. Knowing them might put you into jeopardy. In fact, it is risky for you just to be here with me at all, far too risky."

She appeared to consider this for a moment. "I'm willing to take the risk."

"Well, I'm not." Cander jumped up from the bed and fetched Alsimae's blouse from the back of the chair where she had left it. He held it out to her. "No, I could never forgive myself if something happened to you because of me."

Reluctantly, Alsimae got up from the bed and took the blouse. "Really, Cander, I think you're worrying over nothing. We're perfectly safe here."

"Can't take the chance. It's unfortunate, but I'm sure that you understand, yes?"

"I . . . understand. I think."

"Good. Get your clothes on. There's no time to waste."

Wearing a slightly baffled look, Alsimae wriggled into her blouse, and Cander guided her toward the door. He didn't want to give her a chance to think too much about what was happening.

After opening the door, Cander peered out into the hall. There was no one there. Perfect.

Cander tried to maneuver Alsimae out the door, but she hesitated stubbornly. Her dark eyes flickered over the full length of his body. "I'll go," she said. "But first, a last kiss . . ."

She pressed her body against him, as she reached up with both hands and grasped the back of his neck, bending his head to her. She gave him a long, lingering kiss, which made his thoughts go vague and fevered. Suddenly she broke from him, pulled open the door, and shot him an ardent look.

"Maybe I'll see you around, sometime," she said, then slipped out into the hall and was gone.

Cander closed the door and leaned up against it, breathing heavily. He was overwhelmed.

14

Cander awoke with something cold and hard pressed against his cheek. Still groggy, he almost tried to brush it away with the back of his hand. Just in time, he realized that there was something wrong, and he opened his eyes.

He was startled to see several dark forms poised over him, illuminated only by the faint glimmer of moonlight that seeped through the window: three men in buff-colored coats, one wearing a red sash and the plumed hat of an officer. This last man was holding a cocked pistol to Cander's face.

Cander sucked in an involuntary breath. *Royalists*, he thought, dismayed. *How did they find us?*

He heard the man in the officer's hat chuckle. "Ah, you're awake," he said. "Get up, get dressed. You're coming with us."

As the man backed away slightly, Cander found his voice. "How did you get in here?"

"Why, with the key," the man replied in a mocking tone. "Now, no more questions. Get dressed, quickly!"

Careful not to make any moves that could be interpreted as suspicious, Cander got out of bed and went to the chair where his clothes were. He dressed hastily. Then, garments still askew, limping slightly on his right foot, where he had not been able to get his heel down all the way into his boot, he found himself being pushed roughly toward the door.

In the hall were more men in royalist uniform. They had Eveline, he was disturbed to see. The woman looked as disheveled as Cander knew he himself must. Even so, she bore herself with a rigid dignity, her face revealing nothing of her feelings.

The royalist officer turned to one of the men in the hall. In a low voice, he asked, "What of the others?"

The other man shrugged. "I don't know."

"Check on them."

Nodding, the man started to lope down the hall. Before he could turn the corner, however, another pair of royalists came around it from the other direction. Looking abashed, one of them said, "The thief wasn't in his room. We looked everywhere."

"Damnation!" the officer said. "The baron isn't going to like that one bit."

"No, sir."

"All of you, then—go see what's happening with the magician."

"Yes, sir." The three vanished around the corner. A few moments later, they came hurrying back, white-faced and uneasy. In a worried voice, one of them said, "Captain, the magician was nowhere to be found. And Sergeant Volz and Merris—they're both dead."

"Dead! *How?*"

"I don't know, sir. There's not a mark on either one of them."

"There was a strange smell in the air," another of the men said. "And I saw a green powder on Merris's coat and mustache."

"*Witchcraft,*" the officer said. "It has to be!" Obviously alarmed, the man pulled on his lower lip. "Best not to take any chances, then. We'll take these two, and forget about the rest. I don't care what Quordane says, by Kobb!"

One by one, the men started down the stairs. Cander tried to hang back slightly, hoping that if he stretched his captors out, an opportunity to escape might present itself eventually. A stiff-armed shove to the center of his back, strong enough to almost knock him off his feet, dissuaded him from that notion.

Two men waited in the gloom of the common room below, watching the procession dispassionately. The first was Gerj Kolin; the second, the man whom Gerj had been talking to earlier in the evening, the man in red.

When all were assembled in the common room, the man in red looked them over with narrowed eyes, and said, "Where are the others? There were supposed to be four."

The royalist officer shrugged, obviously uncomfortable with

the subject. "Gone. Not here. The magician killed two of my men and escaped. The thief was nowhere to be found."

"This is not good! You were supposed to take them all!"

"We tried. We did all that we could."

"You can explain that to the baron. I'm sure that he'll be suitably impressed."

Gerj Kolin said in an agitated voice, "What's this? You said that you would get them all. You promised me. Now what? Two of them are still on the loose. What if they should decide to come back here after me?"

The man in red appeared unmoved. "I'm afraid that's your problem, Kolin. Deal with it. Needless to say, I'm as disappointed with the results of the night's adventure as you are."

"Oh, are you?" Gerj asked, a sarcastic edge to his voice.

Dismissing Gerj's distress with no apparent difficulty, the man in red said, "I suppose that we must deal with affairs as they are, not as we would have them. We'd best be on the move. We have an appointment to keep."

Rough hands seized Cander and thrust him toward the door. Turning his head, he saw that Eveline was being impelled in a similar manner, and no less roughly. Her face was no more expressive than it had been upstairs, her bearing even more regal. Attempting to emulate her admirable restraint, Cander choked back his anger and resentment.

There was no denying that things were bad. They might have been worse, of course. At least Kemp and Digrippa had gotten away. Cander expected that they would try to free them, eventually; Digrippa would not abandon his own sister.

Still, this was not a happy moment. Cander doubted that he and Eveline would be well treated by their captors, and there was always the chance that the royalists would dispose of them before Digrippa could contrive of a means to liberate them. Perhaps the only comfort that Cander could take from the situation was that, as it happened, he had not lied to Alsimae when he had turned her away from his room.

Cander turned a final baleful gaze on Gerj Kolin, who had betrayed him. Gerj had been a royalist agent all along, that was clear, but that did not make his actions any more palatable. Cander had deluded himself into thinking that they were friends.

Gerj caught Cander's gaze. At least, he showed the good grace to look embarrassed. "Sorry, Cander. Just business. I hope that you won't take it personally."

I wouldn't count on that, Cander thought grimly.

* * *

The wind blew cold mist into Kemp's face. Feet bare, shirt and waistcoat open and billowing, he hung onto the eaves with numb fingers, his toes jammed painfully into a shallow crevice in the wall of the inn. He shivered, wondering what to do next.

It might be safest, he thought, to stay where he was, high above any danger. The trouble with that was, he did not know how long he could stand the constant exposure to the cold north wind. No, better to climb down and then make his way to the safety of the surrounding woods. Unfortunately, he was not quite sure of how to go about that. There wasn't much of a moon, and what light there was served only to confuse the eye with shadows and distortion. He knew that he would have to find his way largely by feel.

Slowly, gingerly, Kemp started edging his way along the roof, as fingers and toes progressively lost their feeling. At last, he reached a place where the slope of the rear porch roof projected out below him. After grasping a stout brace, Kemp stretched out first one leg, then the other, until he was dangling over the porch, supported only by the hold he had on the brace. As much as he tried to extend himself, however, his toes still swung several inches over the roof. If he just let himself drop, he knew, there was a good chance that he'd go right through the porch roof. But there seemed little else that he could do at this point; he doubted that he even had the strength to pull himself up again.

So, drawing a quick breath and holding it, he let go of the brace. He fell for the merest fraction of a second, and then his feet came down on the rough shingles. He heard, and felt, the roof crack under his weight, but it held. The rake was steeper than he had expected. His feet started to slip out from under him, and he realized that he was at risk of stumbling off the edge of the roof. Leaning back slightly, he stiffened his knees, desperately fighting his natural momentum. A nasty splinter pierced one of his big toes, and the soles of his feet burned as if they'd been gone over with coarse sandpaper; but he managed to stop himself.

Wincing and mouthing black curses, he sat down on the shingled surface and inched his way to the edge. After pausing to pull half an inch of wood from his toe, he leaned over and surveyed the ground below.

It appeared that he had about eight feet more to drop, and there was no easy way down. Kemp sighed. He was getting too old for this. At least, there were no obstructions below to worry about; Gerj Kolin kept a tidy inn.

Kemp got onto his hands and knees, then backed first his feet and then his knees off the end of the roof, so that he was kept from falling only by the weight of his torso and his outstretched arms. Gradually he allowed more and more of his body to slip over the edge, until he could grip the outer lip of the overhang and dangle free. After swinging his legs out away from the structure he let go and dropped. He absorbed the first shock of the landing with flexed knees, then crumpled to the ground and rolled, his momentum almost taking him to his feet again.

In a low crouch, Kemp held very still for a moment, senses straining to pierce the night, afraid that the noise he had made would attract untoward attention. Hearing nothing, and seeing no hint of movement, he arose. Dusting himself off, he moved stealthily around the back of the inn. Just before he'd absconded, he'd thrown his coat and boots out the window. They had to be nearby.

Upon coming to the place that he estimated to be below his window, he searched the ground carefully. He located the coat first, then one boot, and finally the other. After making a bundle of them and clutching it to his chest, he made his way to the border of the neighboring woods. His heart was beating much too fast, he realized.

The coming winter had already denuded most of the tree branches, and the ground was littered with dead, dry leaves, which crunched loudly under his tread. Barefoot, in the dark, he found the sensation disagreeable. Finally he could stand it no longer.

After pulling on his coat, Kemp sat on a fallen log and prepared to put on his boots. He scowled. No stockings. He had forgotten them. *Well. Nothing to be done about that now.*

Kemp drew on his boots, wriggled his toes unhappily. The big toe that had taken the splinter throbbed.

Hanging his head slightly, in order to peer under a low, wavering branch, he looked back toward the inn. The windows, most curtained or shuttered, shed only the faintest of glows. Visible against the moonlit sky, inky smoke leaked from several of the chimneys. The structure, which in daylight had seemed so inviting, had taken on a distinctly forbidding aspect.

Kemp did not know exactly what was happening. He had been sleeping comfortably, when he had been awakened by suspicious noises at his door. Another person might have thought nothing of them until it was too late, but Kemp had spent his life expecting men to come for him in the night. He had acted without hesitation. By the time that he heard the sound of a key being turned in the lock, he was already halfway out of the window. Hanging precariously outside, buffeted by chill winds, he had seen them, their distinctive uniforms. How had they known where to find him?

More important, what had happened to his companions?

He had to find out.

Picking his way carefully through the brush and fallen branches, Kemp circled the inn. All the while, he kept wondering what it was that he expected to accomplish. Under the circumstances, the most prudent thing to do would be to simply disappear into the countryside. He had been lucky to escape, but he could not expect his luck to hold forever. Why, then, was he going out of his way to put himself in further jeopardy? For all he knew, the royalists might start searching the woods for him at any moment.

He only knew that he was unwilling to see Lalerin and Quordane succeed in their machinations. He could not run away while there was still a chance that he could do something to frustrate them. *Stupid,* he thought. *Really stupid . . .*

His father had warned about this sort of thing. Kemp could almost see him now, seated in his favorite booth, in his favorite tavern. "Son," he had said, "one day you may become *earnest* about something, about a woman, a cause, an undertaking. You may in fact become so earnest about this thing that you will be tempted to forget natural caution and self-interest. I urge you to resist this temptation. Earnestness is the dangerous shoal upon which the lives of even the most practical and prudent of men may be wrecked. Believe me, it can do you no good."

His father would be sadly disappointed with him, if he were alive to see him now.

After working his way along behind the screen of trees, Kemp finally came to a vantage from which he could see the front of the inn. A pair of lanterns hung from sconces beside the main door, and a third was mounted on a black iron pole in the yard, each contributing to a wan yellow glow. In the open area between the inn and the stable, a large party of people and horses were assembled. There were at least a dozen buff-coated royalists, struggling to control their agitated mounts. In their midst were two others: Cander Ellis and Eveline. They were on horseback, but the reins to their mounts were in other hands. They were obvious captives.

Kemp noticed that Digrippa and his servant Vedrai were nowhere to be seen. That meant that either they had eluded the royalists, or that they had been killed. All in all, Kemp thought it more likely that they had evaded their would-be captors, who in his estimation had proven themselves to be remarkably inept. If they had taken the simple precaution of sending a man or two around to the back of the inn to keep watch, Kemp himself would not have escaped so easily, if at all.

In quick order, the royalists managed to organize their party. Uttering harsh cries, which sounded sharply in the chill air, the men spurred their horses from the yard, turned past the stable, and set off down the road, taking their captives with them. The clatter of hoofbeats receded into the night.

Clenching his fists in frustration, Kemp watched them depart. In a moment, they would be gone, and then what would he do? He had managed to evade capture, but of what use could he be, alone and on foot? Perhaps it would have been better if he had allowed himself to be taken. With his skills, he might have been able to effect some good. But now?

The stable, he thought. If he could reach it without being seen, maybe he could steal a horse and follow before the trail went entirely cold.

After leaving the shelter of the woods, Kemp made his way to the stable as discreetly as he could under the circumstances. The need for haste made him less careful than he might have been otherwise. He doubted that the royalists had left anyone behind to keep watch, since that would have been the prudent thing to do. At most, he probably had only Gerj Kolin to worry about—for he was nearly certain that it was Kolin who had arranged the evening's activities. Somebody must have sold them out to the royalists, and Kolin was the likely candidate. Who else could have known who they were, even?

After unlatching the door by pulling on a knotted thong that entered the stable through a small hole, Kemp opened it wide enough to slip inside. It was dark within, so much so that even eyes adjusted to the night could not easily pierce the gloom. He had to leave the door open a crack in order to be able to see at all. The comforting earthy smells of hay, of horses, filled his nostrils. He heard the horses stirring in their stalls, and the small snorting sounds that they made.

Kemp moved toward the stalls, careful not to stumble on the

uneven dirt floor, passing alongside a small carriage, its sleek black-lacquered lines glimmering softly, even in the dim light. As he entered the area between the stalls, he suddenly heard a sound and realized that there was somebody behind him. The nerves at the back of neck tingling with dread, he spun about quickly and drew back his fist to deliver a blow.

There *was* someone there, a dark-cloaked and hatted figure, almost—but not quite—invisible in the darkness. As Kemp lashed out with what he hoped would be a preemptive blow, the figure stepped away with an airy effortlessness, out of his reach. The force of his swing almost pulled Kemp off of his feet. He managed to recover, and, lowering his head, he prepared to drive himself straight into the figure's midriff.

"Peace! Enough!" the figure hissed. "You have no fight with *me*, Kemp."

Kemp hesitated, eyes straining to pierce the darkness. That voice . . . He knew it. *Vedrai*.

Feeling a little foolish, Kemp lowered his cocked fist and stood up straight. "Vedrai," he said. "Thank the heavens, it's you! You also eluded the royalists, then."

"Why should they bother with a servant?" the man said dryly. "They had more important quarry to worry about."

"They have Cander and Eveline," Kemp said hurriedly. "I don't know about Talmis. Have you seen him?"

Vedrai nodded slowly. "He sent me to get horses, while he makes sure that the royalists don't elude us. You can be of help. There are saddles and harness over there, by the wall. Bring them to me."

Frowning, Kemp said, "Without a horse, how can he possibly track them? They are long gone now. It would be impossible for him to follow on foot."

"No time for that, no time! Make yourself useful, Kemp, or they will give us the slip for certain."

Compelled by the edge of urgency in Vedrai's voice, Kemp pushed back his curiosity and hastened to do as the man asked. There would be time enough to satisfy his questions later, he supposed. If not, they would not matter.

Working quickly despite the hampering darkness, Kemp and Vedrai saddled three of the horses and led them to the front of the stable. Vedrai peered out through the narrow opening that Kemp had left in the door and finally declared the way safe. While Kemp held the horses, Digrippa's servant put his shoulder to the door and swung it open. *"Quickly!"* the man said in a fierce whisper, as he took the reins of one of the horses and boosted himself up into the saddle.

Following his lead, Kemp mounted his horse. Uttering low exhortations, the two urged the horses from the stable, past the inn, and out onto the road. Vedrai took the lead, and Kemp followed, trailing the riderless horse by the reins. An exalting thrill of freedom sped the blood in his veins.

Behind him, Kemp heard a voice shout, *"Stop! Come back!"* It was Gerj Kolin's voice, he realized. A rich, satisfying chuckle bubbled up in Kemp's throat, as he thought, *Small chance of that, Gerj!*

Suddenly a gunshot rang out. At almost the same instant, Kemp heard something whine by his ear. Ahead of him was a gnarled old oak. Abruptly one of its branches, as thick as Kemp's wrist, shivered, cracked, and toppled. Attached to the tree by only a few fibrous strands, the branch swung ominously in the wind.

Crying out, Kemp ducked low over the neck of his horse, hearing the animal's quick, snorting breaths. There was no second shot, however, and a moment later the road turned behind a dense copse of trees. Even so, Kemp remained unwilling to sit upright in the saddle.

They rode at a gallop for perhaps fifty or sixty yards, and then slowed as they approached the place where the road they followed intersected with the main road. Kemp saw, suddenly, that there was a person standing there, at the side of the road. After a moment, he recognized the person as Digrippa. The magician stood rapt, gold-headed walking stick clenched in both hands, face upturned and eyes closed.

Vedrai pulled to a halt beside his master, and Kemp came abreast of him. Digrippa showed no awareness of their presence. Kemp waited a moment, then said, "What's the matter with him?"

"Shh! Be still!" Vedrai hissed. "He has detached his soul from his body and sent it in search of those we seek. You must not disturb him."

Kemp frowned and nodded. He had been witness to so many extraordinary occurrences recently that he no longer even questioned them. A minute passed, two. Kemp began to throw apprehensive looks over his shoulder, afraid that there might be some pursuit from the inn. It occurred to him that they could hardly make themselves better targets than they already had. At last he ventured, "The trouble is, Gerj Kolin might be coming after us."

Through dark lashes, Vedrai regarded him with cool disdain. "If so, we will just have to deal with him."

"How? I don't happen to have a gun. Do you? *He* certainly does."

The man gave no response, save for a slight sniff.

Grinding his teeth in frustration, Kemp watched Digrippa anxiously. The magician's countenance remained devoid of expression for several moments more. Then, all of a sudden, his facial muscles quivered in a most singular manner. It appeared to Kemp as if Digrippa's personality was being drawn down little by little over the blank and pliable features, giving them life: forehead first, then eyes, cheeks, and mouth. Digrippa took in a sharp inhalation of breath, and his eyes fluttered open.

"Vedrai, Kemp," he said, without even appearing to look at them. "You are here. Good. We've little time to waste. They are heading at speed toward the border. If we expect to catch up with them, we will have to ride as if there are demons at our backs."

With that, the magician took the reins of his horse from Kemp, inserted a foot into the stirrup, and swung up into the saddle. Tucking his walking stick under he right arm, he said, "We must be careful. There are many royalist troops on the road, and more moving through the woods."

"Did you detect any sign of Lalerin?" Vedrai asked.

"Perhaps. There was a large coach escorted by a company of riders, half a league ahead of those who took Eveline and Cander. I didn't want to risk getting too close. Doctor Stahlgrave might be with Lalerin by now, and it is possible that he may be able to detect me in my incorporeal form."

"What of Cander and your sister?" Kemp put in quickly. "Are they all right?"

Digrippa gave a dark grimace. "I would presume so. Nothing will happen to them, save that it is by the order of Lalerin or Quordane.

"Which is why," the magician continued in a tense voice, "we must free them before they can be brought before either of those gentlemen. At that point, their situation will become more . . . unstable. Are we ready, then? It is to be a long, arduous night."

Kemp and Vedrai murmured their assent, and the three set out upon the road to Branion, riding swiftly. The wind, cold and wet, gusted across their path; the lights of the Inn of the Three Crows faded behind them.

Kemp was surprised to find a certain happy satisfaction in his heart. It felt good, for once, to be part of something greater than himself.

15

The sun rose slowly over the tops of trees, dissolving both the thin overcast and the chill morning mists that hung tattered on the branches of the surrounding woods. Hands bound behind him with a length of coarse rope, dampness seeping through the seat of his breeches, Cander sat in the midst of the grassy meadow and tried not to be depressed.

The meadow was aswarm with activity. All morning long the royalist troops had been assembling there, in parties of a dozen or less, until now they numbered some sixty or seventy strong, most with their horses. The pristine turf had been dug up in places, and cook fires built. Smoke drifted across the meadow, hanging close to the ground, irritating Cander's nose and eyes. He hoped that he would not have to sneeze. Lacking the use of his hands, that could be awkward.

The situation was becoming increasingly untenable, Cander knew. The more royalists that there were around them, the more difficult it would be for Digrippa and Kemp to rescue them. It would seem impossible already—were Digrippa not Digrippa. Cander gave Eveline a speculative sidelong glance. The woman sat beside him on the turf, bound as he was. Self-possessed and apparently unconcerned, she appeared to be drowsing—although it was hard to know for certain, since he could see only the profile with the eye patch. The morning sun was yellow on her face.

Cander wondered where they were, exactly. In Branion, was all he knew. They had crossed the border in the early hours of the morning, long before the first glimmer of daylight had appeared in the eastern horizon. Shortly thereafter they had turned onto a road that meandered through the densely wooded hills. Cander had found himself turned around and confused, so that by the time the sun had breasted the rolling horizon, he no longer had any idea of where they were in relation to the main road. Now, even if he managed somehow to escape his captors, he would have no way of knowing in which direction he should run.

Cander attempted to twist his hands within his bonds. They were tight, too tight to hope that he could free himself. Indeed, he found that his fingertips were already numb from the pressure on his wrists. Issuing a slight sigh, he resigned himself to waiting, while trying to work some feeling back into his fingers.

Thus engaged, Cander watched a small carriage drawn by a matched pair of greys appear upon the narrow ribbon of road at the bottom edge of the meadow. He saw it leave the road and roll up onto the green carpet of the meadow, jostling from side to side, before finally coming to a halt. Presently the driver clambered down from his box and opened the door in the side of the carriage.

A peculiar individual emerged from the carriage. He presented a disturbingly vulturine aspect: gaunt, long-necked, slightly stooped. His white, closely cropped hair stuck out in feathery bristles; through it, his pale scalp could clearly be seen. Hugging a plain wooden coffer to his small, rounded belly, he peered about the meadow. His eyes, enlarged and distorted by a pair of thick, wood-framed glasses, looked in the direction of Cander and Eveline, and hesitated a moment.

Cander recognized the man. Only weeks before, after all, he'd had occasion to follow him across most of Gahant. "Doctor Stahlgrave," he said.

Eveline stirred, and her head swiveled in Stahlgrave's direction. "Yes."

"You know Stahlgrave?"

"We are . . . acquainted," she said tersely, her voice strained. Intrigued, Cander attempted to study her reaction, but what he could see of her face told him nothing.

Stahlgrave, meanwhile, labored his way across the meadow, to where most of the royalist officers and the man in red stood together before the fire. He exchanged words with them for a few minutes, but all the while his eyes kept being drawn back to Eveline and Cander. Eventually he left the small group and worked his way to where the two were seated.

Standing over Eveline, he looked down upon her with an expression of satisfaction. "So," he said, "we meet again, Eveline. I must say that your circumstances are remarkably reduced from the last time, *ha*. Not so proud now, perhaps, my dear? What, have you nothing to say?"

"It's good to see you, too," she said dryly. "It appears that the passage of time has done nothing to improve your disposition."

The man scowled. "Say what you will, it means nothing to me. Surely, though, you must admit now that you were wrong and that I was right? You may never have a clearer demonstration of the uses of power. I am free, and allied with strong friends, while you are a helpless prisoner."

"Crow if you like, Stahlgrave. It isn't over yet."

The man licked his wrinkled lips. "It soon will be. With the Society's help, Lalerin will prevail. Then will we share fully in the spoils of his victory. We will be as princes, all of us."

"Assuming, of course, that you can trust Lalerin to live up to his end of the bargain."

"He will not dare betray us."

"A king comfortably lodged upon his throne will dare much. You would be surprised."

"*Enough!* Stubbornness is a poor virtue. Admit your error, and we may overlook your indiscretions. You can still be useful to us."

"To speak with perfect candor, Doctor Stahlgrave, I feel only pity for you—for you and for all those who have labored to corrupt the Society into what it now is. Two centuries of accumulated wisdom, and you only have the wit to use it for your squalid political purposes. It's pathetic, really. Lalerin makes you all his thralls, but you cannot see it."

A flush of blood managed to work its way into Stahlgrave's chalky cheeks. Making a furious sound, he reached down, seized the cord that held Eveline's eyepatch on, and snatched it up and away.

The woman blinked and squinted for a moment, apparently dazzled. Then she glared up at Stahlgrave, her mouth tight with displeasure.

Cander was not sure what he had expected to see under that mysterious eye patch, but the eye that had been hidden beneath it appeared clear, blue, perfect. The way that the eye tracked, and the manner in which Eveline blinked from the light, made it clear to him that there would be nothing wrong with the sight in that eye. Why, then, the patch? It was puzzling.

"Look at me, Eveline," Stahlgrave said. "Look at me with that remarkable sight of yours. What do you see?"

"Nothing to speak of," she replied, her voice chill.

Stahlgrave's face pinched into a simian snarl. He drew back his hand, as if to strike the woman. Without really thinking, Cander pulled back his legs, aimed, and kicked out at Stahlgrave, striking him on the side of the knee. The knee twisted slightly, and the man fell to the ground, dropping the wooden casket he held.

The casket bounced once. Its lid popped open, and the contents spilled out onto the ground—the shoots of an herb, pale green in color, leaves faintly streaked with crimson. Immediately they seemed to wilt and fade in the wan morning sun.

Uttering a hoarse exclamation, Stahlgrave got on his hands and knees and commenced scooping up the tender stalks and returning them to the casket. When he had them all, he shut the lid with a sigh. Pressing his eyes closed, he murmured a phrase over the casket, in a voice too low for Cander to understand.

The man climbed unsteadily to his feet, hugging the casket to him with both arms. Glaring fiercely at Cander, he lashed out at him with a booted foot. His aim was less than perfect, however, and Cander managed to roll aside at the last moment, so the foot merely grazed his ribs. It hurt, but only a little, and it did no real damage. There was no reason why Stahlgrave should know that, though; it would only encourage him to try again, perhaps with better aim. Cander made a good show of grimacing and writhing on the ground.

Stahlgrave looked down on him with apparent satisfaction. *"Ha!"* he said. "Perhaps that will teach you not to interfere with your betters." He gave a spiteful giggle. "Though, I fear, the lesson comes very near the end of your life."

The man returned his attention to Eveline, who stared back at him with obvious loathing. "I do not have any more time to waste on you," he said stiffly. "In time, you will come to regret your intransigence, I have no doubt."

Chin held at a lofty angle, Stahlgrave turned and made his way back to his carriage, walking quickly, with odd little steps. He called out a few peremptory words to his coachman, who lounged nearby. The man hastened to open the carriage door and help Stahlgrave into the passenger compartment. After shutting the door, the coachman clambered up onto the box, took the reins in one hand, a whip in the other. Snapping the whip over their flanks, he urged the team of horses out onto road again. The coach rolled behind a line of trees and disappeared.

Eveline struggled to her knees and leaned over Cander. "Are

you all right? Are you hurt?" Her hair had come unbound. It hung, sweet-smelling and silken, over her face, the ends brushing Cander's own cheeks. He looked up, feeling as if he were surrounded by a billowing tent of reddish gold silk. He was sure that he could read concern in the woman's eyes, and he felt satisfaction at finally being able to wrest some emotion from her. The turnings of fate were indeed strange. Never would he have thought that he might someday consider getting booted in the ribs a fortunate occurrence.

Even as he congratulated himself, however, he noticed Eveline's expression alter. Something cool and austere pushed aside the concern. "Ah," she said, "I see. A trick. Very clever, indeed." Straightening abruptly, she shifted away from him.

After rolling back and forth on the ground a few times, Cander managed to heave himself up into a seated position. Somehow, she had figured out that he wasn't really hurt. He wondered what had given him away. Normally, he flattered himself that he was a tolerably good actor.

"I hope that you don't think that I was trying to trick *you*," he said. "That was for Stahlgrave's benefit."

"I'm sure it's as you say." Eveline looked at Cander, and there was something in her gaze that inspired a vague shiver of dread along his spine.

"Speaking of tricks, I'd be interested to hear the reason for that eye patch. It's obvious that you don't need it."

"You're wrong. I most decidedly do need it."

"You're no more blind in that eye than I am."

"I never said that I was."

"Then why the patch?"

"Perhaps because without it I can see too well."

Cander started to laugh, but thought better of it. She appeared to be serious. "Explain that one, please."

The woman sighed. "That would be difficult. You have no basis by which to understand."

"Try."

She sighed. "Simply put, then—I have through long practice of certain ancient and secret disciplines taught this eye to see beyond the appearance of things, to penetrate the merely material, to the essence of all things. To the truth."

"Hmm, that sounds very high-flown and obscure to me. What is it, specifically, that you can see?"

"That rather depends on what I am looking at. I can detect hidden forces that are invisible to most mortal eyes, the innate magical properties of certain objects, the divinity that manifests itself in sacred places, the frightful shades and specters that crowd the night. And when I look at a person, I can see, as a vague and shifting aura, the outer manifestation of that person's soul. From that aura, I can divine something of the person's inward nature and emotional state—and other things besides, which are nearly impossible to describe."

Cander stared at the woman, profoundly disquieted. Was she telling the truth? If so, he did not know if he would ever feel comfortable around her again. He'd built his life around his mastery of illusion. To be with someone who could penetrate those illusions with a glance made him feel exposed and unworthy.

He said, "If that eye is so talented, why do you keep it covered most of the time? For that matter, why train only the one eye?"

"Ah," she said in a soft, sad voice. "Long ago I discovered that it is distressing to have to always see the truth. Imagine seeing, wherever you look, all of the pain, deceit, and cruelty that there is in the world, and never being able to stop seeing it. It can be terribly . . . wearing."

She paused a moment, then said, "Besides, people tend to find this eye disturbing. They seem to sense its abnormal force, and it makes them uneasy. Even with it covered, some sensitive souls become nervous in my presence. It is not particularly pleasant for me."

Cander considered this for a moment, and he felt a responding twinge of pity. He realized that if Eveline looked at him now, his sentiments would be apparent to her—the pity and, yes, the discomfort—and he didn't particularly want that. He decided that he had better change the subject.

"What, exactly, was it that you and Stahlgrave were talking about?" he asked. "I gathered that in the past you two must have had some sort of dispute, but for the life of me I couldn't figure out what it was about."

Eveline look at him sharply, and he had to force himself not to recoil from her gaze. Melancholy softened her features. "Why not?" she said at last. "I swore not to speak of the business of the Society of the Dawning Sun, but the organization to which I made that promise to doesn't seem to exist anymore."

"You are a member of the Society, then?"

She inclined her head, in affirmation. "Our disagreement concerned the internal politics of the Society of the Dawning

Sun. You see, when the Society was born, more than a hundred years ago, its sole purpose was to preserve the ancient lore and disciplines of magic in a world that was coming more and more to embrace the mechanical and the materialistic. Its first members were magicians and scholars, but over time it began to recruit from people of wealth and temporal power, and its nature began to change. Not long ago, there emerged a strong element within the Society that wanted to use its accumulated knowledge as an instrument for worldly influence. Talmis and I resisted these changes for as long as we could, and when it became clear that we had lost the internal struggle, we withdrew from it, determined to oppose it from the outside."

Cander listened to her with interest. At last, the motives of Eveline and Talmis Digrippa were beginning to make sense to him. "And when I came to you with my peculiar story about the closing of the Chandler's Theater and the apparent involvement of a member of the Society . . ."

"It caught our interest."

"So," Cander said pensively, "the Society of the Dawning Sun has thrown in its lot with the royalist cause."

"Yes."

"Disturbing."

"Very."

Cander gave the woman a sidelong glance. "By the way, what *did* you see when you looked at Stahlgrave?"

"Someone who does not have long to live, and yet who has lived too long, for his soul has shriveled up like a raisin."

After spending a moment to gather his courage, Cander finally asked the question: "And what do you see when you look at me?"

He heard her laughing softly. "A man who is not as bad as he thinks he is, nor as good."

The three men lay on their stomachs atop the low, wooded ridge that overlooked the meadow where the royalists had assembled. Cander and Eveline were about as close to the center of the meadow as they could be, surrounded by dozens of armed men—a fact that did nothing to improve Kemp's native lack of optimism. The situation seemed hopeless.

Beside Kemp, Digrippa gazed down on the meadow for a long time, eyes narrowed against the midmorning glare. "Hmm," he said at last. "Do you have any ideas, Kemp?"

"*Me?* You're the magician. And from the look of things, it will *take* a magician to separate them from the midst of that army."

"What, do you expect me to scatter the royalists with a well-placed thunderbolt?"

"Something like that would sure come in handy."

"Sorry, Kemp, but you have an unrealistic opinion of my humble abilities. Not a single thunderbolt in my quiver. How about you, Vedrai? Any thoughts?"

"None so far."

"Well, this may not be easy . . ." Gazing out over the meadow, Digrippa stroked his chin thoughtfully.

Kemp, meanwhile, dourly considered the situation. He was tired, hungry, and not in the best of moods. They had ridden all night, in constant danger of running into a royalist patrol. What would happen to them if they did run into one was brought home with brutal force when they crossed the frontier into Branion, an hour or so after midnight. They'd found the road open, the barrier that had earlier blocked it abandoned to one side, the company of Protectorate soldiers who had guarded it nowhere in evidence. Dismounting, Kemp and Digrippa had explored as far as the margin of the woods, where at last they had found them, shot dead, all of them, and covered by brush. Kemp had no doubt that the same thing could easily happen to them.

The grisly memory of the Protectorate border guard reminded Kemp of something that he figured he really ought to tell Digrippa. It might mean nothing, but . . .

After clearing his throat, Kemp said, "Talmis, there's something that I think you should know. I'm not sure, mind you, but I have some reason to suspect that Cander Ellis is working as an agent of the Protectorate."

Digrippa gave a faint chuckle. "My dear fellow, *of course* he is! But don't tell him that you know. It would disillusion him no end."

"You *know?*"

"Quiet, I'm getting an idea. Mm, yes. It just might work." The magician pointed with his chin at the meadow below. "What say you, Kemp? How'd you like to walk alone and unarmed into the midst of that?"

Kemp looked from Digrippa to the meadow and back again. "How'd you like to sit on a sharpened fence post?"

"Come, come, that's not the eager spirit that I've come to expect from you! You have nothing to worry about. Trust me!

We'll have to find you appropriate garments, of course, but that should be easy enough."

"What are you talking about?" Kemp asked suspiciously.

"Come on, we've got to get a little closer to the meadow for what I have in mind to work. I'll explain as we go."

While Vedrai minded the horses a short distance away, Kemp and Digrippa watched and waited at the edge of the meadow, well concealed by the trees and the scrubby brush. From time to time, inevitably, one of the royalist soldiers would leave the rest of the group, disappear into the woods, and return a few minutes later. Kemp observed three such occurrences, but each time the man in question entered the woods too far away for them to be of use. Squatting among the brush, thighs starting to ache, Kemp began to question the wisdom of Digrippa's plan.

Finally, though, one royalist soldier—a big, sloppy-looking man, with paper powder cartridges attached to his crossed shoulder harness—approached the woods not far from their hiding place. Kemp and Digrippa exchanged looks, and Digrippa gave a curt nod.

They worked their way toward the soldier, moving through the brush as quietly as they could. As they went, Digrippa opened up his coat and selected a slender ivory tube from his breast pocket. Both ends of the tube were sealed with small lead plugs. As the unsuspecting soldier entered the woods mere yards away, Digrippa removed the plugs and gingerly held the tube out before him.

The soldier had unfastened his breeches and was standing with them around his knees, when Kemp and Digrippa stepped around from behind a large tree. Dumbstruck, the man gaped at them for a moment. Then, as he struggled to pull up his breeches, he drew the breath to call out. Digrippa swiftly put the tube to his mouth and blew into it.

A faint cloud of greenish dust shot from the end of tube, enveloping the soldier's head and shoulders. The man gasped, eyes rolling up in his head. He wavered on his feet for an instant, then toppled face forward onto the ground, where he lay very still.

Digrippa held Kemp back. "Wait," he whispered. "It will take a moment to dissipate . . . all right, it should be safe enough now. Get his uniform."

Kemp hesitated. "Are you sure it's safe?"

"Of course."

Kneeling beside the insensate royalist, Kemp commenced to strip off his garments. "If this doesn't work," he said breathlessly, "I'm coming back to haunt you."

"That's all right, dear fellow. Then I'll just have to exorcise you."

Kemp shot the magician a tart look. He saw that the man, having dropped the ivory tube, was manipulating the head of his walking stick in a particular manner. After a moment, the top half of it sprang open. Holding his right hand above it, with a look of determined concentration, Digrippa made a subtle gesture. A tiny spark of reddish light drifted up from the open head of the walking stick and hung just below the magician's outstretched hand. The spark wavered, growing slightly larger and fainter.

Digrippa caught Kemp's stare. He smiled. *"Ulthants,"* he said. "All that I've been able to collect through months of careful work. Thousands of them."

Minutes later, outfitted in royalist uniform, Kemp emerged from the woods and strolled across the meadow. He hoped that he would not attract any undue attention. Examined closely, his disguise would probably not pass muster. The soldier he had taken it from was a much bigger man than he. The breeches hung long and baggy on him. The coat sleeves enveloped his hands almost to the second knuckle. He could only hope that he didn't look quite as ridiculous as he felt, or he wouldn't get far.

Kemp made his way unchallenged to the center of the meadow, to within a few yards of where Cander Ellis and Eveline were seated. Maintaining a nonchalant pose, he tried to catch their attention with his eyes. Cander looked directly at him once, but then his gaze slid by without recognition.

Look at me, idiot! Kemp thought anxiously.

After several more tense moments, however, Eveline glanced in his direction. Her eyes locked with his, and she quirked up her brows. Then, nodding, she nudged Cander with her shoulder and spoke a quiet word in his ear.

Good, Kemp thought, turning his attention elsewhere. Most of the royalist horses had been gathered in one spot, where a single man kept watch. Several of the horses had not had their bridles removed.

Kemp moved in the direction of the horses, willing himself invisible. When he was quite near them, he looked back toward the woods. He could just barely make out Digrippa's dark form amid the shrubs and drooping branches, and then only because he knew exactly where to look.

Kemp gave a slow nod.

A moment later, he saw the small red spark leave the woods and drift over the meadow. If he had not known it for what it was, he probably would have thought that he had looked at the sun an instant too long.

Ulthants, Digrippa had called them.

A short distance from the edge of the woods, a group of a dozen royalist soldiers were warming themselves before a fire. The *Ulthants* hovered over them for a moment, then glided downward, alighting on the crossed harness of one of the soldiers, which was strung with powder cartridges.

A tiny wisp of smoke arose from one of the cartridges, and then from another. *Crack! Crack! Crack!* One by one, the cartridges burst into smoke and flame, sending shreds of burning paper into the air. Terrified, the soldier gave a jump, then threw himself to the ground and commenced rolling and writhing, his frantic fingers struggling to remove his harness.

All eyes were now on the unfortunate soldier, even those of the man who was supposed to be watching the horses. Kemp slipped in behind him and grasped the leads of two of the horses, swinging up into the saddle of one of them.

Gesticulating wildly with one hand, he cried, *"Hiya ha! Ha!"* The other horses, already nervous from the explosions, scattered in all directions, rearing and snorting.

"You there!" called the man who had been set to watch the horses. "What are you doing? Stop it!"

Not answering, Kemp rode directly at the man, who, after giving out a feeble squawk, threw himself to one side. His cries of outrage faded rapidly behind Kemp.

He rode straight for Cander and Eveline. He was relieved to see that they had managed to get to their feet. After reaching into his boot, he took out his knife. He was suddenly terrified that it would slip from his nervous and sweaty grasp.

Once he pulled up behind Cander and Eveline, he leaned over in the saddle and cut the ropes that bound their hands. While Cander scrambled onto the back of the other horse and pulled Eveline up behind him, Kemp looked out across the meadow, which was now overhung with puffs of dark, acrid smoke. A second man's harness had begun to erupt, and he made a wild, grimly amusing dance of consternation. Even this, however, could not prevent some of the royalists from turning their attention in Kemp's direction.

Turning his horse, Kemp said, "Follow me!" He urged the horse toward the nearest loop of the road. From the corner of his eye, he could see Cander and Eveline following behind.

"Stop them!" a voice shouted from somewhere. Royalists converged on them, hands attempting to grasp the horses' harness. Kemp drove his way mercilessly through the throng, swinging his knife at anyone who got too close.

They reached the road. Without hesitation, Kemp turned onto it and prodded his horse to a gallop. Shots rang out; he heard one ball whine past his ear and saw another skip over the surface of the road ahead, kicking up a puff of dust.

Even after they had made it safely behind the line of trees, the royalists kept up a ragged fusillade. Limbs cracked and lead shot sank with dull thuds into stout trunks, or ricocheted from them.

Kemp did not slow. He rode on, anxious to make his appointment with Vedrai and Digrippa.

16

Softly keening, the north wind whipped over the barren ridge, stirring the sere tufted grasses. Coat held tight against his throat, Cander peered over the gnarled rocks into the shallow canyon below. Although it was not yet noon, the flat, grey gloom of the sky made it seem nearly dusk. The royalist camp below, bordering on the dismal, lichen-blackened ruins of the ancient temple, was lent an aspect of insubstantial unreality that Cander found disturbing.

Standing in a neat group, sides shivering in the wind, a dozen multicolored tents held the land nearest the temple. To one side of them was an area where the common soldiers gathered around numerous firepits; to the other was a makeshift horse enclosure, hastily built of rope and tall posts. Nearby were two coaches. Cander recognized one of them, the smaller one, as the coach belonging to Doctor Stahlgrave.

Digrippa had climbed up beside Cander. Supporting his weight on stiffened forearms, the magician craned his neck to see down into the royalist camp. After a few moments, he lowered his head and sat with his back to the rocks. "Cander," he said, "you're usually good at this sort of thing. How many do you estimate that there are?"

"Three, maybe four hundred."

"Hmm. Four against four hundred. Not very favorable odds, are they?"

Cander saw no need to reply.

Digrippa stretched up to take another long look at the royalist camp. At length, he said, "Hmm, Eveline should take a look at those ruins. I'd like to know *for sure* whether or not this is the right place." Turning, he gave a quick glance at Eveline, where she stood, along with Kemp and the horses, a few yards down the slope. He beckoned to her with a two-fingered gesture.

After leaving the horses tethered to a gnarled shrub, Eveline picked her way up the rough slope. Kemp followed, grasping at the tall, spiky grasses to pull himself along. As soon as both had attained the ridge top, Digrippa said to Eveline, "Take a look. What do you see? Is this the place?"

Cautiously Eveline raised her head. She was silent for a long moment—then, her complexion becoming more than usually pale, she said, "Yes, this is the place."

She sank back behind the rocks. Her expression reminded Cander of that of an acquaintance of his who had just watched a companion get killed by a runaway carriage. "What did you see, exactly?" he asked.

"I can't describe it, really. Imagine if you could see hunger—an old hunger, inhuman and wicked. That is something like what I see."

Kemp ventured a look below. "Well, I know who that carriage belongs to," he said at length.

"Stahlgrave," Cander said, at the very same instant that Kemp said, "Lalerin."

They exchanged bemused looks, as Digrippa declared, "Well, it appears that all the major players are here. The question is, what are we going to do now?"

Nobody spoke.

After dark, they decided to risk a fire. The overcast had blocked out the stars and whatever moon there was, so it was unlikely that the royalists would notice the thin tendril of smoke that twisted from it. Knees drawn up before him, Cander sat on the ground, watching the yellow-orange tongues of flame flicker about the few miserable sticks of wood that they had managed to gather from their barren surroundings. He felt tired, and hungry, and unspeakably grubby.

For three long days they had shadowed the movements of the royalist troops, avoiding patrols and concealed lookouts, as the terrain grew steadily rougher and more barren. They'd had only hard brown bread to eat, from the saddlebags of their stolen horses, and now even that was nearly gone. They'd slept on the ground, exposed to the biting autumn cold, with only a thin blanket apiece. During this time, Cander's ambitions had narrowed to a remarkable degree. The only things he wanted from the world at that moment were a decent meal, a bath, and a bed.

It was unlikely that he was going to be getting any of those things in the near future.

Looking over the small fire, Cander saw Digrippa scribbling thoughtfully on a creased sheet of paper. The magician looked up at the sky and scowled. "I've been trying to work out exactly where we are. I *think* I know. If I could just see the stars, I could be sure."

This caught Cander's attention; he had a keen interest in finding out where they were. After rising to a crouch, he moved awkwardly to Digrippa's side of the fire and sat down beside him. "Let's see," he said.

Digrippa tilted the paper toward him, so that he could see that the magician had drawn a remarkably detailed map. "See," the man said. "Here are the hills where we are now. That much we know for sure, since they represent the only high ground in this region of Branion."

"True, but these hills stretch for quite some distance along the border. It doesn't narrow our position much."

"Yes, of course. Look, though. Here is the Inn of the Three Crows, and here the main road to Branion. We know that we stayed with this road for some distance, then turned onto a side road, which proceeded roughly north and west. The only road that answers that description curves like so, toward the town of Oraskal, yes?"

"That's so."

"Then, two days ago, we left the road and went due west, deeper into the hills. I estimate that we must have been about *here* at the time, and certainly no farther than *here*. We went slowly from this point on, since there was no road to speak of, and we were trying to avoid being seen by the royalists. Let's say that we went a half a league, total. That would put us here."

Cander nodded. He couldn't fault the man's reasoning. "Suppose you fill in some of the nearby towns, for reference."

"All right. Albian should be about here. Morulin here. Oraskal here." Digrippa made three marks at various, widely spaced points about the border of the hills.

Kemp stirred restlessly from his place by the fire. "But what difference does *any* of this make? Shouldn't we be doing something at least moderately useful? Like trying to figure out how to stop Lalerin?"

Digrippa shrugged. "I am simply attempting to satisfy my intellectual curiosity. The exact location of this temple has long been an interest of mine."

"It may be more important than that," Cander said suddenly.

Three faces swiveled mutely in his direction. "Yes?" Digrippa said. "How so?"

Self-conscious, Cander felt a warm flush rising to his cheeks. "I happen to know that the Protectorate has assembled a force at Morulin. If I can get there and fetch them back here in time—before Lalerin can complete his ceremony—then perhaps we can put a stop to it."

Cander had fully expected the others to raise some awkward questions. How did he know about the army at Morulin? How could he expect to convince them to follow him into the wild hill country? Could he even be sure that the Protectorate officers would agree to see him? He had prepared plausible explanations for all of these questions. To his surprise, though, he never got to use them. All three of his companions simply stared at him, each with the same slight, superior smirk. It made him uneasy.

"Hmm," Digrippa said at last, "yes. It seems a reasonable enough idea. Let's see, the sort of magical operation that the royalists are contemplating is best conducted on the first day of a waxing moon, and that comes four days from tomorrow, I believe. Four days. It is conceivable that, if you ride hard, you could reach Morulin and return with a detachment of light cavalry in time. It would be a close thing, at best."

"It would seem to be worth a try, though," Eveline said.

"Indeed, yes. Why not?"

Cander looked from one face to the other. He was amazed that they should be so easily convinced, without even raising any of the objections that came naturally to mind. "It's settled then," he said. "Tomorrow morning I shall take the best of the horses and set forth for Morulin."

No one tried to argue him out of it.

Because they were so near the royalist encampment and there existed a danger that a stray patrol might come upon them in the night, it was decided that they would take turns keeping watch. Too tense to sleep, Cander volunteered to take the first watch.

While the others wrapped themselves in their blankets and tried to sleep, Cander climbed to the top of the ridge, careful not to stumble and fall in the darkness. Standing atop that summit, he looked down upon the royalist encampment. The smoldering campfires were tiny red jewels on a fabric of velvet black. Cander could barely distinguish the tents belonging to Lalerin and his officers; the ruins of the old temple appeared only as a barely apprehended shape, low and starkly massive. Even so, it took on a dire presence in Cander's mind, sinister, cloying, grotesque. He told himself that fatigue and the late hour were merely playing on his fancies, but he could not quite make himself believe it. It seemed too real.

Gradually a dull sense of futility descended upon him. It suddenly seemed impossible that he could reach Morulin, avoiding royalist patrols and natural barriers alike, and return with reinforcements in time to do any good. He knew that it was unlikely that he could expect any help from Shalby or Walthorne anywhere along the way. As he saw it, his trail must have ended at the Inn of the Three Crows. They would have no idea where he was.

Fatigue pressed in on him. Consulting his watch, he saw that it was past midnight, time to rouse Kemp for his turn as sentinel. He delayed for a while longer, unable to work up any great enthusiasm for stretching out on the rocky ground and covering himself with a smelly horse blanket.

As Cander wound the watch and returned it to his waistcoat pocket, he saw Kemp stir under his blanket and sit up. After a moment, the small man got to his feet, dusted himself off, and looked about him. Appearing to notice Cander, he clutched his coat to his chest and clambered up the slope, coming at last to stand beside the taller man.

The two men nodded brusquely to each other. "Any trouble?" Kemp asked.

"No." They spoke softly. At that quiet hour of the night, any loud sound might be heard in the royalist camp and make their presence known.

"I'll take my turn, then."

"Good." Cander tarried, still not ready for sleep. He tried to think of some innocuous topic of conversation, but the one thing that came to mind wasn't entirely innocuous. After a moment's consideration, he ventured, "Kemp, understand that I don't mean any disrespect, but I really am curious to know how a man of your apparent skills came to be a prisoner in Tranding Gaol."

Kemp gave him a hard stare. Gradually his gaze softened, and a small, sly smile appeared on his lips. "All right, I'll tell you—if you promise not to tell anyone else. It, ah, isn't something that I would like to spread around."

"I won't tell a soul."

"Very well, then. It really was a stupid thing. I was robbing the house of an important official of the Protectorate. I had spent several weeks setting up the job, and I knew that the official and his wife were at their country home, leaving only a few servants in the house. So, it was late at night. I'd let myself in by way of a back door, found my way to the official's private chamber upstairs, and located and pocketed some gold coins and a few choice pieces of jewelry. Flushed with the pride of accomplishment, then, I started to leave by the same way that I had come. On the way to the stairs, though, I came upon a door that was open a crack. There was a light behind it. I peeked through the crack, and I saw her—a comely young maidservant. Naked. She was taking a sponge bath by candlelight. It was a hot night, you see, and she was probably trying to refresh herself, so that she could sleep. Well, I was so enchanted by the sight that I lingered there longer than I probably should have. The young woman looked in my direction and must have spotted me, for she screamed. Loudly, very loudly. I ran to the stairway and, in my embarrassment and haste, took a misstep, which sent me head over heels down the stairs. I must have hit my head, for the next thing I knew, I was waking up in my cell in Tranding Gaol."

The man paused, then added thoughtfully, "It was truly a lovely thing to behold, but I doubt that it was worth all the subsequent trouble that I've gone through."

Cander made a strangling noise as he attempted to suppress the laughter that, if let loose, would boom out so loudly that it would wake everyone for miles around, he was sure. His eyes blurred with tears, and he could feel the heat of the blood that congested in his face. It was really quite painful.

Kemp gave him an acerbic look. "I thought that you might enjoy that one. Just remember your promise."

Finding his breath at last, Cander said, "*Oh!* Oh, that is wonderful! Don't worry, though. I'll keep your secret to myself. We are both men of the world, are we not?"

The next morning, shortly after dawn, Cander stood gripping the reins of the horse he had chosen for his journey. The overcast had lowered in the late hours of the night, until it now clothed the hills like a gauzy mantle. Cander could not decide whether or not this was a good thing. It would make it more difficult for the royalist patrols to see him, certainly. But of course that cut both ways: He would not be able to see them, either, so the risk of stumbling unawares into a disagreeable situation was increased.

The others had gathered around him, their breath contributing to the mist. "Good luck," Digrippa said, face impassive, hands cupped over the head of his walking stick. "Remember, you'll have to ride hard and fast, if you expect to return in time to do any good."

Cander nodded. "I know."

Eveline smiled at him, teeth even and white. "Fare well, Cander." Ever since Stahlgrave had stripped her of her eye patch, she had gone with both eyes uncovered. Even now, Cander felt uncomfortable whenever she looked at him. It was small of him, he knew, but still . . .

"Thank you," he said, keeping his gaze slightly averted.

He grasped the pommel of the saddle and put a foot into the stirrup, then drew himself up onto the back of the horse. It stirred uneasily, and he gentled it with a firm hold on the reins and a touch to its neck. "If all goes well," he said, "I'll be back in four days' time."

"May it be so," Digrippa said. "In the meantime, we shall see what can be done here."

Cander let his gaze glide over the others, each in turn: Digrippa, Eveline, Vedrai, Kemp. The latter two stood a slight distance away, wreathed by curling mist. Vedrai wore his usual cynical half smile, his eyes cool and glittering. Kemp, giving Cander a slow nod, showed a more encouraging aspect.

There was nothing left to say. Cander maneuvered his horse to the start of the trail that led down out of the hills. There he paused, suddenly struck with the brave image of himself astride that great black horse, looming large in the pale fog. Cander raised his chin slightly, to present a more gallant attitude. He held the pose for a moment, then finally urged his mount forward.

If he was to die, he thought, at least there were four people in the world who would remember how splendid he had looked at the last.

17

As it gusted over the ridge, the wind kept pushing Kemp's hair into his face. Stubbornly he kept trying to pull it back, wishing that he had a hat.

The man stared down at the royalist camp, as he had for the better part of an hour. In the back of his mind, a course of action had been forming, but he resisted it still. He was a careful, cautious man; he hated being forced to improvise and leave things to chance.

As Kemp mulled over his plan, he continued to watch the royalist encampment, trying to get a sense of how it operated, whether the perimeter of the camp was watched or the tents guarded. He was gratified to see that the royalists seemed as feckless as ever; to all appearances, they had neglected to set guards anywhere.

Kemp centered his attention on the tents that bordered the ruined temple. Little by little, by watching the various comings and goings, he had begun to sort out which tent belonged to whom. The big one in the center was Lalerin's, he was certain, and next to it was the one belonging to Quordane. Slightly removed from the others was Doctor Stahlgrave's tent. In it, lights had burned far into the night, so that its side had shone with a strange, diffuse glow.

These were the only tents that mattered. Kemp knew that the box he had stolen from the Black Tower had to be in one of them. The question was, which one? A strong case could be made for any one of them. The box contained items woven with magic, which was surely Stahlgrave's province; the items, however, belonged to Lalerin; yet it was Quordane who seemed to be running the show, and it was Quordane who had taken the box from Kemp's hands.

As Kemp puzzled over this crucial yet insoluble problem, he saw the flap to Lalerin's tent flutter. From it emerged a young dark-haired woman attired in proper, expensive traveling clothes. Behind her came a young boy, quiet and unnaturally grave, dressed in a style that was far too old for him. They were too far away for him to see their faces, but he knew who they were—Ceris and the unfortunate Prince Garadon, Lalerin's son and intended victim.

The woman paused outside tent. Bending over Garadon, she carefully straightened the boy's jacket and smoothed down his hair. Taking his hand, then, she strolled along with him among the multicolored tents.

Watching them, Kemp was more than ever certain that Ceris could know nothing of what Lalerin had planned. What would she do when she found out? It wouldn't matter. She was a woman alone amid a small army gathered in this place for only one purpose. She could do nothing to stop what was going to happen.

Kemp balled up his hands and squeezed them as tightly as he could. Something had to be done, something had to be done . . .

Ceris and Garadon went behind Quordane's tent, disappearing from view, and at that moment Kemp became aware that there was someone behind him. A quick glance told him that it was Digrippa. The magician knelt down beside him on one knee, giving out a soft grunt. "See anything interesting?"

"I saw Ceris and Prince Garadon. They . . . were out walking."

The magician nodded and said nothing.

After a momentary silence, Kemp said, "There's something I've been wondering about."

"Yes? What is it?"

"Well, Lalerin is supposedly here to sacrifice his son to the god Brani, and so gain the god's favor . . ."

"That is true."

"So why is it necessary to sacrifice his legitimate son and heir? What I mean is, why not beget a bastard for the purpose? If you know what I mean. It . . . would be less traumatic, if no less horrible."

"The gods are not stupid," Digrippa said. "They know when a sacrifice is really a sacrifice, and when it isn't."

A slight shiver worked its way up Kemp's back. "Brani must be the cruelest of all the gods."

"Not really. There are crueler. If you are lucky, though, you will never encounter them."

"I hope I do not!" Kemp was silent for a moment, lost to dark, foreboding thoughts. At last, coming to a decision, he said, "I've been thinking."

"Yes?"

"Well, we can't just wait here, doing nothing, hoping that Cander gets back in time. He might not, you know."

"Can you suggest an alternative?"

"It occurs to me that what I've stolen once I can steal again."

Digrippa studied him through heavy-lidded eyes. "The idea does you credit, Kemp. It's dangerous, though. If they discover you, they won't hesitate to kill you."

Kemp shrugged. "I should've been dead by now, anyway. Besides, I am good at what I do. I won't be discovered."

"If you are determined to do this thing, of course, I won't try to stop you. I just hope that you know what you're doing."

"I have given this some thought."

"Yes, I'm quite certain that you have." Digrippa was silent for a moment, though he kept staring at Kemp, eyes keen with calculation. "You are clever with your hands, are you not? That is supposedly a hallmark of your profession?"

Smiling faintly, Kemp took a silver coin from his pocket and held it in his right hand, palm down. After flipping the coin to the top of his hand with his thumb, he walked it end over end from one finger to the next; when it reached the last finger, he quickly pulled his hand out from under it and then snatched it from midair. He turned his fist palm up, opened it. It was empty. "I am moderately proficient, yes."

"Very good. Very good, indeed. *Well.*" Digrippa pulled something from his coat pocket and held it out for Kemp, who recognized it as the gold medallion he had taken from Quordane's desk. "Since you are going into the royalist camp, there's something that I'd like for you to do, if you get a chance. You may not, but . . ."

"What is it?"

"If the opportunity should arise, try to substitute this medallion for the one Quordane wears around his neck. I don't want you to go out of your way, or to endanger yourself, but if you happen to get the chance . . ."

After taking the medallion, Kemp held it before him. There was something about it that disturbed him, as if it carried with it an emanation of danger and evil. He could not recall that it had invoked this reaction in him before. Kemp squinted thoughtfully at Digrippa. "You've done something to this, haven't you? Changed it, somehow."

The magician inclined his head once.

"What?"

"You can't reveal what you don't know," Digrippa said simply.

At length, Kemp slid the medallion into his pocket. "All right. If I can do it, I will. No promises, though . . . I get the feeling that you have prepared for Quordane a prank that I might well appreciate."

Smiling, Digrippa said nothing.

Once again wearing his royalist uniform, Kemp worked his way over the ridge and down into the encampment, taking advantage of whatever natural cover he could find in the blighted landscape. Breathing heavily, forehead slick with perspiration, he came off the ridge about a quarter of a mile from the royalist camp. After pausing to order his garments, catch his breath, and focus his thoughts, he started up the road. He no longer made any attempt to conceal himself. He would be brazen. Dressed as he was, if he behaved as if he belonged where he was, who would gainsay him?

Mustering all of his nerve, Kemp strolled into camp. He walked purposefully but without haste, doing his best not to attract attention to himself. He avoided the center of the camp, where the assemblage was most dense. Undoubtedly there were some royalists who would recognize him from his rescue of Cander and Eveline, he knew. He could only hope that none of them would notice him.

In all, this was riskier than he would like. He preferred operating at night, when the darkness could conceal his movements, but in this instance that would be impossible. At night, the tents would all be occupied. Even if he waited until everyone was asleep, it was unlikely that he could search them all without someone becoming aware of him and raising the alarm.

At last, he reached the tents, but felt no sense of relief. Indeed, this was where it would get really tricky, since he would have to guess if and when each tent was unoccupied. If he made a wrong judgment and walked in on somebody, it would be more than embarrassing.

Still doing his best to look as if he had some purpose, he made a pass by each of the tents that interested him. He heard voices coming from Lalerin's tent, but both Quordane's and Stahlgrave's tents were silent. Strolling again by each of those, he could detect no sign of habitation.

After withdrawing to the edge of the tented area, Kemp contemplated the ruins of the Gwyndi temple, jumbled blocks of blackened stone woven with briars, while he considered whose tent he would try first. Quordane or Stahlgrave? Stahlgrave or Quordane?

Having no basis by which to make an educated judgment, he made his decision based on the fact that he was, quite simply, more afraid of Quordane than he was of Stahlgrave.

After marching purposefully up to Stahlgrave's tent, he hesitated a moment before pulling the flap aside and risking a look inside. *Let this be easy, for once,* he thought fervently. *Let the tent be empty. Let the box be there.*

Inside, the light was dim, but it was apparent that the tent was deserted. Relieved, he entered and drew the flap shut behind him. Near the far wall was a straw sleeping pad piled up with quilts. Closer to hand were several small, leather-covered trunks and a folding table cluttered with a number of peculiar artifacts. Kemp moved to the table and examined the objects it supported. There were several jars filled with various powders and fluids, a small alcohol burner, a length of twisted copper tubing, several oddly shaped glass vessels. The bottom of one of the vessels was coated with a greenish-black tar. Gingerly he lifted the vessel, sniffed at it, and nearly gagged. He thought it remarkable that a smell that putrid could come from so small a container.

Eyes watering, he set the vessel aside and turned to the two trunks. The first of these was open and empty, the second closed and locked. After drawing his dagger and working the blade under the hasp holding the lid shut, he pulled sharply. The lock snapped and came loose. Inside he found a crimson robe, several old books, and some odd bits of apparatus similar to that on the table.

Frustrated, Kemp scowled. There was no sign of the box containing the antique dagger and crown. As he closed the trunk's lid, he gave the tent a cursory inspection. He did not find what he was looking for.

After a quick glance out through the flap, Kemp left the tent— and nearly ran straight into Quordane and Lalerin, who were at that moment emerging from Lalerin's tent, flanked by guards. Fortunately, the men were looking in the other direction. Absorbed in conversation, they did not appear to notice him.

Kemp wheeled quickly and started away toward the horse enclosure, fighting to keep his rising fear under control. He was certain that at any moment one of the men would challenge him, or raise an alarm. When, after several moments, that did not happen, he braved a glance over one shoulder. He saw that the men were headed away from him, toward the center of the camp. It was obvious that they were unaware of him.

Making an effort to breathe normally, Kemp tarried beside the makeshift horse enclosure, which had been lashed together with ropes and sticks. He watched Quordane, Lalerin, and their escort disappear behind the last tent. Now, he knew, it was time to search the other tents, before they could return. Unfortunately, he could not force himself to move. It was too dangerous, too bloody dangerous . . .

Kemp took three breaths, slow and deep, while he rebuilt his courage. Finally he turned and strode back toward the tents. *I have time*, he thought. *It's in and out, no worry.*

Lalerin's tent was first. Kemp approached it cautiously, giving circumspect glances about him. Seeing no one, he parted the flap and stepped inside.

Immediately he was surprised by how lavishly appointed the tent was. There were three sturdy camp beds, two of them close together, the third standing isolated. Kemp could not help wondering whose bed was the isolated one—Lalerin's or the child's. He guessed Lalerin. He could easily imagine him choosing to sleep apart from his wife and child.

In addition to the beds, there was a small desk, facing the tent opening, a round-backed chair behind it. There were no fewer than four large traveling chests, of the sort that had hinged panels in front, which folded back to reveal numerous small drawers and compartments. A lacquered cabinet with brass carrying handles stood beside the desk, supporting a gold flagon and several matching goblets. On the desk itself was an expensive silver jafar service.

"I see that you like to travel light, Lalerin," Kemp muttered darkly. He stood where he was for a long moment, unable to decide where to begin looking. Finally he moved to one of the traveling chests and began, one by one, going through the drawers, finding nothing but various articles of clothing, in silk and linen. After rapidly sorting through the contents of the first chest, he moved on to the next, where the search was no more fruitful. The third chest contained women's clothing. Kemp could not help feeling vaguely indecent as he searched among the lacy frills and silken undergarments.

He was finishing with the last of the drawers when he heard the tent flap rustle behind him. A sudden chill fluttering on the back of his neck, he turned slowly and saw Prince Garadon standing just inside the tent, peering at him with grave interest. Unsure of what to do, Kemp essayed a nervous smile.

Suddenly, in a clear voice, Garadon announced, "*Mother, there's a strange man in our tent.*"

The flap stirred, was swept back. Ceris entered, in a gown the color of a summer sky, the collar of the finest Liln lace. Kemp gaped at her, struck dumb by her sudden appearance. There was something about her that disarmed him entirely.

She looked at him, frowning. "What are you doing here? Do I . . . know you?"

"We met once," Kemp answered. "I wasn't dressed in this uniform at the time."

Squinting, she said, "Yes, I remember now. At Baron Quordane's house. You had some business with my husband."

Kemp smiled broadly. "Yes, that's it."

"Of course, that doesn't quite explain why you are going through the things in my chest."

The corners of his mouth drooping, he said, "No, it does not. I'm . . . looking for something."

"Indeed? In my underwear?"

"Ah, that is a mistake. I am looking for something that belongs to your husband."

"That is no explanation. I think I'm going to call for help now."

"*Don't do that.*"

"Why shouldn't I?"

Why indeed? Kemp toyed with several possible lies, ultimately dismissing all of them as unconvincing. He decided that he had no alternative but to risk the truth. If it turned out that she already knew about Lalerin's plans, then he would be finished—but, even applying the full measure of his cynicism, he could not believe that of her. "If you do, you will regret it," he said steadily. "I don't think you realize the danger that you are in."

"What are you talking about?"

"First, send the boy outside. There's no reason he should hear this."

The woman contemplated Kemp for a moment and appeared

to come to a decision. "Very well. If you try anything when we are alone, though, I'll scream."

Kemp shrugged. "As you say."

Ceris knelt down next to the young prince. Straightening the collar of his coat, she said, "Darling, go outside for a few moments. Your mother wants to talk to this gentleman."

"Yes, Mother."

"Don't go far. Stay right outside."

"Yes, Mother."

The boy went out through the flap. Ceris straightened and fixed Kemp with a frosty gaze. "Now," she said, "speak."

Kemp hesitated. He knew what he needed to say, but how could he make it believable to Ceris? In truth, he found it hard to believe himself. At last, he ventured, "Have you been told why you are here, in the middle of nowhere, beside a ruined temple?"

A pause. "No," Ceris admitted. "My husband doesn't confide his purposes to me."

Did he detect a trace of bitterness in the woman's tone? If so, that would give him something to work with. "There *is* a reason. You must know that. It was certainly not a mere whim that brought you and your son here, along with hundreds of armed men."

"Suppose you tell me what you think that reason is."

"Not think—*know*. I know. Your husband is ambitious. He would do anything to regain the throne of Branion, even that which would be unthinkable for most men."

As he spoke, Kemp studied Ceris, hoping to gauge her reaction. The woman's gaze remained level; she said nothing. Encouraged that she did not attempt to refute him, Kemp continued, "Lalerin has brought you and Garadon here for a reason, and for a reason he has kept you ignorant. This is a place inhabited by an old god, a terrible god. Your husband hopes to enlist the god's help in his effort to regain his throne, but the god requires that he first make a sacrifice."

Kemp paused long enough to take a deep breath. "His son. The life of his son. That is what the god requires."

The woman's eyes grew large. For several moments she appeared to be unable to speak. At last she said, "You're lying. My husband wouldn't . . . Not even he."

Noting that her denial lacked fire, Kemp was encouraged to think that, given time, he could convince her. "I'm sorry to say that he would. Can you think of any other reason why he would bring you and Garadon to this place?"

"No, but . . ."

"There is a box, leather-covered, so wide and so long," he said, indicating the dimensions with his hands. "It contains an iron crown and a dagger. This is the thing that I am looking for. Without it, Lalerin will be unable to do as he plans. Garadon would be safe. Have you seen it? Can you tell me where it is?"

Ceris bit her lower lip and said nothing.

"If you know, you must tell me. You *must*."

Suddenly a new voice sounded, a distressingly familiar one. "Tell him nothing. He is a madman—and an enemy." The tent flap quivered, went back. The speaker, Baron Quordane, entered the tent, followed by Lalerin, Garadon, and the two guards.

Propelling young Garadon toward his mother, Lalerin said, "You should not let the boy wander about unsupervised, Ceris. I would not like it if some unfortunate accident befell him."

Ceris scooped up the boy and held him protectively to him. "Why is that, Husband?"

"That is an impertinent question, Ceris," the man said coldly.

Quordane, meanwhile, stepped forward to confront Kemp, giving a smile that made the thief feel sick to his core. "Well, well," the man said, "Kemp. I can't tell you how happy I am to see you again."

"I wish that I could say that the feeling was mutual."

"Where are your friends, Kemp? I am quite anxious to renew my acquaintance with them, also."

"Far from here, alas."

"Is that true?"

"Would I lie to you? I owe you so much, after all. Someday I hope to repay you in full."

Quordane chuckled. "We shall see. Come, Kemp, I have plans for you."

Glumly Kemp assessed his situation. It was not good. At best, he could expect a quick death—at worst, slow torture, followed by a lingering death. And it would be in vain, he knew. He had failed to find what he was looking for; he had not interfered with Quordane's scheme in the least.

There was only one thing left for him to do.

Quordane stood several short paces away; Lalerin and the guards were more than a yard behind him. If he moved quickly, Kemp could have his satisfaction.

Giving a doleful shrug and hanging his head, he took a shuffling step toward Quordane. The baron started to turn away—and, at that instant, Kemp leapt upon him, grabbing the collar of his coat and wrenching it hard. It was a pleasure to see Quordane's smug expression turn to shock, as the man uttered a brief squawk of alarm.

Pushing his shoulder into Quordane's chest, Kemp bore down against him with all his weight, carrying him over onto the ground. Kemp straddled the fallen baron, then, trying to get his hands around the man's fat throat. For effect, he kept shouting "Swine! Swine! Swine!"

Quordane rolled back and forth, trying to get out from under the apparently enraged thief. He put up his arms in an effort to protect his throat. He cried, "Get this madman off of me! *Get him off!*"

Strong hands seized Kemp, a pair on either arm, and hauled him from the prostrate man. Kemp struggled against them—but not too vigorously.

Quordane sat up, glaring at Kemp. He must have bitten the inside of his lip, because there was a thin streak of blood next to his mouth. Daubing at this with the knuckle of one finger, he said in a dire voice, "You shall regret this. After we have fed the boy to the god Brani, you shall be the dessert."

Kemp heard Ceris utter a faint gasp.

"Take him out," Quordane said. "Beat him soundly—but take care not to kill him. A worse fate awaits him. Be sure to check his boots. He keeps a knife there."

As the two guards pulled Kemp staggering from the tent, the thief covertly slipped his closed fist into the side pocket of his coat and let the gold medallion drop. He had already taken the precaution of unstitching the bottom of the pocket. He felt the medallion slither down into the lining of his coat, where a casual search would not find it. He hoped that the substitution he had made would be worth the pain it was going to cost him.

18

Cander did not see the trap until it had already closed around him.

He had been riding for so long that his body—particularly the part that met the saddle—had begun to go numb. The sun was dropping low in the sky and many of the trees that crowded the road were darkening and merging. As he passed a copse of slender trees clad in autumn's gold, he saw the men, where they had concealed themselves among the trees—but unfortunately not before they had also seen him.

There were four of them. They wore dull breastplates over dun coats and carried long-barreled muskets. As soon as Cander turned the bend in the road and came even with them, they stood up from behind the fallen tree that had concealed them. Three of the men shouldered their weapons, while the fourth called out, "*Halt!* Stop where you are."

A sudden surge of alarm clearing away most of his fatigue, Cander evaluated his position in a single instant. He realized that he could do one of two things. Either he could make a break for freedom, or he could do as he was told. He quickly rejected the first option. There were three guns pointed at him, his only weapon was an old saber strapped to his saddle, and his horse was hardly fresh. His chances of getting away cleanly were poor at best.

Cander halted. Hoping that he could bluff his way through, he put on an expression of innocent terror. "Please, sir," he said in an abject voice, "tell your fellows not to shoot. I will give you all my money. I don't have much, but whatever I have is yours."

The man frowned. "We're not robbing you, fool."

Putting on a perplexed look, Cander said, "What, then? What do you want from me?"

"Come to the side of the road. Slowly."

Cander did this, and the man giving the orders stepped closer to him and scrutinized him with care. "Who are you? What business do you have on this road?" he demanded.

"I am a gentleman, sir. My name is Thaddus Krowel, and I am traveling to Oraskal for the harvest fair."

The man squinted up at him. "Hmm, maybe," he conceded. "But you fit the description of someone we were ordered to stop. Get down from your horse, and then we'll try to sort this out."

Cander tried not to let his distress at this show. He knew that if he got off his horse, he would immediately lose whatever small advantage he had. But what else could he do?

"Bedloe, look!" said one of the other men. "Someone else comes."

Looking around, Cander saw that a man on horseback was approaching from the opposite direction than he himself had been going. The man rode a grey horse with a white blaze and wore a full grey cloak. The cloak billowed out over the horse's hindquarters in back but was clasped firmly shut in front, at a level just above the saddle's pommel, making the man's hands invisible.

Although it took a few moments for Cander to be able to see the man's face clearly, he recognized him instantly, by his posture and by the color and cut of his cloak. The ways of the world were indeed strange, Cander thought. He would never have imagined that there could ever be a circumstance in which he would be this happy to see Shalby.

Face as phlegmatic and composed as ever, Shalby slowed as he approached Cander and his captors, pulling up beside Cander. He flashed a smile. "Greetings, Nephew," he said, focusing on him an alarming degree of cordiality. "What seems to be going on here?"

Though dubious, Cander decided that he might as well follow Shalby's lead. He returned a big, stupid grin. "Hello, Uncle. I'm glad to see you. These gentlemen have confused me with someone else."

Shalby turned his attention to the man called Bedloe. "Is there something wrong here? Why have you detained my nephew?"

"Your nephew?" Bedloe asked guardedly.

"Indeed, yes. We were to meet here on this road and journey onward together."

"Your nephew, if that is what he is, fits the description of someone we were ordered to detain."

"A mistake. Just look at him. He's a very common-looking fellow, surely."

"Perhaps, but we still need to make sure. I think it best that you *both* get down off your horses now, so that we can make proper inquiries."

"I'm afraid that I can't do that."

"I'm afraid that you'll have to. Otherwise, my men won't hesitate to shoot you dead."

Shalby sighed. "And I was so hoping that this wouldn't get unpleasant." Suddenly a pistol projected from the front of his cloak. It was an uncommon weapon, Cander saw, a five-barrel pepperbox; it could fire five shots without being reloaded.

Eyes going wide, Bedloe shouted out a frantic warning. The men with the muskets hesitated a crucial second, clearly unsure of what was happening—and this was their undoing. Shalby swiftly leveled his pistol, firing off first one barrel and then another. The pistol spat fire and black smoke.

Cander heard the sound of metal being struck hard, once, twice. He saw the breastplates of two of the men deform and breach at the center. One of the men fell promptly backward and lay there on the ground unmoving, face slack and ghastly pale; the other spun around, casting off his musket, and dropped mechanically to his hands and knees.

In that same instant, Cander's horse reared and tried to bolt. He managed to restrain it with a strong hand on the reins—though he might not have, had the horse not been a cavalry charger, trained not to panic at the sound of gunfire.

From the corner of his eye, he caught sight of Bedloe fumbling with the pistol that was stuck into his sash. Knowing that he could not allow the man to get his gun out, Cander quickly drew his saber from its sheath and slashed out wildly. A shock of impact communicated itself through the blade and into his hand. With a peculiar sense of detached horror, he saw the edge of the blade cleave halfway through Bedloe's neck and continue on in a beautiful arc, blood dripping from it like a scattering of rubies. Bedloe crumpled to the ground, head canted off to a bizarre angle.

Cander heard the sharp report of a gun and an instant later the heavy sound of something falling to earth. Shalby's horse made a wild sound, reared, and took off at a gallop down the road. There was no one in the saddle. Jerking his head around, Cander saw that Shalby lay facedown at the edge of the road, not moving. Standing beside his fallen fellows, wreathed by black smoke, the remaining royalist soldier was struggling with powder horn and rod to reload his gun.

Filled with a heady mixture of fear and rage, Cander urged his horse to leave the road and charged directly at the man, holding his gory saber high. The royalist, taking one look at Cander, went deathly pale, flung his musket aside, and bolted abruptly into the woods.

Pulling up before the screen of trees, Cander watched the man's energetic retreat. The royalist leapt over rocks and fallen branches and caromed around tree trunks in his eagerness to get away. As it became plain that the man no longer represented any threat, Cander returned to the roadside.

Everything had happened so quickly that it was hard to believe that it had in fact happened at all. Stirred by the wind, a pall of smoke hung over the road and intertwined itself with the overhanging branches. Four bodies lay motionless on or about the road: the three royalist soldiers, and Shalby.

Cander shivered, appalled by the sight. Suddenly conscious of the saber still clenched in his hand, he lowered it slowly and returned it to its sheath. Ignoring the royalists, all of whom were obviously either dead or near death, he dismounted beside the fallen Shalby and knelt down on one knee.

The man in grey lay facedown on the margin of the road, legs slightly splayed, arms under his torso, cloak twisted and askew to one side. Cander thought that he must be dead, too. Then he saw that he was still breathing.

Touching the man lightly on one shoulder, Cander said, "Shalby, can you hear me? Shalby? Are you hurt?"

Shalby stirred, making a rusty-sounding grunt deep in his throat. Slowly, laboriously, he turned himself over onto his back. There was a grimace on his face, and he had gone quite pale beneath his tan. "What do you think?" he muttered through bared teeth.

"Where were you hit?" Shalby did not answer, but suddenly Cander could see the ragged hole in the man's waistcoat and the spreading stain around it. "Hold still," he said, unfastening waistcoat and shirt and gingerly pulling them from the wound. The shot had caught Shalby in the left side, near waist level,

Cander saw. Blood was leaking from the wound, but there was not as much of it as he had feared there might be.

"Can you sit up a little, Shalby? I need to see if the ball went through, or if it is still in there somewhere."

Eyes bleak and unfocused, the man nodded and wrenched himself up on one elbow. A grimace tightened his mouth.

After drawing back the man's waistcoat and shirt, Cander saw that there was a matching wound in back, somewhat higher than the first. Taking into account the angle of the shot, that was as it should be. "Mm, that's fortunate. At least, it seems to have passed through. I don't think that it hit anything vital."

Face slick with perspiration, in spite of the cold, Shalby said, "Have you found them?"

"Them?"

"Quordane, Lalerin. The crown."

"Oh, *them*. Yes, certainly. I was on my way to find Walthorne when I was stopped."

"Why are you wasting time here, then? *Go*."

"I can't just leave you here, Shalby. You're—well, you've been shot."

"I'm well aware of that," the man said in a mordant tone.

"Without help, you could bleed to death. Or die of shock or exposure."

"Don't worry about me. I'm . . . fine. For once, just worry about doing your job. Do I really have to remind you what's at stake here?"

"Please don't."

"Then *go*, damn you."

"No."

"You're being a stubborn fool."

"Am I now?"

"Every moment you delay is the moment that may bring our downfall. *Leave me.*"

"If you don't shut up, Shalby, I may just have to throttle you."

The man sneered. "Try it."

With his arms bound so tightly with ropes that not even he could hope to wriggle free, Kemp lay curled on his side, forsaken on the damp, cold grass. Every breath brought pain. Quordane's men had been uncommonly diligent. He could still taste the blood.

More than anything else now, he just wanted to sleep. He had to force himself to stay alert. He knew that there was not much time left. Whatever was going to happen was going to happen soon. All day he had watched the royalists making their hurried preparations, and now it appeared that they were nearly finished.

Crowned by a somber purple sky streaked with high, dusky clouds, the temple of Brani had been laboriously returned to life. Wind-whipped torches planted before and beside it carved a small world from the surrounding gloom. Enclosed on three sides by towering megaliths of green stone, the central court had been cleared of brambles, brush, and debris. In the center of it was a massive slab hewn of the same glossy green stone as the megaliths. Stretching perhaps ten feet in length, the slab rose to the height of a man's waist, if he was a tall man. On one end of it a number of articles had been set out: a huge bronze brazier, a cup, several corked jars, an archaic dagger and an iron crown. The slab was an altar, Kemp had realized.

Beside the slab stood Lalerin, Quordane, and Stahlgrave. They wore identical ankle-length robes, of crisp white linen, complex sigils sewn in crimson thread on the left breast. Stahlgrave was barefoot.

The royalist troops had been brought together before the temple, where they waited with an air of perplexed expectation, seeming to sense that something extraordinary was about to happen, but not knowing what. Their voices merged into a constant low rumble in Kemp's ears.

Kemp himself lay unheeded five or six yards from the royalist tents, at a place where the torchlight shaded by subtle degrees into the darkness. He had no doubt that Quordane would know exactly where to find him when the time came, and that gave him no pleasure at all.

His hopes of Cander returning with help in time to do any good had long since dwindled away to almost nothing. It seemed clear that he could not trust matters to providence. If there was to be a last-minute miracle, he would have to manufacture it himself. But how?

As Kemp fretted over this question, he noticed a small group leave the tented area to his left and march quickly in the direction of the temple. At first, the darkness made it impossible to make out the individual members of the group, but as they moved toward the temple the dancing torchlight revealed them in full. He saw that at the center of the clique was Ceris and her son, surrounded by stern-faced royalist officers. One of these kept one hand on the woman's arm as they walked. Kemp had the certain impression this was not out of courtesy; the stiff attitude that they both maintained suggested that it was a gesture intended more to control than to assist.

Skirting the area where the common soldiers stood waiting, they approached the temple from the side and climbed several high cyclopean steps, hauling young Garadon up them as if he were a sack of flour. They stopped behind and to one side of the altar stone, near the base of one of the towering megaliths. Surrounded by her somber custodians, Ceris stood by rigidly, her hands gripping Garadon's narrow shoulders. Her lips were pressed together into a rigid line. Her eyes were veiled by hopelessness and fear. Garadon seemed to sense her unease. He kept squirming around to look up at his mother, his face intent and questioning.

Quordane gave a glance back at Ceris, Garadon, and the others, then he whispered a word into Stahlgrave's ear, who nodded. Stepping forward, Quordane cleared his throat, held up his arms, and began to address the assembled troops in a loud voice:

"*Men!* Soldiers in our most just cause! Hear me! We have assembled here for one purpose: to crown Lalerin, the rightful ruler of Branion, in the manner of his ancestors, and to consecrate him in the name of Brani, the ancient and terrible god of this land. When this is done, Brani will lend his strength to our cause. The land itself shall rise up to help us. We shall sweep the traitors from Branion, and Lalerin shall rule in Lorum. We shall be invincible. Brani is great! Cry all hail to Brani!"

After an uncertain pause, the shout went up from the assemblage, echoing out into the night: *"Hail Brani!"*

"Cry all hail to Lalerin, your king!"

"Hail Lalerin!"

Face flushed, eyes shining, Quordane stepped back behind Lalerin, while Lalerin and Stahlgrave moved to the altar. Stahlgrave took a pinch of powder from a shallow bowl and scattered it over the brazier. White smoked boiled up from the brazier, to be scattered by the gusting wind.

After taking a gold cup in both hands, Stahlgrave held it out before Lalerin. "Lalerin, son of Carelinas," he said, "do you consent to be consecrated in the name of Brani?"

Lalerin's face was pinched and grave. "I do so consent."

"Do you promise to serve His will, no matter what sacrifice He may demand?"

"I do so promise."

"Drink, then, of Brani's pleasure." Stahlgrave held the cup to the younger man, who took hold of the cup's base and tilted it to his lips. Lalerin drank deeply, draining the cup of its contents. A red trickle ran from the corner of his mouth and glistened on his chin.

After taking the cup from Lalerin and setting it on the altar, Stahlgrave proclaimed a short phrase in a guttural language that Kemp did not recognize. The magician threw another pinch of powder from the bowl into the brazier. He took up the iron crown and passed it three times through the smoke, all the while repeating a phrase in a subdued voice.

As all this was occurring, Kemp was struggling to think of something that he could do to stop it. He had noticed, when Quordane had first begun his address, that the royalist soldiers had started to gradually edge toward the front of the temple, leaving him forgotten at the periphery of the assembly. No one was paying any attention to him. If he could work his way over to the tents, there was a chance that he could find something sharp and free himself from the cords that bound him. He wasn't sure what he might do then, but at least he would be in a position to do *something*.

Even after he had come to his decision, though, he hesitated. If he were to be discovered trying to escape, the royalists would hurt him, and they had already shown themselves uncommonly adept at hurting. But then again, if he did nothing, they would doubtless hurt him anyway. He really had nothing to lose.

Staying curled on his side, he started working his way slowly toward the tents, moving like an inchworm: swiveling his kinked legs in the direction he wanted to go and then pushing the rest of his body after them with his shoulder. This was a slow, laborious process, and his current physical condition made it quite painful. The question that he contemplated as he squirmed his way across the field was not whether or not he had broken ribs, but rather how many of them were broken.

Once he reached the line of the first tent, he would be able to get to his feet. There was too great a risk of being noticed if he tried to do it before then.

Still well short of his goal, Kemp ran out of strength. His thoughts grew vague and fleeting, and he was afraid that he might faint if he did not rest a moment. After rolling over onto his back, he tried to catch his breath, while stealing a look over one shoulder at the temple.

He saw that Lalerin now knelt beside the altar. Stahlgrave

held the crown over his head, all the while muttering something in that guttural tongue. Something else had changed, something that he could not quite place. All seemed to be as it was before, but it was also . . . different.

The darkness surrounding the temple was more complete than it had been. It seemed to be almost a physical presence now, oppressive and hostile. It pressed relentlessly on the bubble of light that surrounded the temple, which in turn appeared brighter now, perhaps by contrast. The wind, which only minutes before had whipped fiercely around the temple, had died away to nothing. All was deathly still.

At last, Stahlgrave placed the iron crown upon Lalerin's head, and a general shout of acclamation went up. Rising slowly to his feet, Lalerin gazed out toward his supporters, mouth twisted with an expression of arrogant triumph.

Kemp could not help but marvel at the man. He seemed reborn—bigger, stronger, and more sure of movement than Kemp remembered him. Vigor and power shone from his face and seemed to animate his slender frame. It was as if the Lalerin he had known before had been but an empty skin, filled now to bursting.

Kemp was not the only one to perceive the change in the man. Though he could now discern little of the host who surrounded the temple, he began to sense in them a growing confidence and excitement, and he felt a fleeting, insidious desire to become one with them, to share in their elation, their sense of purpose.

Stahlgrave took the archaic dagger from its place on the altar. Holding it in his right hand, he passed it three times through the smoke that was drifting up from the brazier. Each time he did so, the blade seemed to gain substance, in a way that Kemp could not quite define. It had seemed an ordinary weapon, of dull lusterless iron; but now it took on a dark sheen, strange and deadly. Stahlgrave held the dagger out lengthwise before Lalerin, who muttered a word and kissed the wicked blade, slowly, in a manner that seemed to Kemp perversely erotic.

Stahlgrave had been chanting all the while. The magician's voice droned through the world, unintelligible, and yet full of implied meaning. The words fell into a dark place in Kemp's mind and filled it with an ancient knowledge that the rest of him could not quite comprehend. He knew that he ought to move, to continue toward the tents, yet a peculiar torpor had overtaken him, and he could not seem to find the will to overcome it.

Stahlgrave gave a beckoning gesture to the men who stood

with Ceris and Garadon. Two of the men put hands on the boy's shoulders and compelled him toward the altar. Ceris attempted to follow, but one of the other men blocked her way with a stiffened forearm. Submitting without a struggle, the woman stood silently by, eyes grown large and woeful.

The men brought Garadon to between Stahlgrave and Lalerin. They then backed away a pace, although they continued to watch the boy with cold, careful eyes. Garadon himself looked from Lalerin to Stahlgrave, obviously curious but as yet unaware of the danger he faced. Lalerin smiled at the boy, in a manner that was probably intended to be reassuring, but which in fact was so distant and calculated an expression that Garadon merely frowned and looked away uneasily.

After turning Garadon to face him, Stahlgrave held a hand before the boy, palm outward, fingers spread. Slowly the hand described a clockwise circle around the boy's face, then came forward and touched on his pale forehead. Garadon stiffened immediately and started to slump forward. Before he could fall, Stahlgrave caught the boy under the arms and lifted him up deftly, depositing him on the altar. The boy lay there unmoving. After a moment, his head lolled to the side, and Kemp was able to see his small features, slack as if with innocent slumber. The horrid contrast between the boy's expression and his plight struck Kemp with an almost physical force, rousing him from his apathy. He knew in that moment that he could not simply watch while events unfolded before him. He had to at least try to do something.

Exerting every bit of will left to him, Kemp renewed his efforts to reach the tents. Realizing that his progress was far too slow, he soon decided to risk being noticed and get to his feet. This proved to be more demanding than he would have thought. Bound as he was, it was hard enough to get his feet under him. With the added impediment of his damaged ribs, standing was nearly impossible. Eventually he managed it, though the effort left him light-headed and gasping for breath.

Glancing back toward the temple, Kemp beheld a scene that caused him to completely forget his many discomforts. Lalerin stood poised over Garadon. On his head was the crown, in his hand the dagger. Stahlgrave stood behind him, chanting, arms spread. The rest of the royalists were chanting, too—in that same strange, guttural language. Kemp wondered how they had all learned to speak in that tongue, even as he found the same words coming from someplace inside of him and attempting to take control of his lips and tongue. He fought the urge, but it was difficult, almost impossibly difficult, to resist it.

Lalerin displayed the sacrificial knife to the assembly. The blade glittered and shone like a flawless black jewel. He called out: *"Brani!* Hear me, O great god! For you I make this sacrifice, and to you I submit all the works of my hand. I beg you to accept my offering. *For you, Brani!"*

After taking the dagger in both hands, Lalerin held it poised, point down, over his unconscious son. The man's lungs were working hard; his chest was heaving fast and shallow, as if from some great exertion. His eyes had a feverish look to them, and his thin lips were twisted and tight.

Kemp blinked, caught in a dark spell from which he seemed unable to free himself. Suddenly Lalerin seemed oddly indistinct, as if shadow had cloaked him, even though he stood at the center of the pooling torchlight. Yet the dagger appeared as clear and distinct as ever, seeming the only feature in the terrible tableau that retained its full share of reality.

Gradually Kemp became aware of the mood of avid expectation that rose from the assemblage like a fog. They were all waiting, he realized, waiting for the blood. He could see it in their rapt postures, hear it in their voices, as they continued their strange chant. Even more horribly, Kemp could feel those same emotions rising from within *himself*. He tried to distance himself from it, but it was a part of him, inescapable. He watched the blade, waiting, and something primitive and corrupt within him willed it to fall. His own arm tensed, as if he held the dagger himself and could plunge it into a helpless victim. In that moment, he lusted for blood, for death.

Time seemed to slow. The torchlight flickered amber red and dismal. Kemp felt ill, as if there were an expanding void in the center of his stomach. His face was hot.

The tip of the dagger poised above the boy twitched almost imperceptibly. It was about to descend, Kemp knew. All was eerily silent in that frozen instant of time, which hung uneasily between life and death, yearning and completion.

A moment later the silence was shattered, and with it the terrible spell that had held Kemp in thrall.

Throughout the ceremony, Ceris had stood compliantly between the two royalist officers, though her eyes darted apprehensively and her hands were clenched and white at her sides. Perhaps over time her acquiescence had lulled her guardians, or perhaps they had become entranced, as Kemp himself had, by the ritual. For whatever reason, when Ceris, giving out a wail of frantic horror that touched Kemp's nerves like a hot iron, leapt abruptly for Lalerin and Garadon, her guardians failed to react until she was already well beyond their grasp.

In an instant, Ceris crossed the space that separated her from Lalerin. So intent was he on what he was doing that he apparently did not see her coming, for he did nothing to avoid her.

Ceris ran headlong into Lalerin, grappling for the hands that held the dagger. "Lalerin, *no*!" she cried as she struggled to catch his wrists. "Please god, you mustn't!"

Giving a low growl, Lalerin twisted to one side, attempting to extricate himself from the woman's clinging grasp. The force of her body had thrown him off balance, however; he did not seem to be able to stop twisting once he'd started. Their legs tangled, and they went down behind the altar, still struggling for control of the dagger.

Kemp could see little of what happened next; only the legs and feet of the two were visible from behind the massive stone altar. For several moments he could see them thrashing, rolling. Then they were abruptly still.

Kemp felt the certain knowledge that something significant had occurred in that instant, but he wasn't sure what it was. The change, though palpable, was elusive. It seemed as if the morbid oppression that had encompassed the temple had collapsed, so quickly and completely that it was hard to believe that it had ever existed at all. Suddenly, even though he remained physically bound, Kemp felt a wonderful sense of lightness and freedom. *Something had happened* . . .

Ceris was the first to rise from behind the altar. Her hands were wet with blood, and the front of her gown was stained crimson. Backing away, she held those hands away from her body in a peculiar manner, as if they were alien things, entirely detached from her. Her face was ashen, and her eyes stared all the while with terrified fascination at the place from where she had risen.

Fingers curled into cruel claws, a hand came up from behind the altar and slapped itself stiffly on the smooth stone. Then a second hand appeared, coming down beside the first. The fingers of both hands dug at the unyielding stone for a moment and then the hands began to press downward. Slowly, agonizingly, Lalerin arose from behind the altar—head first, then shoulders, and finally torso.

The man wore a look of plaintive bewilderment, as if he could not quite comprehend what had happened. Kemp saw then, with a sick shock, that the handle of the dagger projected from under the man's ribs, surrounded by a spreading stain of wetness, a deep red blooming on the white robes. Lalerin worked his mouth silently, seemingly unable to find words or breath. Then his eyes rolled up in their sockets. He fell forward onto the altar at his son's feet, and moved no more.

For a long moment, all was silence. The assembled royalist host seemed too shocked to speak or move. Even Stahlgrave and Quordane stood by dumbly. Quordane's mouth hung open, as if caught in a frozen shout.

The moment passed. The royalists began to murmur among themselves, and several isolated cries sounded, despairing, lost in the night. Quordane came suddenly alive. His gaze fell upon Ceris, who stood numbly where she had stopped, several paces from the altar. "You," he declared, voice thick with passion. "You did this. *You.* You've ruined . . . *everything.*"

Quordane's hands came up, knotted with frustrated rage. He began advancing upon the woman, menace oozing from every pore. Ceris just stared at him, unmoving, apparently transfixed by the realization of what she had done.

Kemp watched helplessly. He tried to twist his hands free of their bonds, but it was useless. They had been tied too tightly.

After closing on Ceris with several long strides, Quordane drew back his right hand and cuffed her a powerful backhanded blow to the cheek. The woman's head flew back. She spun around half a turn, then fell to her knees. Quordane lunged at her, hands grappling for her throat, eyes ablaze with murderous intent.

Ceris made no real attempt to escape Quordane. She did try to keep him from closing on her throat, by throwing her arms up in his face and pushing him away, but Kemp knew that she could not keep him at bay for long. Her one chance lay in putting some distance between Quordane and herself.

"Get *up*, Ceris!" Kemp found himself shouting. *"Run!"* Kemp heard hostile murmurings from the royalist host and suddenly realized what he had done. When he glanced about him, he was acutely discomfited to find that people were looking at him. They did not appear at all pleased.

Seeing dark shapes closing on him from several directions, Kemp decided to take his own advice and run. After turning toward the tents, he loped away at top speed. Unfortunately, it was dark, and the ground was deeply pitted and littered with rocks. Still several yards short of the nearest tent, he caught his toe on something and was unable to regain his balance. He met the ground with his face, so hard that for a moment his senses fled. When they danced back from the vague hinter regions, they brought with them a dull, nauseating pain.

Kemp lay where he fell, knowing that he could not regain his feet before his pursuers reached him. He prepared himself for what he knew must come next.

What happened next, though, was not exactly what he had expected.

High above, somewhere to his right, there came a long, thin whistle. An instant later he heard a distant boom, followed almost immediately by a much closer explosion. A fine shower of dirt and small stones pelted down on him.

"What the *hell*—" he cried, turning over onto his back—which, if he had paused to think about it, was probably not the smartest thing he could have done. He saw a plume of smoke rising from the ground perhaps thirty feet away. Disorganized and shouting, the royalists were fleeing from the spot.

What was that? Kemp asked himself, even as a second high whistle oscillated in from the same direction as the first. Fire and smoke erupted this time from just to one side of the temple. A dull boom echoed through the hills. At that moment a fearful realization caught him by the throat and squeezed. He knew exactly what it was.

Artillery.

19

The royalist forces were in disarray.

Half a dozen shells had fallen into their midst, resulting in a blind, unreasoning panic. Men ran this way and that, shouting, cursing, crying. Kemp saw one man walking slowly toward him, and at first he admired the man for his calm amid all the chaos. Then he saw that the man was starting to stagger and that blood was flowing from a terrible gash just over the left ear. When the man was perhaps a yard and a half away, his legs slid out from under him and he sank slowly to the ground, looking as if he had simply decided to go to sleep where he was. He did not move after that.

The really good thing about this, Kemp reasoned, was that he need never fear a nightmare again. What nightmare, after all, could compare to this?

Painfully Kemp managed to get to his knees, and then to his feet. He looked toward the temple, but the smoke kept him from being able to see anything but the tops of the dolmen stones. He could only hope that the shell bursts had distracted Quordane from his dire intentions.

For his own part, Kemp knew that he had to find something with which to sever his bonds. He couldn't do much without the use of his hands.

Walking bent over at the waist, so as to stay as low as possible, Kemp quickly covered the ground that separated him from the tented area. As he went, he felt wetness leaking along his cheekbone and gathering in the deep fold bracketing his nose, until at last a single incarnadine drop fell and spattered on the toe of his boot.

He was making his way toward Lalerin's tent, where he figured there would be something sharp with which to cut through the ropes that bound him. He saw the tent before him. Lamplight showed through its quivering sides, beckoning him onward, though he felt his strength fading with every passing moment.

Almost there . . .

Suddenly he heard another whistle high overhead. In that same instant he realized that this shell was going to come down much closer to him than any of the others. The only thing that kept him from throwing himself to the ground was the near certainty he felt that if he did he would never be able to get up again.

He did not actually see the shell hit the tent before him, but he saw the tent shudder and heard the explosions, and drew the logical conclusion.

The tent was collapsing, he saw, its supporting poles blown out from under it. For one moment it looked like an enormous brightly colored jellyfish, then it flattened and flames burst forth from its center and began consuming it.

Kemp watched the spreading fire. "Wonderful," he declared dolefully. "Just wonderful."

Abruptly a voice very near to him said, "Close one, what? A very near thing."

Kemp swung around quickly in the direction of the voice, but saw nothing. "What? Where are you?"

A figure appeared before Kemp, strangely murky and distorted, as if seen through a dark crystal that was being constantly rotated to present different facets. The figure was a man. He was holding a gold-headed stick over his head like a torch. *Digrippa!* The man lowered the stick, and as he did so, he grew more material in form, until he was entirely solid and of normal appearance.

"Good heavens," Digrippa said mildly. "You do look like you've had a rough time of it, Kemp."

Deciding not to comment on Digrippa's extraordinary appearance, nor on his startling command of the obvious, Kemp essayed a smile, but could manage only a sickly grimace. "Mm, I shan't bore you with the details. Can you cut me loose?"

"Hmm? Oh, I see. Yes, I think so."

Kemp presented the magician with his back. He felt a blade sawing at the ropes that bound him at the wrists. The ropes gave way, and his hands fell heavily to his sides. There was little sensation left in them, and what there was was not pleasant. He tried to wipe away the blood from his cheek, but it felt like he was daubing at his face with some dead thing.

"Did you manage to replace Quordane's medallion?" Digrippa asked.

"Yes. It cost me dearly to do so. I hope that it is going to be worth it."

The magician gave a grim smile. "*Excellent*. Don't worry, Kemp. I think that you'll be gratified by the result of your labors."

"Where's Eveline?" Kemp asked.

"Nearby, never fear."

"It appears that Cander has managed to do his part."

"Indeed, it would so appear. Well, no time to waste! I'm off to find Baron Quordane." The magician raised his stick, and as he did began to fade away again.

"*Wait*. I'm coming with you."

Digrippa hesitated, caught halfway between being and not-being. "Are you sure, dear fellow? I'd say that you've done more than your share."

"I'm sure. I want to see this."

"Very well. Take my hand, and I will extend my protection to you."

Kemp took the man's proffered hand. This was not as simple a thing as it might have been. His own hands were starting to come back to life, and he was treated to an excruciating pins-and-needles sensation whenever he moved them. Kemp ground his teeth and tried to think of something else.

The moment he touched Digrippa's hand, a peculiar feeling crept through his body, a feeling of dislocation, as if he had been cut off from the world. Sounds seemed muffled and remote, and everything looked flat and drained of substance. As Digrippa raised his stick higher, these perceptions became ever more pronounced and disturbing.

They walked away slowly from the tents, into the fearful pandemonium that lay beyond. The shells had stopped falling, it seemed, but the disorder they had engendered still remained. Dense clouds of acrid smoke drifted over the field. Men milled about aimlessly, looking shocked and afraid, while their officers bawled out orders, which were generally ignored. One of the falling shells must have breached the horse enclosure. Kemp saw several horses cantering uncontrolled through the throng. Some of the royalists were attempting to control the excited steeds, but that was proving difficult, as they lacked harness and had no interest in being controlled.

Kemp heard a distant thundering of hooves. At first he thought that this came from the greater body of royalist horse, somewhere beyond the tents. It soon occurred to him, however, that it sounded too organized to be coming from a mass of panicked and riderless horses. Also, it was getting louder, and quickly.

As Digrippa led him through the center of the royalist host, Kemp turned a look over one shoulder. There was nothing. Nothing. Wait . . . *There!*

A dozen or more horsemen burst suddenly from around one of the tents, riding swiftly and in close formation. Several instants later a second dozen came into view around the other side of the tents. All wore the red coats of the Protectorate guard.

Kemp's delight at this sight was tempered by the realization that he was at that moment in the very middle of where any fighting would occur. He drew a deep breath and clutched Digrippa's hand tighter.

"Oh, Mother," he said.

The horsemen closed from two sides. Sabers held high, they waded into the royalist mass. At this critical juncture, if they had decided to make a fight of it, the royalist forces might well have pushed back or dragged down the closing cavalry, who appeared badly outnumbered. Instead, the royalists chose to break in the face of the advance. Abandoning equipment and any lingering sense of order, they swarmed away from the Protectorate horsemen, literally falling over each other in their eagerness to escape. Isolated and abandoned, those few who tried to stand their ground quickly fell before the flashing sabers of the Protectorate.

More of the Protectorate horse was arriving on the field by the moment. They immediately joined the fray, plunging into the dissolving royalist ranks. Clutching Digrippa's hand as if it were a lifeline, Kemp walked unnoticed and unaccosted through the middle of the melee. Past him horses galloped and men ran panicked, yet none of these touched him, though many came perilously close. He wondered why. Was this part of the spell that Digrippa had extended to him? He supposed that it must be.

Suddenly he saw a man astride a grey stallion, where he has pulled up some yards before him. It took a moment, but Kemp finally recognized him. It was Cander Ellis.

Cander wore the immaculate crimson uniform of an officer of the Protectorate. On his head was a plumed hat, in his hand a gold-hilted saber. He looked quite dashing, Kemp noted with a twinge of envy. Dashing or not, however, he did not appear anxious to close with the fleeing royalists.

Kemp called out, "Cander! Over here! Over here, man!"

Grimacing, Digrippa tightened his grip on Kemp's hand. "*Shh*. Enough. You'll give me a headache. He can't hear or see you."

Indeed, Cander showed no awareness of his calls. A few moments later, he appeared to see something that interested him at the far end of the field. Giving spur to his steed, he galloped ahead, jumping a fallen stone column woven over with dead vines, and was soon lost to the smoke and confusion.

It was a rout.

Cander guided his nervous horse through the enemy camp, while firelight illuminated the fleeing royalists in brief, disconnected flashes. He saw immediately that the enemy had no intention of putting up any resistance. Their will to fight had been broken, more thoroughly than he would have supposed possible, even in his most optimistic moments. The brief bombardment that had preceeded the cavalry, produced by four small horse-drawn cannons, should not have had this great an effect. It was astounding. So far, the royalists had not even noticed that they outnumbered their opponents by more than four to one.

Sixty-five cavalrymen. That was the extent of the force that Walthorne had been able to spare. Sixty-five cavalrymen, a handful of gunners, and Cander. Even taking into account the surprise factor, who could have guessed that it would go so well? Certainly not Cander.

Even though the situation seemed well in hand, Cander could feel fear and anxiety running cold currents through him. He did not have to remind himself that it would take only one royalist to stand his ground and fight, one stray shot, to bring him down. He was far from safe.

After drawing his horse to a halt at the top of a small rise, Cander surveyed the field. To one side were the tents of the royalist officers, fire spreading swiftly among them, driven by a brisk wind from the north. At least three of the tents were involved now, and the yellow-amber glow that they shed sent flickering shadows rolling across the field. To the other side was the temple, black smoke billowing up before it and wreathing its weathered cyclopean piers.

Were we in time? he wondered. *Did we come soon enough to stop the horror that they had planned?*

Cander caught sight of something then. At the far edge of the temple, where it blended into a stunted, winter-barren wood, a figure moved quickly, dimly illuminated by the distant fires. A woman.

Eveline.

She ran along the outer margins of the temple ruins, past tumbled stone blocks and canted columns, her red-gold hair trailing behind her. She appeared to be in pursuit of someone, but Cander could not see who. Within moments, she had reached the first of the trees and disappeared behind it. He saw her then only in elusive flashes.

Curious as to what the woman was after, Cander spurred his horse toward the woods. As he rode, he carefully kept the tip of his saber interposed between himself and anyone who ventured near, friend and foe. This was enough to keep him from being accosted until he could reach the edge of the woods.

Pausing for a moment, he peered up the slope into the blackness of the woods. Seeing nothing dangerous, he urged his unwilling horse up the rocky grade. Twisted branches heavy with mistletoe reached out to him.

Cander heard a rustling in the underbrush just ahead. Suddenly he saw someone emerge from behind a dusky tree trunk and move lightly across the slope. He realized who it was.

"Eveline," he said in an urgent whisper. *"Eveline, it's me."*

The woman paused where she was. She gave Cander one quick glance over her shoulder, appearing not at all surprised to see him. "Cander," she said. "Good. I need you. Get down from your horse and come with me. He went this way."

"Who? I've seen no one but you."

"Quickly!"

Frowning with annoyance, Cander did as she asked. After swinging down out of the saddle, he looped the reins around a low branch, sheathed his saber, and scrambled up the steep, rocky slope after Eveline. His nostrils tingled from the dust his booted feet raised.

Upon reaching Eveline's side, he quietly repeated his question: "Who is it that we are after?"

"Stahlgrave. He's attempting to escape this way."

"Are you sure? I—"

Just then the brush a few yards up-slope started to thrash. Cander could see it shuddering and moving aside in a narrow path that led directly to the top of the rise, but he could not see what was causing the disturbance. *A wild animal, most likely*, he thought.

"There!" Eveline exclaimed triumphantly. "We have him now!" She sprang forward, pursuing the tremulous weeds up the hill.

"Eveline, wait! It can't be Stahlgrave. There's nobody there."

"He's a *magician*," she called back at him, as if that one phrase answered all questions.

After a moment of awkward indecision, Cander sprinted after the woman, immediately catching one foot on a thorny vine and almost falling flat on his face as he did so. Staggering on his other foot for a moment, he cursed richly while he pulled himself free. By this time, Eveline had reached the crest of the hill; she disappeared behind it before Cander could resume the pursuit.

Heedless of the many small hazards that faced him in the darkness, he raced after her. His labored breathing sounded loud and harsh in his ears.

As he came to the top of the rise, Cander caught sight of Eveline again. She had stopped several yards down the slope, and she seemed to be struggling with something—something that was not there. She'd thrown her arms around empty air and was attempting to restrain it, though it was apparently putting up a terrific fight.

Taking it on faith that the woman had not suddenly gone mad, Cander made his way quickly down the side of the hill. As he neared, Eveline said sharply, "Hit him, Cander!"

He frowned. "How? I can't see anyone."

"Aim at my stomach. Hard as you can."

"But—"

"*Do it!*"

Cander gave a small, apologetic shrug, drew a breath, and threw a halfhearted punch at Eveline's stomach. It never got there. Something stopped it first. From nowhere, a muffled *oof* sounded.

"*Again,*" Eveline said. "Harder."

Cander drew back, then struck with all his strength at the same spot. Again his fist struck something before it could reach the woman. He heard a gasping sound.

Eveline abruptly let go of whatever she had been holding. Cander followed her gaze as it tracked slowly down to the ground. His eyes caught a disconcerting flicker, and suddenly he saw a figure at their feet, doubled over and panting for breath.

"Stahlgrave," Cander said.

Eveline's lips showed an enigmatic smile. "He could make himself invisible to mortal sight, but he could not evade *this*." She tapped one finger lightly on her temple, beside one fathomless eye.

"Thank you for your help, Cander."

Hand in hand, Kemp and Digrippa advanced upon the temple of Brani. The smoke thinned and parted before them. The long altar stone took solid form first, and then that which lay behind it. As before, the young prince Garadon seemed to sleep peacefully atop the altar. His mother lay in a heap on the ground. For one terrible instant, Kemp thought that Quordane had done it, had killed her. Then he saw that her shoulders were rising and falling rapidly, as she gasped or sobbed. Apparently the bombardment and arrival of the Protectorate forces had distracted the baron from his intentions.

Quordane himself had retreated behind the five royalist officers who stood to the right of the altar stone. These officers, almost unique among their fellows, were attempting to put up a defense against the converging cavalry, wielding both sword and pistol. It was hopeless, however. One officer had already fallen. As Kemp watched, three more fell to Protectorate gunfire. One after another they slumped lifeless to the stone floor, their previously immaculate uniforms showing spreading stains of red.

Apparently realizing that he was in an untenable position, the last royalist officer threw down his weapons and put his hands up over his head, waving them around, so all would be sure to see.

"*Coward!*" Quordane exclaimed with a black scowl. Kemp believed that if he'd had a gun, he would have shot the man himself.

By this time, Kemp and Digrippa had made their way to the outer skirt of the temple. Digrippa lowered his walking stick, and Kemp again felt that strange inward churning, as they became visible once more. After dropping Kemp's hand, the magician quickly climbed the three steep, roughly cut steps that ran all along the front of the temple. Kemp followed, rather more warily.

As Digrippa came to the top step, he shouted, "*Quordane!* Over here, Quordane!"

The baron's gaze swiveled around to include Digrippa and

Kemp. Immediately it filled with boundless hatred. "You," he stated scornfully.

"Surrender, Quordane. You can't escape. You're finished." As if to underscore Digrippa's point, a half-dozen Protectorate horsemen chose that moment to come riding out of the swirling smoke and converge on the front of the temple.

Quordane took this in with a bland flicker of his eyes. "Finished? I think not. I'll concede you the day, Digrippa. That's all."

The baron began backing away toward the rear of temple. As he did so, he loosened the collar of his shirt with one hand and pulled out the medallion that hung from his neck. He was smiling as he took the medallion in his hand, smiling as he pronounced those strange words that Kemp had first heard outside the Chandler's Theater.

"No," Digrippa said in a curiously flat and unemotional tone. "Don't do it. Stop."

Ignoring him, Quordane reached the end of his incantation, then stood by serenely, waiting to be whisked away to safety. A moment later, a troubled and perplexed look came to his face, as it became clear that something had gone wrong.

Instead of the dark slash in the substance of the world that had opened over him that night in Lorum, a small pinwheel of white light had appeared above his head. It spun rapidly, casting off long beams of painful brilliance. Little by little it slowed and then finally stopped. For one moment it hung frozen in space. Then, with sudden violence, it burst asunder, sending out a blazing pulse of heat and light in all directions.

Staggered and half blinded, Kemp saw Quordane get thrown to the ground by the blast. The baron shook his head, obviously stunned, and looked above him. His eyes widened in dismay.

The fissure in space had appeared over him at last, but it was not dark. An intense flickering radiance showed from it, reminding Kemp of a series of lightning flashes seen obliquely through a second-storey window. He wondered briefly what it was that Quordane beheld there, in that shimmering aperture.

Then he saw.

Two fiery hands reached down out of the void, each one bigger than a man. They grasped hold of Quordane and lifted him into the air, making an appalling sizzling sound when they touched him. "No!" the man shouted, squirming violently against the hands. "Let me go, *let me go!*"

Remorseless, the hands held the struggling man in an implacable grip, as they drew him up and into the place from whence they had come. Quordane's garments were beginning to smolder and smoke as he disappeared into the bright chasm.

Kemp heard the man's anguished wail, shrill and weirdly echoing, as the gap overhead shuddered and its edges drew together. Soon all that could be seen of it was a dim point of light. An instant later even this was gone. Quordane's terrible wail was abruptly, mercifully, truncated.

Kemp stared straight ahead for a moment, suppressing a shudder. Then he gave Digrippa a speculative look. The magician's face betrayed no emotion, though Kemp knew full well that he had arranged this awful end for Quordane. Did he feel satisfaction, regret?

At last Kemp spoke. "Dead?"

"Hm?" Digrippa gave him a distracted look.

"Is he dead?"

"If he is lucky, dear fellow. Only if he is lucky."

Kemp heard a soft moan. Face streaked with tears and blood, Ceris was trying to get to her feet, though she appeared at the end of her strength. "Garadon," she kept saying, in a faint, breathless voice, "Garadon . . ."

Climbing the last of the temple steps, Kemp moved to help her.

20

Walthorne had converted the Morulin town hall to his own uses. The building, though not impressive by Lorum standards, was the largest and finest that the provincial town could offer. Naturally, the Lord Protector had claimed it for his own. Most of the nearby buildings had been similarly invested by the commands of various elements of the army: Cavalry, Engineers, Dragoons, Supply. Even many of the outlying houses had been claimed as billets for common soldiers. Cander did not know what the locals thought of all of this, but he could hazard a guess.

Cander and his companions—Kemp, Digrippa, Eveline, and Vedrai—were kept waiting for a long time in the building's spacious foyer. Standing close together, the five watched the soldiers and somberly clad clerks bustle by, and said little.

Finally a gaunt-cheeked clerk dressed all in black appeared and beckoned to them. He led them down a short corridor, past a massive door, and into a large chamber with stark white walls and a high ceiling. Walthorne was there, standing behind a cherry-wood table piled high with documents. Cander could tell at a glance that Walthorne was in a rare good mood. The Protector even smiled a bit as he met Cander's gaze. "Ah, you're here," he said. "Come in, come in! Reymes, close the door behind you. There's a good fellow."

Face studiously grave, the clerk stepped out into the hall, pulling the door shut behind him. Walthorne waited until the heavy door settled completely into its frame before letting his gaze play over Cander and the others, saying "You have done well, all of you. Branion owes you a great debt. Thanks in large part to your efforts, Lalerin and his supporters are finished. The

Protectorate is safe, at least for now. It's a shame that the nation can never know what you've done."

There was a pause. Finally Digrippa said, "Why can't it?"

"It's been decided that it would be unsettling to the populace to know the full facts of this matter. Something will have to be said, of course, but I expect that it will be as little as possible. Something to the effect that a royalist plot had been discovered and foiled, leading to the death the pretender to the throne, Lalerin."

"I think you're making a mistake there," Digrippa said, frowning. "If you can't trust your citizens to know the truth, how will they even know what truth looks like when the next crisis arises? By keeping them ignorant, you'll only be buying yourself future trouble."

Walthorne cocked his head. "An interesting philosophical point, no doubt. However, Branion is not ruled by philosophers, but rather by practical men."

"I'm speaking practically. If you tell people the truth now—"

"But we *are* telling them the truth—or as much of it as they need to know."

"Yes, but—"

"*Enough,*" Walthorne said in a warning tone. "The decision has been made. I do not wish to discuss it further."

Seeing Digrippa start to open his mouth, as if to continue the argument, Cander hastily attempted to change the subject. "So: I assume that the royalists have by now been defeated entirely."

Walthorne nodded, seeming to warm to the new subject immediately. "Those who came across the border are now either dead or prisoners. Those who remain in Gahant are no great threat. If Lalerin and his officers had survived to lead their troops toward a common objective, matters might have been different. *However.*" The man gave a veiled smile.

Kemp spoke up abruptly. "A question. What has become of Ceris and Garadon? I've not seen them since they were taken away by your troops."

Narrowing his eyes, Walthorne gave the smaller man a suspicious look. "They are well. They will be kept safe."

"Where?"

"You do not need to know that."

"But I want to know. I insist."

"If you must know, they are at this moment being escorted

under heavy guard to the Black Tower, where they will be held until it is determined what should be done with them."

"The Black Tower? Why? They are innocent of any wrongdoing."

"That hardly matters. They still represent a danger. Ceris is the Pretender's wife, Garadon his son. Either of them could be used as a focal point for future trouble."

"That is hardly *their* fault."

"No indeed. More's the pity."

"Will they be killed?"

"Oh, I very much doubt it. We're not savages, after all."

"But they are not to be given their freedom."

"I'd hardly think so. As I say, they represent too great a danger to the Protectorate."

"Ever?"

Walthorne ignored this question, giving Cander a pointed look. "Who *is* this person, Cander?"

Cander knew that look. He felt an icy chill running along the back of his neck. "No one, Protector. No one that you need concern yourself with."

"What is his *name*?"

"Kemp."

"Tell Master Kemp that he presumes too much upon my amiable nature."

"I'm sure he means no harm."

"Hm, perhaps not. I must say, though—you certainly have recruited a contentious lot for your agents."

Cander cringed inwardly at this, but a quick look at his companion showed no discernible reaction to Walthorne's suggestion. That was odd, when he thought about it. "Sorry," he said.

"At any rate, I have no time for this. You may go, all of you. You have my gratitude for your good work, and so on . . ."

"Most gracious, Protector."

"Wait," Kemp said loudly. "I believe that I asked a question."

"Quiet," Cander said, putting hands firmly on the thief's shoulders and propelling him unwillingly toward the door. *"Not now."*

They were well outside the building before Kemp turned on Cander with a sneer of disdain and said, "Why did you stop me? There were questions that needed to be asked. Are you nothing more than Walthorne's lackey?"

Stung, Cander answered in a measured voice. "Have you forgotten who you are, Kemp? If so, let me remind you. You are a condemned thief. Do you really want to draw attention to yourself? From *Walthorne*, of all people? What, do you actually expect him to respond to moral arguments? If what you want is to commit suicide, I'd just as soon not be around when you do it."

Kemp opened and closed his mouth, apparently unable to dredge up an adequate response. Finally he said, "You're right. It is useless to argue with the likes of Walthorne." With that, he turned and strode off quickly down the street, the anger still readily apparent in the set of his back.

When he was well away, Cander said, bemused, "What's the matter with *him*? He hardly seems himself."

Eveline answered, "Isn't it obvious? He's fallen in love with Ceris. A little bit, at least."

"Good Lord! Do you really think so?"

"I know so."

The certainty in her voice made him look at her. He saw that she still wasn't wearing her eye patch. He'd almost forgotten. Feeling suddenly exposed and self-conscious, he had to look away. At the edge of his sight, he saw Eveline appear momentarily confused. Then he could see the realization strike her. Her face set in a bleak expression, and her hand came up and touched her brow, partly covering that eye.

Cander felt a sharp-edge remorse. He knew that he should not have reacted the way that he had, but he could not seem to help himself. Why could he not accept the power of that eye? he wondered. No easy answer offered itself to him.

Digrippa looked from Eveline to Cander and back again. "Well, Cander," he put in rapidly. "What are your plans now?"

"Hmm? Oh, I must get back to Lorum as soon as possible. I have . . . business. And you?"

"I imagine that Eveline and I will loiter about these parts for a while before returning. Rest and fresh air seem to be the order of the day, eh? And I suppose we'll have to keep Kemp from getting himself into trouble."

"That sounds like a good idea. Well, I guess we'll meet again in Lorum."

"No doubt, no doubt. In case we don't see each other again before you leave, be sure to have a pleasant journey."

"Thank you, I will." The two men clasped hands, rather tentatively. "Take care."

Glancing obliquely at Eveline, Cander said to her, "Good-bye, Eveline."

"Good-bye."

Cander turned then and started away. He knew when he was being dismissed.

He was several paces away when Digrippa called out, "One more thing, Cander!"

Cander stopped and turned back to face the pair. "What?"

"You did well. Be happy."

"I'll . . . try."

Immediately upon leaving Eveline and Digrippa, Cander made inquiries concerning transportation back to Lorum. After learning from Walthorne's clerk, the phlegmatic Reymes, that a coach bound for the city would be leaving early the next morning, he managed to inveigle himself a place on it.

So it was that he found himself standing on the steps of the town hall at an hour when the meanest private of the army was still warm and asleep in bed, as the autumn mist wrapped its chill, amorphous tendrils about him.

As he stood waiting for the coach to arrive, he could not evade a morbid sense of hollowness, incompletion, and loss. He knew that he ought to feel differently. They'd won, hadn't they? They'd done what they had set out to do. And yet the victory seemed muddled and unsatisfying. What, really, had changed? The Protectorate would continue as it had before, no better or worse. Lor Brunnage would be released from Tranding Gaol, and the Chandler's Theater would be allowed to reopen. In all, Cander's life would return to what it had been a month or two before—except that he would carry with him the knowledge that somewhere an innocent woman and her child would be imprisoned, probably for the rest of their lives.

Too, he was vexed and disappointed that his parting from Kemp, Digrippa, and Eveline had gone so badly. But what had he expected? They had shared an extraordinary adventure; now it was over. Their lives would continue along separate paths.

Cander shivered from the cold, trying to pull his neck down into his cloak as far as it would go. He had no doubt that his grim mood came in no small part from fatigue and the melancholy weather. He would be glad to be in Lorum again. Rest, work, and good companionship would make him whole again, or so he hoped.

At length, he heard the distant sound of hooves on the dirt

streets of Morulin. Looking up, he saw a black coach trundling toward him along the main street. He was surprised to see that it was accompanied by an armed escort: two riders before, three behind.

When the coach finally pulled to a halt before the town hall steps, Cander abruptly realized that he recognized it. A queasy sensation blossomed in the center of his stomach.

The black-lacquered door to the coach swung open, revealing a dim, dancing light and several shadowy forms. Cander hesitated a moment, unwilling to take the required two or three steps to reach the coach.

Finally a narrow, pale face with a pointed white beard thrust itself out through the open door, and Cander's worst fear was confirmed. "Well, come along, Cander," Walthorne said crossly. "We don't have all day."

Restraining a sigh, Cander moved to the coach, climbed up inside, and settled onto the seat opposite Walthorne. There was someone sitting next to him. A glance told him that it was the clerk Reymes.

"Um, thanks for ride."

"Think nothing of it," Walthorne answered in a disinterested voice. Then, after a pause: "You will find a loaded pistol under your seat. If by chance we should come under attack, you will of course be expected to defend me to the death."

Cander studied the man for a moment. He did not appear to be joking. "Of course."

The coach lurched into motion. As it swung around the town's central plaza and headed west, Cander came to the uncomfortable realization that on this journey he was to fulfill Shalby's normal function, as bodyguard and chief hatchetman.

Shalby.

Cander said, "I haven't had a chance to ask yet. How is Shalby doing?"

"As well as can be expected, I daresay. The physicians say that he should be himself again in a few weeks. Indeed, he seems well on the road to recovery already. He had nothing but complaints about you, by the way. He felt—with some justification, I must say—that you should not have endangered your mission by stopping to aid him. However, in light of Shalby's value to me, and your ultimate success, I have decided to ignore the matter."

Cander snorted.

After lifting the corner of the leather flap that covered the window, Cander peered out at the passing houses, silent and dark at this hour of the morning. Aimlessly his mind fretted over the vexing events of the last several weeks.

At last, he lowered the window flap. He gave a speculative glance to Reymes and said, "May I speak openly, Protector Walthorne?"

"Hmm? Yes, of course. You may say anything in front of Reymes. He knows where all the bodies are buried, so to speak."

"I was wondering whether you were able to extract any more useful information from Rensloe Fant, or whatever his real name was."

"From poor Jursen Palintine? Quite a bit, actually. After he had been with us for a few days, he couldn't say too much. Even now, he is helping us root out the royalist sympathizers within the Protectorate." His voice assumed a confidential tone. "I will tell you that they go quite high, all the way up to Jey Cordelay, First Secretary of the High Council."

"Jey Cordelay? Now *that* I find surprising."

"As did I."

Cander cleared his throat. "Now that this affair is concluded, I assume that you'll live up to our agreement."

"And what agreement is that?"

"The order closing the Chandler's Theater is to be rescinded, and Lor Brunnage and all other members of the Company are to be released from Tranding Gaol. Remember?"

"Oh, that. Of course. It is of no consequence now. Tranding Gaol is likely to become overcrowded in the next few weeks, in any event."

It took three full days to reach Lorum—three days of excruciating boredom, watching the countryside slip by in a blur—bare-limbed forests and bleak, unplanted fields—while listening to the drone of Walthorne's voice as he dictated letter after letter to the ever-attentive Reymes. Cander tried to sleep, but the constant jostling made that difficult, and it seemed that whenever he managed to drop off for more than a few moments the coach stopped for food or a change of horses.

It was late at night when the coach finally trundled to a halt at a deserted corner several blocks away from where Cander lived. Walthorne bid Cander good-bye with customary indifference, and Cander emerged from the coach into a cold drizzle. Shoulders hunched, he started away down the dark street. Behind him, he heard the sound of ponderous wheels and receding hooves on rain-slicked cobbles.

When he reached home and at last closed and locked the door behind him, he immediately threw his damp coat over the back of a chair, pried off his boots, and fell into bed. He slept for ten hours, went out to the local tavern for something to eat, then returned home and slept for eight more.

True to his word, Walthorne arranged for the release of Lor Brunnage and the reinstatement of the Chandler's Theater. A messenger bearing the necessary documents appeared at Cander's door shortly after breakfast on that second day. Wasting no time, Cander hired a cab and journeyed out to Tranding Gaol. After some delay at the main gate, he was allowed in and brought before Warden Farenbras.

The old man perused the release papers carefully, the text, the signature, the heavy seal affixed to the bottom, all the while making doubtful little sounds deep in his throat. At last, he let the papers flutter to his desk. "These appear to be in order," he said, with apparent regret.

Cander waited just inside the main gate for Lor to be brought up, feeling thoroughly oppressed by the low vaulting of blackened stone that surrounded him. He hated this place, truly hated it; he hoped never to have to set foot inside it again.

Accompanied by a lone guard, Lor Brunnage finally appeared at the far end of the shadowed court. He was unsteady on his feet, pounds thinner, and filthy. Even the dim light available in the enclosed court made him blink and squint. He was quite close before he apparently saw and recognized Cander. When he finally did, tears came to his eyes. "Cander," he croaked. "Is it true? Am I really free to go?"

"It's true," Cander said, taking the man by the arm. "You're free."

The guard unlocked the outer gate and pulled it open. Iron hinges shrieked, as if in protest. Taking small, slow steps, Lor and Cander made their way through the gate and into the street beyond.

Cander helped Lor into the waiting cab, then climbed up beside him. After taking a moment to catch his breath, Lor lifted up the window flap and looked out. "So much light," he murmured.

Letting the flap fall, the man sat back with a sigh. "I can't tell you," he said, "what it is like to breathe fresh air again."

Cander suppressed the urge to tell the man that the air around him wasn't exactly fresh, and wouldn't be until he took a bath and changed his clothes. Being in the enclosed cab with Lor made Cander's eyes water. "You want fresh air? Here, let's roll up that window flap."

"No. It's too much, too much."

The cab pulled away and slowly gained speed. After a moment, Lor said, "I'm afraid to ask, but I must. What of the Chandler's Theater?"

Cander smiled. "All cleared up. We can reopen whenever we like. I have the papers right here." He dropped the heavy packet into Lor's lap.

Lor gingerly plucked the packet open with thumb and forefinger, glanced over the contents, and smiled. After carefully refolding the papers, he left them balanced on his stomach and put one hand over them. A faint smile clung to his lips for a long while.

Finally he bestirred himself. Tugging on his filthy waistcoat and giving Cander a sidelong look, he said, "You realize, of course, that you still owe me a play."

Two days later, Cander finally stood before his desk and spread what he'd already written of his play before him. It wasn't much, he had to admit—the first act and four scenes of the second.

That only left four and a half acts to go. Though daunted by the size of the task, Cander knew that there was nothing to do but push up his sleeves and have a go at it.

After hiring a local youth he knew of to bring him meals and carafes of lukewarm jafar at regular intervals, Cander set to work. As he had expected, it was difficult going at first. A long time had passed since he had last put pen to paper, and he had rather lost the thread of the thing. After the first day, however, he and the play began to mesh, and it seemed part of him again.

The play was intended to be a light, frothy comedy, a lark, a bit of frippery, full of remarkable coincidences, improbable events, and mistaken identity. In a way, it was a relief to concentrate the whole of his mind upon something so inconsequential, for it served to distract him from the troubling events of the past month. He took pleasure in the work, and in the tools of his trade, the heavy cream-colored paper, the quill pen, the inkpot, and the penknife. He wrote from early morning until late at night. When at last he fell into bed, aching and unable to string even two more words together, his mind still raced, unwilling to be stilled. In the morning, he began again.

Ten days later, he was finished. He penned the final *exeunt all*, set the page aside, and put a fresh sheet before him. Twirling the quill pen between thumb and forefinger, he thought for a moment, then finally bent to give the play its name: *A Fool's Revenge*.

After gathering up the pages of the play, Cander straightened them and set them aside. As far as he was concerned, it was all ready for the copyist. He supposed that he should feel happy that it was done, but a certain restless dissatisfaction clung to him.

At length, he decided to walk off his excess energy. Exercise and fresh air would do him good. He selected an old blue coat with red cuffs and matching piping from the wardrobe, then went out, finding a miserably cold and blustery day awaiting him. The streets were only lightly populated, and most of those whom Cander saw abroad were either huddled in overhung doorways or walking with a brisk purposefulness. As his nose and cheeks lost their feeling, Cander quickly became disenchanted with the notion of a stroll.

Without really thinking about it, he flagged down a passing cab and instructed the driver to take him to Digrippa's house. The odds were that Digrippa and Eveline had not yet returned home, but he found himself strangely anxious to see them.

When the cab pulled up before Digrippa's disreputable manse, Cander climbed out and told the driver to wait. He made his way up the narrow path to the door and started to knock, when he saw that the door was open a crack. Holding the doorknob with his left hand, he tapped lightly on the door with the right. When no answer came, he pushed the door open and stepped into the foyer. "Hello?" he called out. "Talmis? Eveline? Is there anybody here?"

He heard steps, ponderous and slow. Looking down the hall, he saw the basement door swing open. Expecting to see Digrippa, he was surprised to see Shalby emerge instead from the doorway. If Shalby was equally surprised to see him, his face didn't show it.

The man came toward Cander, his gait uncharacteristically stiff. He carried a gnarled walking stick, but did not seem to need it, and hardly used it.

"Where are they, Cander?" Shalby asked in a deep, ominous voice.

"Digrippa and his sister? I don't know. I thought that they might be here."

"What about the other one? The one called Kemp."

"Again, I don't know. I haven't seen him since Morulin."

Shalby carefully scanned his face. "Is that true?"

"No, Shalby. I lied, and now I'm going to admit it to you."

There was a long pause, as the man continued to study Cander. At last, he said, "Very well. So you don't know where they are."

"What's this all about? Why the interest?"

Shalby appeared uncomfortable with this subject. He hesitated a moment, then said, "Something has happened. Protector Walthorne wishes urgently to speak to them."

"*What* has happened?"

"Lalerin's woman and her brat have disappeared from the Black Tower. They . . . had help. We think that it came from Kemp and the other two."

Cander nearly laughed, but managed with some difficulty to keep a straight face. "Disappeared? I say, that is awkward, isn't it? What makes you think that Kemp had anything to do with it?"

"Walthorne has had your friend Kemp thoroughly investigated. I think that you know well enough that he is uniquely qualified to break into the Black Tower. And, from what Walthorne said, he was quite keen to see Ceris and Garadon free."

"I can see how suspicion might fall on him," Cander conceded. "But why does it include Digrippa and Eveline?"

"They were seen with a waiting carriage outside the Chandler's Theater on the night of the disappearance. I know that you are aware of what import that has."

Cander made a noncommittal sound.

"If any of them attempt to contact you, I trust that you will report the fact. And lest you start to admire your friend's idealistic zeal, you should know that on that same night that Ceris disappeared a fortune in jewels was taken from the Black Tower."

"*Ha!* It just keeps getting worse, doesn't it? I rather doubt that any of them will be anxious to get in touch with me, though. I'm afraid that I was unable to entirely conceal my relationship with Walthorne from them. They're none of them fools." Cander gave a glance about the foyer. "And if Digrippa did have anything to do with this, I doubt very much that he'll be coming back here."

Shalby sighed. "You're probably right."

A pause. Cander said, "Apart from that, how do affairs stand?"

"Well enough, I suppose. I am healing. The Society of the Dawning Sun is to be outlawed, and we are now attempting to root out its members from positions of authority. It is important to be tidy at times like these."

"No doubt."

Shalby gave Cander a pensive look. "Speaking of which, we are planning a little foray across the border in a few days, to take care of the Inn of the Green Crow and its owner, the royalist spy Gerj Kolin. I thought that you might like to come along."

Cander considered this for a moment, and was surprised, when he thought of Gerj Kolin, by how much resentment he still felt. "Yes," he said. "By all means."

They crossed the frontier with Gahant just before midnight—Cander, Shalby, and a dozen other men, most of them grim, hard-bitten dragoons in civilian clothing. They rode two abreast along the desolate, wind-swept road, the darkness of night sealing them into their own little world, until at last they reached the Inn of the Green Crow, which slept unawares under a lowering blanket of woodsmoke and cold mist.

Cander dismounted before the inn's main doors, but he did not enter the building with Shalby and the others. He preferred not to take part in what was to happen next. He supposed that it was foolish to have such qualms. Did it matter whether he dirtied his own hands, or just stood by and let happen what would happen? Still . . .

He stood there in the lonely courtyard, his breath blooming white in the frigid air; he listened to the muffled sounds of violence emanating from the inn: the shouts, the cries of alarm, the thumps and crashes. Finally the door flew open, and Shalby and his men reemerged, driving before them the inn's guests, white-faced and perplexed, in various stages of undress. Among them was Gerj Kolin, barefoot and clad only in a nightshirt. A trickle of blood ran from the corner of his mouth, and the right side of his face was already starting to swell. His hands were behind his back, held there by one of Shalby's dragoons, who kept propelling him relentlessly forward.

Abruptly Gerj's gaze fell upon Cander and held there. He sneered, eyes burning with fierce contempt. "Well, Cander, you have me. Is it true what they say, that revenge is sweet?"

Cander was aware of a peculiar mix of emotions within him,

satisfaction alternating with furtive shame. Seeing Gerj again reminded Cander of their friendship, and all at once it was difficult to blame the man. They had both been playing the same secret game, after all; Gerj had merely been on the wrong side. Still, Cander liked to believe that he would have behaved differently in Gerj's place, that he would not have betrayed his friend's trust so absolutely. Whether or not this was actually true was difficult to say.

Cander tried not to let his uncertainty show. "Not my call, Gerj," he said. "I merely wanted to be here to see it."

The other man gave a thin smile of ironic detachment and spat blood at his feet. He said nothing more as he was led away.

The door to the inn had been left open. Through it, Cander could see a vague, shifting glow, and then the smoke. At first it was only a thin pall, but it quickly grew dark and threatening. As the black smoke started to pour out through the doorway, Cander caught sight of the flames for the first time. He felt the rush of escaping heat on his face.

He was sad to see the Three Crows' destruction. It had been an agreeable place; the world would be the worse for its loss. *Ah, well,* he thought regretfully, *nothing is forever.*

As Shalby called for everyone to move back, his men formed a loose cordon and started forcing the unwilling onlookers away from the burning inn. Turning, Cander quickly scanned their faces, now illuminated by the spreading flames. After a moment, he spotted her, Alsimae. The woman was dressed in a thin white nightdress; her flaxen hair hung loosely about her shoulders, and her cheeks were flushed from the chill wind. She looked quite beautiful. Feeling a small pang, Cander went to her.

The woman's eyes registered his approach with surprise. "Cander!" she exclaimed. "Where did you come from?" And then in a tone of mild censure: "You disappeared without saying good-bye."

"I didn't disappear, actually. I was disappeared. That is to say, I didn't have any choice in the matter."

Alsimae frowned, obviously dissatisfied, but unwilling to press the point. "Do you know what's happening here? Who are these men? Why are they burning down the inn?"

"It's best that you don't know who they are. As for why, let's just call it politics." He sighed. "Everything is politics."

"*Politics!*" she exclaimed, anger apparent on her face. "I'm to lose my livelihood and everything I own because of *politics*?"

Cander gave a helpless shrug.

"What am I to do *now*?"

Cander could not think how to answer, so he didn't. Unfastening his cloak from around his throat, he said, "You're cold. Here, take this." He settled the cloak around her shoulders. Her face looked pale against the darkness of the cloak.

Alsimae clutched the cloak to her throat. "I suppose that I'll have to go back home again now," she said, more to herself than to Cander. "I'll have to. There's nothing else to do. Nothing."

A thought that he had never before contemplated suddenly seized hold of Cander. "There's one other thing you could do," he found himself saying. "You could come with me to Lorum."

"With you?"

"Yes."

"To Lorum?"

"Yes."

Alsimae regarded him closely, her eyes searching over his face. "I don't know. Are you asking me this just because you feel sorry for me?"

"No. I'm asking because I've grown fond of you. We do get on well together, don't we? Come with me. I'll show you Holyrod Palace at night, when it is lit by a hundred lights, and the view from the Grand Prospect. We'll dine beside the river, at a cozy little place I know, and stroll along the Plaza of Fallen Heroes. We'll have a grand time." If Cander was initially uncertain of the wisdom of what he was suggesting, he had quite convinced himself by the time he finished his speech.

"Are you certain, Cander?"

"Absolutely."

Alsimae raised her chin slightly. "Very well," she said with an air of gracious dignity. "I will go with you."

"Kiss me then, and then we'll be off."

She did.

Sharing the same horse and, indeed, the same cloak, Cander and Alsimae crossed the border into Branion. At the first way station, they traded in their horse and caught the regular coach to Lorum. It was snowing when they arrived, and the city was lovely beneath its mantle of new-fallen snow. Alsimae's eyes took in everything with unveiled wonderment, and through her Cander was able to see the city anew. As days turned to weeks, he would show Alsimae everything that he had promised, and more.

Spring came, and *A Fool's Revenge* opened at the Chandler's Theater. Its immediate success emboldened Cander to implement the scheme that he had devised earlier; he entered into an agreement with a local printer to publish the text of his play, and even went so far as to invest his own money in the project. Fortunately, the printed play moved briskly from the Lorum bookstalls, and even found favor abroad. With his share of the profits, which were considerable, Cander was able to buy and furnish a comfortable house on the edge of the fashionable Layton district. This, too, was fortunate, for in the early winter, Alsimae bore Cander a child, a daughter.

All during this time, change worked its way through the Protectorate. The Society of the Dawning Sun was outlawed and its properties confiscated. Of its members, some found themselves in Tranding Gaol, and others were forced underground. That year many a lofty individual fell from power and was ruined. The public journals mentioned little of that, and nothing of the disappearance of Lalerin's wife and son, along with a substantial portion of the crown jewels, but there were rumors everywhere. Not surprisingly, Digrippa and Eveline never returned to their house at the river's edge.

Cander did not see Kemp again until four years later, in the spring.

About the Author

Craig Mills was born in 1955, in Alameda, California, and grew up in nearby Fremont. He attended California State University at Hayward, majoring in Drama, before setting out for New York City along with his future wife, Dorrie, in a 1959 Dodge Step Van packed to the roof with their possessions.. He lived in Manhattan for three years, where he acted in a number of off-off Broadway plays, held the usual assortment of odd jobs, took classes, and wrote his first novel, *The Bane of Lord Caladon*. Currently, he lives just south of San Francisco, in a house that would overlook the ocean, if it were a lot taller.